Tom Clancy's
POWER PLAYS

WILD CARD

CREATED BY
TOM CLANCY
AND
MARTIN GREENBERG

WRITTEN BY
JEROME PREISLER

PENGUIN BOOKS

Tom Clancy's
POWER PLAYS

WILD CARD

PENGUIN BOOKS

Published by the Penguin Group
Penguin Books Ltd, 80 Strand, London WC2R 0RL, England
Penguin Group (USA) Inc., 375 Hudson Street, New York, New York 10014, USA
Penguin Group (Canada), 10 Alcorn Avenue, Toronto, Ontario, Canada M4V 3B2
(a division of Pearson Penguin Canada Inc.)
Penguin Ireland, 25 St Stephen's Green, Dublin 2, Ireland (a division of Penguin Books Ltd)
Penguin Group (Australia), 250 Camberwell Road, Camberwell, Victoria 3124, Australia
(a division of Pearson Australia Group Pty Ltd)
Penguin Books India Pvt Ltd, 11 Community Centre,
Panchsheel Park, New Delhi – 110 017, India
Penguin Group (NZ), cnr Airborne and Rosedale Roads, Albany,
Auckland 1310, New Zealand (a division of Pearson New Zealand Ltd)
Penguin Books (South Africa) (Pty) Ltd, 24 Sturdee Avenue, Rosebank 2196, South Africa

Penguin Books Ltd, Registered Offices: 80 Strand, London WC2R 0RL, England

www.penguin.com

First published in the Unites States of America by the Berkley Publishing Group 2004
First published in Great Britain in Penguin Books 2004
3

Copyright © RSE Holdings, Inc, 2004
All rights reserved

The moral right of the author has been asserted

TOM CLANCY'S POWER PLAYS: WILD CARD
This is a work of fiction. Names, characters, places, and incidents either are the product
of the author's imagination or are used fictitiously, and any resemblances to actual persons,
living or dead, business establishments, events or locales is entirely coincidental.

Printed in England by Clays Ltd, St Ives plc

Except in the United States of America, this book is sold subject
to the condition that it shall not, by way of trade or otherwise, be lent,
re-sold, hired out, or otherwise circulated without the publisher's
prior consent in any form of binding or cover other than that in
which it is published and without a similar condition including this
condition being imposed on the subsequent purchaser

ACKNOWLEDGMENTS

I would like to acknowledge the assistance of Marc Cerasini, Larry Segriff, Denise Little, John Helfers, Brittiany Koren, Robert Youdelman, Esq., Danielle Forte, Esq., Dianne Jude, and the wonderful people at Penguin Group (USA) Inc., including David Shanks and Tom Colgan. But most important, it is for you, my readers, to determine how successful our collective endeavor has been.

—Tom Clancy

PROLOGUE

MORPAIGN SUPPOSED HE MIGHT HAVE KNOWN it would turn to his advantage. When all was said and done, he could rely on his sharp nose for profit, and his knack for finding opportunity even in ill circumstance, to take him far along in the world.

Looking out over the water, Lord Claude Morpaign truly might have realized the flames would burn a pathway to bigger and better things. But he didn't pause to consider the larger picture, not right at once, standing there in his moment of stunned discovery. His thoughts, like the merchant vessel, were on fire, seething with inexpressible anger. There had been no call for the sea wolf to flex his muscle in so brutal a manner. He could have made a persuasive offer without setting the ship ablaze and, worse, putting two able-bodied slaves to their violent deaths. Whatever the reasons, his tactics were excessive . . . unless the killing and destruction were carried out solely for his own relish, putting his bloodthirsty nature into full view.

While Morpaign would never have certain evidence of this, the suspicion later grew strong within him. And no man's heart would prove more like Redbone Baxter's than his own in the final reckoning.

Leaving the main house at twilight, Morpaign had anticipated an uneventful, matter-of-course run. His chief overseer, Didier, had met him at their prearranged spot with a team of slaves handpicked for their trustworthiness and experience working in the tunnel. As usual, a separate pair of slaves had brought a horse-drawn wagon around the skirts of the forest, ready for their fellows to emerge from down below. Once the load was on the wagon, the entire group would ride a short distance up the strand and transfer the barrels from their carriage to waiting longboats. From there the laden boats were to head out toward the New England–bound merchant vessel under Morpaign's attentive eye.

Routine as routine could be, such was his business at the start.

The head of the tunnel was just past the edge of the woods near the southern boundary of Morpaign's vast estate, its opening screened by tropical underbrush and covered with a mat of packed sod and twigs. Thirty or forty feet beyond the entrance a stone chimney top projected from the forest floor amid the obscuring vegetation.

Didier had led the group through the woods in his tattered, begrimed muslins and laborer's cap, a lantern swaying in his hand as dusk fell heavily over the island. He'd come to the loose section of turf, flapped it back, raised the hinged trapdoor underneath, and descended some narrow wooden stairs, followed in single file by the slaves.

Morpaign took up the rear, careful to avoid brushing his embroidered silk dress frock against the moist, grubby walls of the passage. Although he'd rather have worn clothes more befitting the night's task, an unexpected late-day visit by his father-in-law, the Spanish governor, had left him rushed and unable to change into them before his rendezvous, squandering much of the afternoon besides.

As he reached the tunnel floor, Morpaign had taken some fair consolation knowing his night would not be likewise wasted.

Still leading the rest by several paces, Didier had moved on through the gloom, removed the candle from his lantern, and, one at a time, lit the oil lamps hanging in niches along the masonry walls to either side of him. Their rag wicks ignited with little *flumps* of displaced air as he went down the line.

"These lamps are quick to take and brighten, never

mind the dank," he said to Morpaign. "The stuff fuel-
ing 'em ought to be bottled and sold."

"So you've urged in the past."

"And will again, seigneur. You could price it
cheaper than whale oil an' still outprofit those who
market it abroad . . . cheaper by more'n half, I'd
think," Didier said. "The pitch lake's near bottom-
less, and skimming barrels of mineral oil from its
surface would take naught but labor that's already
been put t'work there dredging caulk. Best of all,
you'd have no middleman showing his eager palm for
a commission."

Morpaign gave the Breton a look of mildly amused
condescension. In his hire for many years, Didier
spoke a coarse rustic French that still sometimes
thwarted an ear attuned to the more refined speech of
Versailles aristocrats. Yet for all his lowbred crudity
he was valuable for his protective instincts—like
some loyal and duteous mongrel dog.

"It is one thing to separate enough of the bitumen
for our own use," Morpaign said. "Show me how to
filter it from that stinking tar in volume and I'll heed
your suggestion." *And praise the superior intellect
behind it*, he thought with a pinched little smile. "Until then I shall be content to market the spirits we've
drummed up beneath the ground."

He waved a fleshy hand toward an archway in the
wall to his right. Large enough for three big men to

pass through abreast, it was swamped with shadows, as was the recess beyond.

The overseer merely shrugged and then turned into the darkened chamber. Putting his candle to its lamps, he motioned for the carriers to join him.

Again, Morpaign went last, in his perpetual caution.

An approximate rectangle, the chamber was much deeper than wide. Charred oak casks lined the walls to either side of Morpaign, resting on their flat, round heads in even rows. In a corner near the entrance was a stall holding some open-framed wooden pushcarts.

Morpaign paused beneath the arch, his nostrils tickled by the smell of burned tinder . . . and more faintly underneath it, the pungent, mingled aromas of cinnamon and bay.

He strode past the carts in the lamplight then, his gaze reaching out to a pair of great brick kettles across the chamber. The double firebox base on which they stood off the dirt floor had been similarly built of bricks; behind it, a shared flue rising aboveground matched the sooty gray stone-and-mortar construction of the tunnel walls. Two wooden barrels, each taller than a grown man, stood flanking either end of the base, their lids connected with an array of thin, curved iron pipes.

Morpaign went over to the assembly and regarded it with quiet satisfaction. His pot distillery was small, its production far surpassed by others in the islands—but it had been barely a year since he'd relocated from Haiti at his father-in-law's invitation, and most of his efforts since had been directed toward settling his household. Even when the still reached peak output, moreover, there would be limits imposed by the need to keep it buried out of sight. While the British navy and Morpaign's hosts from the Spanish capital were generally at violent cross-purposes, it was ironic that they might have a common will to block his illicit trade.

He rubbed his chin in thought, his back toward Didier and the slaves. "How much of our stock is ready to go tonight?"

"There are twenty-two aged barrels in the storeroom, besides the fourteen you see around us," Didier said.

Morpaign did a hasty mental computation.

"Over six thousand liters of spiced, total," he said. "Very good."

"Oui," Didier said. "We'll be moving the rum in two or three trips. And I expect those rowers will have to do the same before our full cargo's loaded aboard their ship."

"My only concern is that the lute has arrived without delay."

"Be a foul surprise if it hasn't . . . though you'd imagine Javier and Leon would've reported such news to us."

Morpaign considered that and nodded.

"Yes," he said. "One would imagine so."

The overseer remained standing behind him. "Will you accompany the first haul, sir, or wait here till the last?" he said.

"I'll go out with the first." Morpaign finally turned from the platform. "It's a pleasant evening, and I would much prefer the ocean air to the closeness of this tunnel."

Didier nodded, grunted his hurried orders at the slaves. "These hard-muscled bulls should get it done in here," he said to Morpaign. "Meanwhile, I'd better take some of 'em into the storeroom and fire up the lamps."

A moment later he turned back through the archway, leading the rest of the men out.

Silent, his arms folded over his chest, Morpaign watched the slaves who'd remained behind with him stoop to their task. Whether on his estate grounds or the Tobago plantation, it was Morpaign's strict rule of house to address the males in his workforce only through his overseers. The slaves for their part were forbidden from ever speaking a direct word to him, or so much as looking him in the cye. And while there were nights when Morpaign found himself gripped by the desire for a closer and more intimate contact with his *négresse* housemaid, Jaqueline—nights when he would slip from his wife's side to her quarters, and tell her how to satisfy his cravings in clear and bluntly expressed terms—he considered this an exception that came with his privilege of ownership, a secret and guarded affair to be kept locked away as if in a hidden strongbox.

But such thoughts had no place in his mind during a run. A touch annoyed with himself for letting them enter it, Morpaign had watched his laborers boost the casks of rum atop the pushcarts, lash them securely together to prevent any from toppling over, and then roll them out into the passage. There they joined Didier and the others, who had left the second chamber with their own creaking, weighted-down carts.

Morpaign brought up the rear as they continued on into the tunnel, bumping through its curves and bends by the trembling light of Didier's lantern.

Half an hour passed before they began their climb to the surface. Morpaign felt a trickle of ocean breeze against his cheek and knew they were nearing the tunnel's outlet, a limestone cave worn into the hills above the beach by time, weather, and constantly percolating groundwater.

The passage floor soon grew steeper and less uneven, the dirt underfoot giving way to a sort of natural stone ramp. The slaves put their backs to hauling the loads the rest of the way up, pushing at the carts with increased effort.

They had been toiling over this last hump, the cave mouth just ahead, when Morpaign noticed an odd red-orange glow staining the patch of sky visible beyond its rough circle. While seemingly at a distance, it was brighter by far than the moonlight . . . bright enough to render Didier's upraised lantern unnecessary.

Puzzled, Morpaign stopped flatfooted. The workers had also come to a sudden halt, jamming the passage before him, the wheels of their heavy carts ceasing to turn and rattle over its bare rock floor. Didier stood slightly below its exit sniffing the air.

Morpaign found himself doing the same. A thick, acrid stench had mingled with the smell of sea salt filtering underground.

"Smoke," Didier said. He sniffed again, wiped his nose with his calloused knuckles. "From a great fire, I'd say."

Morpaign gave no comment. The fool had stated the profoundly obvious. Something was burning. Something *large*. Not on the hills, or the beach, but beyond, upon the water.

He scuffed past the slaves and barrel carts, ignoring his own policy of address to urge them out of his way, heedless of soiling his fashionable coat against the cave wall.

"Move aside," he said. "*All of you, aside now.*"

Pushing his ample frame around Didier, he hurried up the remaining few feet to the tunnel's mouth, left it a step ahead of the overseer.

The sight he encountered outside the cave stole the breath from his lungs.

Just ahead of him, Javier and Leon lay sprawled on

their backs near the horse carriage, blood sheeting over their faces from ugly gaping wounds between their eyes. Perhaps ten or twelve coarse, bearded men in short jackets and sailor's slops ringed the wagon in a loose knot. All of them were armed with cutlasses—some of the blades drawn, some still in belt scabbards at their sides—and a few shouldered muskets or blunderbusses as well. Another man stood nearer the cave entrance, his poised appearance and almost officerlike garb distinguishing him from the rest. Clean-shaven, his black hair pulled into a pigtail under a colorfully plumed bicorn hat, he wore a single-breasted frock, waistcoat, breeches, and knee boots. Tucked into a leather bandolier across his chest were five flintlock pistols, three on his right hip, two on his left.

A sixth was in his hand and aimed at Morpaign.

"Damn my eyes," Didier muttered. He pointed down at the murdered slave hands, his mouth agape. "Will you look at *this*?"

The man in the bicorn hat was silent, paying no attention to him, holding his weapon steady on Morpaign, keeping it level with his heart.

Morpaign lifted his gaze from its barrel to the gunman's face.

"What have you done here?" he said, his lip quivering with shock and outrage.

A moment went by. The man creased his brow in mock confusion, as if only then becoming aware of the bodies.

"Ah, your chattel, forgive me," he said in French. "'Twas unfortunate they had to be put down, but I saw no surer way to prevent them from warning you of our arrival." He shrugged. "My men were gentler with the sailors they took captive."

It was Morpaign's turn to stand without response, his eyes shifting back to the weapon that had been trained on him. He'd kept enough of his wits to notice the ornate cartouches on its gold-plated barrel . . . notice that and a good deal besides. At the extreme right corner of his vision, he could see the lute burning offshore, enveloped in fierce, ragged shrouds of flame, black blots of smoke swirling upward into the night from its lofty spars and crosstrees. A square-rigged brigantine with wide, sweeping sails sat in the water off to starboard, dark figures milling about its upper deck, cannons turned toward the beleaguered charter vessel.

Morpaign had instantly known there would be a Jolly Roger fluttering high atop the brig's masthead, known it must have slipped into the bay to take the merchantman while it rested at anchor, coming up broadside with its batteries trained and ready . . .

"Permit me to introduce myself," the gunman said, speaking English this time. Then he paused and seemed to catch his tongue: "*Je suis désolé. Permettez-moi de me présenter—*"

"I know who you are, pirate." Morpaign glanced at the flames out in the cove, felt a different sort of angry combustion inside him. "Redbone Baxter's notoriety precedes him."

The man with the flintlock shrugged again.

"The names of pirates *and* gentlemen carry many leagues in the wind, Lord Morpaign," he said. "In fact, I've grown to believe they travel furthest going in a shared direction . . . but only while the wind continues to blow strong."

Morpaign had managed to regain some of his composure. "You spout nonsense and riddles," he said.

"No." Baxter shook his head. "I make you a proposal. A straightforward offer of partnership."

Morpaign stood looking at him with disbelief. The man had attacked his charter, brought a raiding party ashore to plunder his shipment, executed his slaves without apparent qualm. How dare he speak now of *partnership*?

"If this is true," he said, "it merely proves your madness."

Again Baxter shook his head.

"Mine is no lunatic idea," he said. "There are stirrings in North America that cannot be quieted by all the rivers of grog the colonists pour down their throats. In Charlestown, where your barrels were to be smuggled past harbor agents to avoid the threepence duties, the Tea Act puts new heat to tempers certain to boil over into rebellion. Whether this comes in months, a year, or two years, I cannot predict. But come it will. And whatever befalls afterward, I have no doubt that George the Third's import taxes will be crammed up his royal arse, rendering extinct those who now profit from running contraband." Baxter paused, showed a hint of a smile. "It would be wise of you to make the most of the present, m'lord . . . and wiser still to prepare for changes that are bound to occur in the future."

Morpaign continued standing there in silence. He had been tempted to give vent to his fury, reject Baxter outright no matter the consequences—but something made him hesitate.

"Let us allow your remarks for a moment," he said. "What have I to gain from linking myself to a bandit's fortunes?"

Baxter returned his stare, his smile growing in size.

"It is through this bandit that you can expand your trade beyond measure," he said. "I have picked my way along smuggling routes known only to a shrewd and adventurous handful, and made contacts who will be become indispensable when the black marketeer's day is done in the Caribbean. The quantity of spiced rum you sell the northern colonists is but a fraction of what I can move. Double your production, triple it, you'll gain buyers from Rhode Island to Georgia. And it needn't end there. Give me raw cane by the cropload, hogsheads of molasses to fill a ship's hold from top to bottom. I can guarantee their ready distribution."

"And your share of the take?"

"An equal cut . . . no more, no less." Baxter's eyes gleamed. "You see, lord, I am ready to check my natural greed for our common purpose."

Morpaign had fallen still again, hands clenched into tight balls at his sides, beads of perspiration gathering in the furrow above his upper lip. His hatred of having to stand at another man's mercy was almost choking in its intensity, matching only his disdain for the brigand's swagger. And yet . . .

And yet despite all that, he could not have pretended to ignore the sharp bite of curiosity, and the tantalizing sense that it might be pursued to some unforeseen and illimitable gain. No, not even at point of gun, with the dead still pouring their blood into the ground under his feet.

"You fail to account for British maritime patrols," he'd said in a deliberately hedging tone. "The cargo once aboard that merchantman is in your hands. Should you have found undeclared goods aboard, they would have been limited to inconspicuous quantities, stowed where they might have slipped past inspection. But a pirate vessel loaded with contraband . . . how could it elude the admiralty?"

Baxter laughed. It was a cold, somehow arrogant outburst that would echo in Morpaign's thoughts very often in times to come, always inseparable from his recollection of molten red fireglow that had risen high into the black roof of the night.

"Now there's the tickler," he said. "I have become the admirality's *arm,* lord. No longer pirate but privateer in its service. With the King's colors flying from my masthead, and a letter of marque in my breast pocket, I am warranted to board vessels hostile to the empire and seize any illicit freight for a prize." He grinned broadly, nodded in the direction of the torched vessel below. "Nothing could be safer from interdiction than a shipment carried under my banner."

Morpaign looked at him for a long moment, opened his mouth to speak . . . and then shut it, his attention drawn by a sudden movement over to his right.

Didier, he realized. The impulsive, loose-lipped fool had turned from the bodies of the slaves, his face contorted with anger.

"That what cleared him to blow the brains out o' our two best and strongest, seigneur?" he blurted, pointing at Baxter. "Or was his trigger finger actin' on its own?"

Baxter's grin pulled in at the edges but remained on his lips. He straightened, whirled on his heel, and swung his pistol toward the gesticulating overseer.

"Noise for noise," he said.

His gun crashed and spouted flame. The horses tethered to the wagons reared up with fear, their tails flicking, front hooves kicking at the air. Morpaign heard Didier scream, saw him fall to the ground clutching his kneecap with both hands.

Baxter spared a moment to glance down at his

whimpering victim, gave out an audible cluck of his tongue. Then he lowered the gun's smoking barrel and turned back to Morpaign, his expression that of someone who had tolerated a fleeting, barely consequential interruption.

"Patch the sorry creature and he will survive— lame but better behaved," he said. "Now I'd hear your response to my offer."

Still struck with astonishment, Morpaign raised his eyes from where the overseer lay bleeding and crumpled near the murdered slaves.

"And if I decline?" he said, gathering himself together.

"I'd consider it a business decision and bear no grudge," Baxter said. He nodded back toward the wagon, the flintlock resting against his hip. "That shipment of rum would adequately curb my disappointment as we part ways."

The two men did not speak for a tense minute, the silence about them penetrated only by Didier's sobs, the stamping and snorting of the horses, and the whispered exchanges of the stunned, frightened laborers inside the cave. They were peering out its mouth at the latest victim to fall before the gun, and Morpaign again found himself doing the same. Writhing in agony, his knee gushing, the overseer was a bad sight. If his wound was not tended soon, he would suffer the worst for his impulsive mouthings.

There was, however, a decision that needed to be

reached first. His mind working, Morpaign gazed past Baxter at his ragtag band of sea rovers. Gathered around the wagon and its agitated team of horses, they returned his scrutiny with hard stares, the light of the flames over the water glinting off their blades.

Through me you can expand your trade beyond measure, Baxter had said. It was a bold declaration, yes. But could anything have made it easier to believe than the brazen ruthlessness of his actions?

Finally Morpaign returned his attention to Baxter, his bunched fists loosening at his sides.

Through wreck and violence, through blood and fire, his path had become clear. And more than that, or so it felt.

In the unreality of the moment, it all might have been a consecration of his destiny.

"Doing business with you," he said with intent slowness, "shall be my pleasure."

Redbone Baxter smiled. Then he holstered his flintlock, slipped another from his bandolier, and held it out by the long gold-plated barrel. Its elaborate scrollwork was similar to what Morpaign had seen on the first pistol, but here he also noticed a gleaming silver butt cap cast as a demonic face with narrow eyes, grotesquely distorted features . . . and, Morpaign thought, a grin of cold, insolent delight eerily similar to the one on Baxter's face.

Or so it appeared to him, at least, in the tricky light and shadows hurled by the soaring, distant flames.

"Take the pistol as a gift, and consider it a symbol of our newborn alliance," Baxter said. "May it endure for many long and profitable years."

Morpaign nodded and accepted the gun.

"Long years, indeed," he said, wrapping his fingers around its demon-headed stock.

ONE

"SEEMS TO ME YOU'VE PROBABLY GOT A COU-
ple'a leakers," said Hendricks, a big, burly, florid-
cheeked guy in his middle fifties wearing a dark blue
uniform with a U.S. Customs patch on the upper left
breast of its shirt. He shook his clipboard at a skid
truck parked on the nearby tarmac. "Better come see
them for yourselves."

Three of the four men standing in a semicircle
around him seemed disinclined to budge an inch.
They were also in uniform, albeit of a type that represented no government agency or legal authority. Still,
their green jumpsuits, orange Day-Glo vests, yellow
hard hats, and Sun West Air Transport employee ID
tags did help get across the message implicit in their

balky expressions—namely that this was not their specific responsibility, not by any interpretation of airline procedures, being they were only cargo handlers whose job pretty much began and ended with clearing out the DC-9's transport hold, which was precisely what they and the rest of their crew had done minutes earlier. It was obvious they'd seen all they would have preferred of the questionable freight, and didn't intend to see any *more* unless and until they were told to move it over to the terminal. Either that or they heard from their boss, Tom Bruford, the other man outside the jet representing Sun West, that they would need to put their aching arms and backs toward doing something else with it . . . though they hadn't the foggiest idea what that *something* might be.

"A couple, well, I don't know. It seems pretty unusual," Bruford said now. An assistant transport manager with the freight forwarder, he was short, thin, tired-eyed, thirtyish, and in his blazer and tie, the only one in the group to be sporting ordinary business attire. "They're stacked one on top of the other, right? I'm guessing it's just spillage on that bottom crate."

Hendricks gave him an irritated frown.

"I used the word 'probably' for a reason," he said. "Do we really need to argue?"

"I wasn't arguing."

"Whatever you want to call it."

"I'm just trying to explain something about the fish crates." Bruford sighed. "They're required to have Styrofoam liners, absorbent pads for drippage—"

Hendricks held up a hand to stop him.

"Before you raise more of a fuss," he said, "you might want to remember the shipment's got six containers in total listed on your manifest, and *I've* got them all sitting on that truck over there, and won't have any choice except to reject the whole goddamn skid load for likely contamination if you won't cooperate."

Bruford opened his mouth to answer, decided he'd better snap it shut for his own good. In his sound and objective critical estimate, the inspector was a hump of the first order. Wait and see, in a minute he'd claim he had cut Sun West some kind of break by conducting his spot check out here on the runway instead of routinely waiting till the crates got inside the Customs building —which happened to be right next door to the freight forwarder's international reception terminal, a hell of a lot more convenient location for everybody involved.

"*Got* to be spillage, but I'll go have a look," Bruford said, and turned toward the skid truck.

Hendricks tagged along with him.

"They're pushed a little over to one side," he said. "I had them separated from the rest, see?"

A Hump with a capital H, Bruford thought. "I can see that, right, thanks . . ."

Dropping back about a foot, Hendricks glanced at the documentation on his clipboard.

"Trinidad," he read aloud in a sour tone. "I noticed that's the shipment's country of origin."

"Right."

"You ask me, whoever carries imports or exports from over there is only looking for trouble," Hendricks said. "Its national health regs, oversight procedures, airport security . . . they're all a joke."

Crouched over the supposed leakers, Bruford was thinking he didn't remember having asked the fat leprechaun for his opinion about that or anything else. In fact, he'd have gotten along just fine and zip-a-dee-doo-dah dandy without it.

As he'd started telling Hendricks, the rugged three-hundred-pound-capacity wooden crates his men had offloaded onto the truck were a standardized type the Trinidadian client, an international seafood wholesaler, always used for moving large fish. Each ordinarily would have three sides pasted with the requisite stickers marking out its point of departure, weight in pounds and kilos, exact contents, and other important information. The contents code labels on these half dozen boxes in particular read "YN/THU-NALBA"—an abbreviation used industry-wide for yellowfin tuna, scientific name *thunnus albacares*.

A quick examination of the skid load Hendricks had cited *did* reveal evidence of a leak in the topmost crate, and irrespective of his feelings about the inspector, Bruford couldn't deny it looked fairly serious. Most of the spillage was at the lower left-hand corner, where he saw a wet, dark red slime that appeared to consist of blood, mucous, and maybe some water from melted packing ice. The heavy goop had run onto the lid of the crate underneath, and then gone dripping down over the crate's side panel, soaking through most of the adhesive markers there and causing a couple of them to warp and peel away at the edges.

That, Bruford decided, was the discouraging part. On the positive flip side, he didn't notice any visible damage to either of the crates, which meant that the problem in all likelihood could be attributed to the upper container's load exceeding its weight limit rather than a break in the wood or insulating material during transport—that second possibility a worst-case mishap liable to spoil the fish inside.

"That fluid's been seeping out so fast you ought to be glad I held back the crates," Hendricks commented from behind him now. "If I'd let them stay together with the rest of your freight, sent 'em ahead to check-in, there'd be botulism and God knows what other germs crawling on everything off the plane. It'd leave you open to all kinds of financial liability."

Bruford had to bite his lip in annoyance. *Yeah, right,* he thought. *Such big-hearted concern.* Hendricks breaking his chops was bad enough. Hendricks chumming up to him, freely offering his sage advice, took the prize cake. As if the guy was doing anybody here a favor. As if he didn't have the slightest inkling freight forwarders were indemnified against that sort of thing. *And* as if it made more sense from a public health standpoint to keep the boxes sitting out in the baking Miami sunlight than to have them segregated inside the terminal's enormous cool room, where their perishable contents could be refrigerated while awaiting inspection.

Bruford sighed, rose from his knees. "You want both crates opened?" he said resignedly.

Hendricks nodded.

"Be safest for everybody involved," he said.

Bruford raised a hand and beckoned over a couple of his waiting freight handlers, one of whom had already pulled a crowbar from his leather tool-belt holster. "The inspector would appreciate a peek inside these two," he said, motioning toward the crates.

The handlers looked at him unhappily.

"Right here, huh?" said the guy with the crowbar.

"Yeah," Bruford said with a commiserative nod. "Here."

The handlers turned toward the skid truck and got to work.

For a minute Bruford stood watching them start on the top crate. Then he turned to Hendricks, figuring he'd see how his theory about excess weight had gone over.

"Suppose the crate's leaking because it was over-packed," he asked. "We going to need to put it on a scale for you?"

Hendricks shrugged.

"Look at it from my position," he said. "There's a big enough difference between its declared and actual weight, it could be an intentional duty violation."

"Or an honest mistake."

Another shrug. "Subject to enforcement either way."

Bruford frowned. He was guessing his question had been answered with the closest equivalent of a solid *yes* available in this piss-pond bureaucrat's lingo. He was also wondering what cosmic sin he could have committed to merit God's having punished him with the ridiculous crap being squarely dished out on his head today. But maybe there was no cause-and-effect explanation. Maybe sometimes you just had put it down to a hump being a hump to his core.

Bruford expelled another breath. Behind him the fish crate creaked and squealed in protest as its lid was wedged upward with the flat end of the crowbar.

He had started turning toward it again to check on his men's progress when the most awful scream he'd ever heard tore through the air from that same direction, shredding through the loud turbine roar of planes that were landing and departing on the airport's busy runways.

His skin erupting into gooseflesh, Bruford whirled

around the rest of the way to discover the brawny six-footer who'd been working at the crate howling his lungs out, *shrieking* like a terrified little kid. He had his back to the skid truck and was pressing his fists into his temples, the crowbar he'd been using dropped heedlessly on the tarmac beside the box's displaced lid. Meanwhile the other handler had remained by the crate, staring into it, his eyes so wide Bruford could see their bulging whites from where he stood.

He rushed forward, thinking maybe he shouldn't be too eager to find out what inside those boxes could have sent a pair of grown men into crazed and seemingly unashamed fits of hysteria, but letting his feet take him over to the skid truck anyway, moving up to it with three or four long, hurried strides.

And then he was standing there looking down into the crate, feeling his stomach seize with horror and revulsion.

There were body parts inside. Instantly recognizable *human* body parts. Bruford's disbelieving eyes picked out a headless torso with white knobs of bone protruding from its arm sockets. Then another beneath it, partially exposed under torn plastic wrapping and a scattered layer of freezer gel packs. One of them had belonged to a light-skinned person. The other to someone with skin that was a very dark shade of brown.

Both looked like they were male to Bruford,

though he couldn't be sure. He had also had no way to be positive the severed limbs packed in the crate belonged to the same two people. The only thing he *did* know before recoiling in shock and aversion was that there was a hacked-up anatomical jumble crammed against the container's bloodstained foam liner. He could see everything, everything, wedged into every possible space, awash in a soup of gore. Arms, legs, feet, other pieces of human beings he either couldn't or didn't want to identify . . .

Everything but the heads, and the hands.

He turned away from the horrible sight, clapped a palm over his mouth to fend off an attack of nausea. He was aware of Hendricks behind him now, peering over his shoulder at the gross butchery inside the crate. His radio up against his ear, the inspector was calling out for assistance in a cracking, excited voice—either from airport security or the police, Bruford was too far out of his skull to tell. He heard a response squawk from the Customs inspector's handset, jerked his head around, and knew at a glance that Hendricks was struggling with the same kind of paroxysms he'd managed to subdue a moment before.

Their eyes met for an instant. The color had drained from Hendricks's cheeks until they turned an ashen gray.

"I told you," he gasped hoarsely, wringing the words through livid, contorted lips. *"Fucking Trinidad!"*

Then he covered his stomach with his hands, dou-
bled over, produced an awful retching noise, and
threw up all over his shoes.

SAN FRANCISCO BAY AREA, CALIFORNIA

"Hey, you!" said Marissa Vasquez without slowing
her jog in the sand. "Watch it!"

Felipe, who'd fallen a step or two behind Marissa,
reacted about the way she would have expected and
ignored her. Of course her zippy tone wasn't what she
might have called high in the intimidation factor . . .

"*Ouch!*" she said, feeling him pinch her rear end
again. "Thought I warned you to quit—"

Before she could finish protesting, Felipe caught
up to her, hooked an arm around her waist, and drew
her into his embrace.

"Sorry." He gave her a slyly playful smile. "Tried
to check myself."

Marissa threw her hands around his neck and
stood facing him on the beach in the chill early morning breeze.

"You're hopeless," she said.

He shrugged and pulled her gently but irresistibly
closer.

"You're also fouling up my pace," she said.

Felipe pulled her still closer, kissed her in the middle of her forehead.

"Bringing me down off my targeted heart rate," Marissa said. And who did *she* think she was kidding? She fell into his arms, her heart racing right along, her increasingly short breaths having more to do with what Felipe did to her—on and sometimes before contact—than the exertion of their run along the shore.

He kissed her again, lightly, his lips touching her left brow, her right, her eyelids, the tip of her nose, then brushing down over the corners of her mouth, and further down to her neck as his hand glided up and up over the front of her running jacket.

Marissa felt ripples of warmth. "Felipe . . ."

He tilted his head back, a glint in his dark brown eyes.

"I think you're heartbeat feels just fine," he said, putting his hand right *there*, cupping it over the firm swell of her breast.

"Felipe . . ."

"Fine as can be," he said huskily, and raised his other hand to her cheek, stroked her hair back behind her ear with delicate fingertips, a few strands at a time, and then guided her mouth to his mouth, and kissed her long and fully and deeply.

Her lips parted wide, hungry for him, Marissa felt his hand slide under her jacket and pressed herself against him to make it clear he could keep right on doing what he was, all the while surprised and further excited by her utter lack of modesty and self-consciousness. The early hour aside, this little beach on the Miller-Knox shoreline was a public place, and before Felipe Escalona entered her life that would have her made her far too uptight to carry on like a teenager having her first heavy make-out session. But this was what he did to her, and was how it had been for her since they'd met here almost a month ago to the hour, both out for Sunday morning jogs on the weekend before Easter.

They were yin and yang, opposites attracting, choose your favorite advice column canard for two very different types of people who seemed to make an ideal fit.

The only child of a Latino entrepreneur who ran a large San Francisco construction and real-estate development firm of his founding, Marissa was a few months shy of her twenty-first birthday, which would roughly coincide with her graduation from UC Berkeley, where she'd studied toward a BA in business administration and a minor degree in political science. Felipe, who was five years her senior, and whose trace of an accent hinted at his Mexican origins—he'd told her that his parents had immigrated from Guadalajara when he was a boy, and that he'd spent a couple of years in his native country earning a master's in Spanish language and literature—made his living as a freelance writer of bilingual educational materials, and was presently contracted with a software designer called Golden

Triangle to work on a program meant for high school classrooms. Easygoing and spontaneous, his tongue partially in cheek (or so Marissa assumed), Felipe insisted the key to his happiness and productivity was wearing sweatpants in his home office, and claimed the prospect of having to put on a suit and tie five days a week canceled out whatever lure a guaranteed wage might present.

By sharp contrast Marissa was pragmatic, sober, and normally controlled to an extreme, traits she believed came straight from her father, a man of strict discipline who had raised her as a single parent since she was ten, when terminal uterine cancer had claimed a still-youthful Yolanda Vasquez to deprive Marissa of a mother's affection. All her life Marissa had found that her success within ruled social and scholastic lines had been the surest way to please him, and pleasing him remained as important to her now as it ever was. She felt the need to channel her considerable energy and intelligence within the structure of an imposed routine, thrived in the academic grid of scheduled classes and exams, and could not envision a career without organizational security and a regular weekly paycheck. On entering the employment market after commencement, she hoped to expeditiously find a position with one of the corporate multinationals that would utilize her specialized academic skills.

In her amorous affairs Marissa's patterns of behavior always had been much the same—partitioned and ordered so as not to upset her normal balance. She'd cared for her two previous lovers and enjoyed the physical aspects of those relationships, but in each case the divide between their sexual intimacies and Marissa's reserved expressions of emotion had left both partners ultimately dissatisfied, and made her wonder if she suffered from an irremediable personality glitch. Yet from the very beginning with Felipe, their sex had been a sort of catalytic conversion, an act of abandon binding her heart and body to his in a wholly fulfilling way she had never believed she would experience.

Still Marissa knew that she and Felipe were really, essentially different from one another in *many* ways . . . just as she undeniably knew she'd fallen in love with him. For three of the past four weekends they had spent together, she had continued to allow that it might be simple infatuation, albeit with a giddy extra charge. But lying drowsily wrapped around Felipe at her Oxford Avenue apartment Friday night, her thoughts getting into a relaxed flow after they had exhausted their passions in bed, Marissa had found it impossible to conceive of losing what he had brought out in her, or sharing it with any other man, and acknowledged then that it was time to release whatever emotional reins she'd persisted in holding onto.

Being who she was, however, letting go of her emotions did not mean she could simply have them bolt the fences. Marissa needed a framework within which to display and share them, and sought unambiguous definition for her relationship with Felipe if she was to feel altogether comfortable with it. If the two of them were not yet a mutually and openly declared, exclusive, official *couple,* then maybe what they were having was just a disruptive sidetrack in the well-coordinated progress of her life, a fling that—like the others that had preceded it—would lead nowhere in the end. In those moments late Friday night after he'd brought her to unprecedented pleasure and gratification, taken her as far out of control as she had ever been, Marissa had drifted off to sleep thinking she wanted to take the next step toward romantic legitimacy and introduce him to her father, whose stamp of approval she strongly desired, even while worrying more than a bit that she might be rushing things. But to her relief Felipe had met the idea with enthusiasm when she broached it the next morning, and, seeing no point in further delay, she'd arranged for them to meet for brunch up at the family home in San Rafael later on today.

Right now though . . . right now Felipe was once again making it hard to think about later on. Or about anything.

Not with what he was doing to her.

He kept his eyes open while they kissed, as did Marissa, their gazes locked, remaining that way until after their mouths came apart.

"We should quit," she said, taking a breath, "before we do something against the law."

"I won't snitch."

"Somebody might see us."

"There's no one else around."

"This is a public beach."

"No one's around," he repeated. "It's six A.M."

"Right about the time it was when *we* met."

She looked at him.

He looked at her.

"I know where," he said. "Let's go back to the car."

"You're kidding."

"No."

Marissa's heart pounded. And those *tingles* coming from all the way down inside her . . .

"Felipe, this is crazy, we aren't through with our run," she said, her last bit of resistance sounding unbelievably lame to her own ears.

He slid his hand from under her jacket and T-shirt now, wrapped both arms around her waist, and pulled her hips against him, held her so close their clothes hardly seemed to give them any separation.

She gasped, swallowed.

"*Omigod.*"

Felipe nodded.

"Forget about running," he said. "Let's go while I can still walk."

She understood perfectly what he meant.

They had driven down from Marissa's place near the Berkeley campus, leaving her Outback in a sandy access road east of the tunnel that cut through the hills below Richmond Plunge. Tucked into a cove past the marina, the beach was a fairly secluded cul-de-sac pocketed in on its landward side by the split and crumbled remnants of an ancient cliff face, with the road where Marissa parked about midway along its irregular curve on the bay shore. Her usual habit was to trot to the cove from the vehicle and then start her laps in earnest, running to one end of the beach, then the other, and then doubling on back toward the access road to wind things up. She and Felipe had been in that final stage of their run when he had gotten to her with his bottom-pinching seduction, and they could see the road through some waist-high beach grass a short distance ahead to their right.

Her pulse raced as they walked toward it, holding hands. Felipe had gotten to her all right, gotten her weak-kneed with eagerness. Reaching the foot of the access road, she could feel whatever was left of her inhibitions sailing off toward the white gulls and cloud puffs overhead like helium balloons snipped from their strings.

Which made the unexpected sight of another parked vehicle a wholly frustrating comedown.

It was a Saturn wagon, one of those sporty new models designed to resemble sleeked out minivans, and it had been angled onto the side of the road opposite her car a few yards closer to the beach. Standing by the closed rear hatch with his back to them was a guy in a windbreaker, jeans, sneakers, and an army green field or baseball cap. He was bent over one of those large red-and-white beer coolers as if reorganizing its contents.

They paused at the foot of the road and exchanged looks.

"So much for us being alone," Marissa said, thinking Felipe seemed especially out of sorts. She sighed, let go of his hand to slip her water bottle from its pouch in her runner's belt, and took a long gulp. "Better have some," she said and handed him the bottle. "It'll cool you down."

Felipe lifted the water to his mouth and drank without a word, still seemingly unable to quite grasp the idea that there might be more than two early birds roaming the beach in the state of California.

He was passing the bottle back to Marissa when the guy behind the Saturn straightened from rummaging around in his cooler and turned to look at them.

His appearance caught Marissa by surprise. For whatever reason—his posture, or the way he was dressed, or maybe because of that oversized two-tone beer cooler—she had assumed he would be a youngish man, but the face under the bill of his cap was far from youthful. In fact it was incredibly ancient. Lined and wrinkled, its cheeks sagging in loose folds of flesh, the slits of its eyes peering at her from above a vulturous nose and scowling lips, it was also infinitely unpleasant . . .

Then Marissa noticed what he was holding in his right hand. What he'd drawn out of the cooler, keeping it briefly hidden from sight by his body as he turned. And all at once her surprised reaction jolted up to one of surpassing shock and fear.

Not at any point in the waking nightmare to come would Marissa be certain whether she realized the man was wearing a mask before she actually saw his weapon, what might have been an Uzi, or something like one. But she knew what was happening the instant she *did* see it, knew it was her fault, all hers . . . and knew that none of the protective structures she'd built to contain her orderly little world had kept the truth from breaking through at last.

The man raised his gun in front of him, and then the rear doors of the station wagon were flying open, and more men were exiting both sides, three of them spilling from the doors, sprinting across the sand toward her and Felipe with miniature submachine guns also in their hands and obvious disguises pulled over

their heads—a bearded pirate, a devil's head, a grinning skull.

Tears began to flood Marissa's eyes, further dis-
torting the grotesque Halloween shop faces, but she
held them back, checking them almost on reflex, refusing to succumb to panic. This was a public beach,
hadn't that been what she'd insisted? A public beach,
where any break in the quiet would stand out. Her
voice would carry, and someone might be close
enough to hear her scream. Driving, walking, on a bi-
cycle. Close enough to hear.

Make some noise, she demanded of herself. *Come
on, make some noise, scream your head off—*

But it was too late, the men from the wagon were on
her in a flash, surrounding her, a hand clapping over
her mouth to stifle her rising cry for help. *"Entra aqui!
A prisa!"* the one with the old man mask shouted to
the others in Spanish, telling them to hurry up. And an
instant later she was grabbed by the arms and shoulders and hustled toward the car with the metal bore of
a gun sticking into her back. Alongside her, and then
slightly ahead of her, Felipe was also jostled forward
at gunpoint, stumbling a little as they pushed him toward one of the wagon's open back doors.

He turned his head toward her, eyes wide, and
started to call out her name, but was punched hard
across the face by the man in the pirate mask before it
could fully escape his lips.

They shoved Felipe into the rear of the station

wagon as his legs crumpled underneath him, and moments later jammed Marissa through the same door, a gunman climbing into the backseat on either side of them, the others rushing around into the front.

This is my fault, she thought again mutely. *It's true, it's my fault, I should have known.*

And then the wagon's motor came to life, and Marissa was jerked back in her seat as it kicked into reverse, cut a sharp turn away from the beach, and went speeding off in a cloud of spun-up sand.

SAN JOSE, CALIFORNIA

"Trinidad," Megan Breen said to Nimec.

"What?"

"And Tobago," Megan said. "With Annie."

"Huh?"

"Annie, your lovely and beloved wife." She regarded him across her desk with mild amusement. "The place I mentioned . . . on Tobago, not Trinidad . . . is called Rayos del Sol. I'm sure you've heard of it."

Nimec sat with a blank expression on his face.

"Testing one-two-three, Pete," Megan said, and pointed to her ear. "Can you read me, or is it cochlear implant time?"

Nimec frowned. "I don't know what you're talking about."

"I'm talking about your hearing. I've noticed it seems to conk out whenever I ask you to do something that conflicts with plans you've already locked in on."

His frown deepened.

"I sat here listening to your Caribbean project update for half an hour," he said. "You want me to run every detail back to you, I'll be glad to oblige."

"Which I guess would make your deafness selective."

Nimec crossed his hands in a time-out gesture.

"We going to talk straight?" he said.

"I'd be peachy with that."

"I'm not getting shipped out to Trinidad. Not with Ricci on our front burner."

"Then we'll shift burners."

"That isn't fair."

"To him or us?" Megan said.

Nimec shrugged.

"Both, I suppose," he said. "Our lead field op being on indefinite suspension is the kind of thing that leaves everybody betwixt and between. UpLink's stuck without a replacement, Ricci can't move on with his life."

She looked at him, her large, intelligent green eyes holding steady on his face. Nimec braced for a difficult contest. He'd been in this spot with Meg before, or in similar spots, and didn't see any easy give in her right now.

"I'm prepared to occupy a solitary corner of limbo for a while," she said. "In a sense, we've been in it for over a month. Tom Ricci's got us in a bind with all three branches of government and every major law-enforcement agency you can name. Even our best friends at the Pentagon have started to distance themselves, which puts our pending defense contracts at risk. And you know the table's set for us to become the target of a public furor the moment any information about his one-man road show on the East Coast is declassified."

"Figure the people whose lives he saved from those terrorists might be a few million exceptions to popular opinion."

"And if it had gone the other way, I don't know that even God in all his mercy could forgive us," Megan said. "Ricci's secretive actions could as easily have made those people casualties, Pete. But that's over and *done*. He took us out of the decision-making loop by going it alone. Now it's his turn to wait outside it while we deal with the consequences." Megan paused. "You need some physical and mental distance from San Jose. A chance to order your thoughts before making a comfortable decision on whether he stays or goes."

Nimec held his silence. Behind Megan, her office window gave a curiously smog-bleared view of Mount Hamilton away to the north. He remembered its rugged flank as everlastingly vivid and imposing from Roger Gordian's office, which was just catercorner up the hall. But then, Meg's window was just that, a window. Gord's occupied an entire side of the room from floor to ceiling . . . really, it might be considered a glass wall. With that much light pouring through, Nimec supposed you would see well into the distance regardless of hazy environmental conditions. Anyway, it was impossible to make comparisons. And unfair. Gord was more or less retired. Megan had gotten a deserved promotion in rank to CEO and was more or less in charge of UpLink International's corporate affairs. The outlook from her office was the one Nimec had here before his eyes these days, and it remained consistent with the view he'd always appreciated next door. How could Meg be blamed if it wasn't as impressively crystal clear?

The simple fact was that, little by little, things had changed. And he'd have to accept it.

"Bottom line," he said after a moment, "you're telling me I need a vacation."

Megan shook her head.

"Wrong," she said. "Though I was afraid you'd see things that way."

"How am I supposed to see them?"

"It goes back to the project update you can supposedly recite back to me by heart," she said. "We've finished wiring Sedco Petroleum's deepwater rigs for fiberoptics. Within a month to six weeks we *should be* finished laying our submarine cables between Monos, Huevos, and Chacachacare—"

"Those islands in that strait over there?"

"Boca del Sierpe, right," Megan said. "The Serpent's Mouth. It separates Trinidad and Venezuela."

"Colorful name."

"Give due credit to Christopher Columbus," she said. "Anyway, we have to get on with some logistical decisions and I don't think we should wait too long . . . for our own sake, and because we owe it to the Trinidadians, who've done everything within their political and economic capabilities to make us feel welcome."

"As in footing a chunk of the bill for our fiber network."

"And hammering out that bargain rate government land lease for our base." Megan smiled wryly. "It's nice to know you really and truly *were* paying attention to me before."

Nimec shrugged in an offhand way.

"So we're looking at either converting our temporary hq on the southern coast to something permanent, or moving the facilities inland and closer to a developed area," he said. "I got that part. I realize there are different security issues depending on which site we choose . . ."

She flapped a hand in the air.

"Your turn to hit the pause button, Pete," she said. "Security could *determine* our choice, and that's the part I may not have stressed nearly enough. By this date next year we'll have upwards of a thousand employees living and working on that base, a substantial number of them with their families. You know, and I know, that what's convenient in terms of transportation, getting supplies in and out, those sorts of things, don't necessarily dovetail with what's safest for our personnel . . . and their well-being's my top concern." She paused. "I want your eyewitness perspective on which site makes the most sense. If you say we ought to stay put, fine, give me a list of suggestions on how existing security systems can be upgraded to the highest possible level. If you think changing locations would be best, I'd like your reasons laid out in a nice, bulleted report I can hand the board of directors along with my proposed budget."

Nimec considered that.

"I might've been sold on the trip if it wasn't for the vacation pitch," he said. "It'd take three, maybe four days for targeted inspections with Vince Scull's risk assessments in my hip pocket. But I can't see how to justify two weeks away from here."

Meg smiled, combed her fingers back through a long, thick sheet of auburn hair. "Pete, you've got to be the only man on this planet who'd fight to avoid this assignment. And you still haven't heard me say 'vacation.'"

"You call staying at some tropical resort *work*?"

Megan looked at him.

"Pull teeth all you want, I can stand the pain," she

said. "You don't need me to tell you Rayos del Sol isn't just another getaway. It's an exclusive resort that caters to the world's most powerful individuals . . . including our own past and present heads of state. It's spread across an entire island in the Serpent's Mouth and has its own international airport and ocean harbor. And lest we forget, it has a security force that's been assembled by a former head of the French GIGN, Henri Beauchart, who would very much like to personally compare notes with our security chief." She looked at him. "We should also keep in mind that its controlling owners include members of the Trinidadian parliament who have ties to Sedco, and are highly supportive of UpLink International's regional presence. They're eager to put their lush native paradise on proud display for us."

There was another pause. Nimec thought some more, tugged his earlobe, leaned forward.

"I've been waiting for you to mention those e-mails you got a couple weeks back," he said.

"My intention was to save them for a last-but-not-least." Megan shrugged a little. "Every aspect of this deal's been written about in the financial press, including the Rayos del Sol/Sedco connection. To be perfectly honest, I'd dismiss the messages as a nasty prank . . . somebody's bush league attempt at throwing a wrench into things . . . if it wasn't for that. Vague claims of accounting, inventory, and shipping irregularities at Rayos del Sol with nothing to back them up. Our nameless whistle-blower didn't see fit to specify *which* inventories or shipments are supposed to be questionable, or even explain why he or she would choose to make the allegations to an Up-Link executive." She gave another shrug. "As I said, it's all so insubstantial I'm tempted to ignore it. But it's probably worth checking out while you're there."

"On vacation," Nimec said.

Megan's eyes were on him again.

"Repeat the word a hundred times, I still won't understand why you find it so abhorrent," she said. "Nor will I concede it's even applicable. You have legitimate professional reasons for making the trip."

"And for bringing along my wife, some fresh cabana shirts, and maybe a jug of suntan lotion."

"No crime, Pete," Megan said. "Your job's taken you to some very unfriendly places. That doesn't mean you'd be cheating your responsibilities by visiting a hospitable clime for a change. This isn't the sort of opportunity that comes around very often. Enjoy it on the company's tab. Bring Annie so she can enjoy it, too, I guarantee it'll do both of you a ton of good—"

Nimec shook his head.

"We've got Chris and Linda," he said. "*They've* got school."

"They also have a grandmother to see they get there and back every day."

He gave another head shake. "Annie's mom lives in Kansas City."

"And she just might be available," Megan said. "In fact, she'd probably love the chance to come visit the kids and spoil them rotten."

Nimec started to say something, stopped, at a sudden loss.

"What makes you sound so sure?" he said after a moment.

Megan held her hands out and wriggled her fingers.

"A mildly psychic hunch," she said, smiling.

Nimec felt as if he was looking at a good-natured hijacker.

He smoothed a hand over his hair, slightly grown out from his preferred brush cut at Annie's insistence. What was it she'd said the other morning? Her remark had come out of the blue—or so it seemed to Nimec at the time—when he'd been readying himself for work, their bathroom's skylit brightness washing over him as he knotted his tie in front of the mirror.

"Ricci's Field," she'd said from over his shoulder. *"Oh how does your garden grow."*

Nimec had glanced questioningly at Annie's reflection, noticed the sobriety in her smile.

"This gray patch," she'd explained, and fondly scratched the side of his head. "We should dedicate it to Tom Ricci. Post a little handmade sign that says how much we really owe him for putting it there."

Looking himself over in the mirror, Nimec hadn't managed to smile back at her.

Now he sat opposite Megan in silence, his eyes returning to the blurry view of San Jose that filled her window. He thought about all the opinions of Ricci he'd heard, more than he could accurately recall. Sometimes he would hear a single person give contradictory opinions in what almost seemed to be the same breath. A lot of them seemed to have equal or nearly equal merit. But only three voices counted in deciding whether Ricci had become an unsalvageable liability. Meg had already gone down on record that she'd had enough of him. Rollie Thibodeau had been cagier about his sentiments, which was pretty uncharacteristic for someone who normally had no trouble expressing himself. But he'd always disliked and distrusted Ricci, and seemed resentful of sharing the title of global field supervisor with him. He also normally aligned with Meg on important decisions involving the company's security arm. That, Nimec mused, left him straddling the fence alone. If a vote were taken that very morning, he was betting it would come out two-to-one in favor of Ricci's permanent dismissal. A delay might be his only shot at a different result, and Nimec wasn't too sure he could find a totally honest and unbiased rationale for why Ricci would deserve it. Or that Ricci, who'd returned none of his phone calls for the past several days, would even *want* to stick around, which might prove to be the real kicker in the end.

Nimec looked out at the somewhat indistinct contours of the mountain a while longer, turning things over in his mind. There were decisions and there were decisions. Some were tougher than others, and with good reason. When you had one that couldn't be reversed and worried endlessly about the consequences of getting it wrong, Nimec guessed that ought to be reason enough to rank it high on the difficulty scale. And maybe knocking a week or two off the calendar was exactly what he needed to get the decision ahead of him right.

Another full minute of silence passed before he brought his eyes back to Megan's face.

"Hope you're okay holding down the fort while I visit Shangri-la," he said with a relenting sigh.

"Fret not," she said. "I'll keep our stockades guarded round the clock."

"You and Gramma Caulfield?"

Megan smiled, reached across the desk, and gave his wrist a fond little pat.

"Leave it to us womenfolk, *pardnuh,*" she said.

TERRITORIAL TRINIDAD

Jarvis wanted to believe the chopper wasn't out searching for him. Even as he opened the motorboat's throttle to push it faster downriver than any boat piloted by a sane man should be moving in the pitch darkness, he was wishing he could convince himself they would not do so drastic a thing, send a helicopter into the air after *him*, a small and unimportant person in their big, important world. Someone who'd not taken so much as an unearned cent from them, and did not let his eyes stray far from the grounds he kept in nice, trim shape for his weekly paycheck. And why not think he'd be found deserving of a fair turn? *An honest, hardworkin' gardener is Jarvis Lenard, we'll make an exception an' let him be,* they might have said. *Save some trouble, ya know. Leavin' aside that bad seed family relation of his, what have we to fear from the man?*

Jarvis had to smile grimly at the thought. And right so. The bird might be whipping over that southern shore for some purpose other than to track him down. Just as the Sunglasses might've come poking around the employee commons for a reason besides his connection to poor Udonis. If he were to give his imagination a stretch, Jarvis supposed he could come up with an explanation that *didn't* involve his cousin for the Sunglasses having asked about him in that menacing way of theirs, wanting to know this and that and the other thing from anyone they could seek out that knew him. Surely he could, and no doubt his words would find an accepting ear . . . but the truth would remain the truth all the same. His mother hadn't raised any fools under her roof, and it was too late in the day to eat a plate full of lies and nonsense, especially those served up raw by his own brain. Not after hiding for almost a week in the bush with only the few supplies he'd taken from his cabin. Not since spending every dollar he'd saved over these past years, every dollar and *more,* to grease the hands of a bald hair parasite for use of his flimsy little seventeen-footer. And most especially not at this moment, while he was shooting along the channel at—what was his speed just now?—Lord Almighty, sixty miles an hour, *sixty* on a moonless night, heading out to the open sea.

The truth was the truth. Right so, right so. It was there in the sky above that Jarvis Lenard had his evidence.

The copter was out prowling the night for him. The Sunglasses never gave up. *Sinister, menacin' bastards, yeh.* Weren't going to quit until they found him, caught him trying to reach the mainland. And Jarvis knew that if they did, he would come to the same bloody end as his cousin Udonis and those men out of Point Hope he'd hired to bring him away safe.

Jarvis glanced over at the left side of the channel, where a forest of mangrove trees had crept toward the water's marshy bank, their air roots groping out over the mud and rushes like slender, covetous feelers. Though the helicopter was not yet in sight, he could tell it was close upon him from the loud knocking of its blades, and didn't need to check the GPS box on the motorboat's control console to know there was a long way to travel before he reached the inlet. Proba-

bly his bow lights would be enough to guide him—
bright new kryptons, they were, he'd received that
much good treatment from the bloodsucking waterfront leach in exchange for emptying his wallet—and
Jarvis supposed he could have found his course
through the river's many twistings and turnings by
second nature after having lived his whole thirty-five
years on earth near its shores. But say he reached the
Serpent's Mouth before daybreak? What lay ahead of
him then? A journey of many miles around the cape,
with a chance he would be coming into Cedros Bay
against the tidal current, all depending how fast he
could navigate.

Could be it would have been none the worse if
sweet Nan hadn't given him a heads-up and he'd
stayed put, just waited for the Sunglasses to come for
him. Could be. But why bother his mind with second
guesses, eh? There were times when you had to make
your choice and to stick to it whatever the outcome.

Jarvis darted along the curving waterway, his bow
high, heavy sheets of spray lashing against the outboard's windscreen as he breasted the surface. Still
he was unable to leave the noise of the chopper behind . . . indeed the sound of its blades seemed closer
than before. Holding steady as he could, he once
again flicked a glance over his shoulder toward the
south bank.

That was when he got his first fearful look at it, a

sleek black shadow which might have blended seam-
lessly into the night except for the tiny red and blue
pricks of the running lights on its sides and tail. The
helicopter whirred in over the mangroves he'd just
left behind, a spotlight in its nose washing the treetops in sudden brilliance. Jarvis saw them churn from
its rapid descent, their interwoven branches beaten
into wild contortions by the downdraft of its rotors.

The long shaft of the beam sliced ahead of the oncoming bird, roved over the trees and across the reeds
to the water. It made a quick sweep over and past
Jarvis, and then reversed direction and locked on his
speeding craft.

Jarvis kept his eyes raised for only a moment before he brought them back to his windscreen, blinking as much from fear and agitation as the somehow
otherworldly glare. His hands clenched around the
butterfly wheel, he shot into high gear and poured on
speed, pushing the outboard to its max, holding onto
that wheel, feeling its jerky resistance and holding on
tight, certain the wheel would tear free of his grip if
he loosened it the slightest bit, spin right out of his
fingers and send the boat careening onto its side.

The helicopter attached its trajectory to him even
as he struggled to retain control. Cutting across the
shoreline to the river, it veered sharply west and then
swooped down low at Jarvis's back, came down in
pursuit like an enormous predatory nighthawk, the

fixed, fierce eye of its spotlight shafting him with brightness. And the *noise,* Jarvis had never heard anything like it. The *knock-knock-knock* of the copter's rotors beating the air had transformed into a deafening roar as it drew closer and closer, and the sound that assaulted him now seemed to outwardly echo and amplify the accelerated pounding of his heart.

And then, out of that clamor, a voice from the bird's public address system: *"Bring the boat to a halt! We mean no harm! I repeat, Jarvis Lenard, we mean no harm!"*

Jarvis raced around a looping bend in the channel, hoping to buy whatever thin slice of time he could, aware that separating himself from the helicopter would be almost impossible.

He felt no surprise when it stuck to his tail as he took the turn, then gained on him, pulling practically overhead, its spot blazing down like the noonday sun.

"We want only your cooperation!" the voice blared over its loudspeakers. *"I repeat, we want only—"*

Jarvis squinted, trapped in the lights, struggling to stay his course while barely able to see what lay ahead. Cooperation, no harm, was that what they'd told Udonis and the rest when they caught them? As if the Sunglasses would find someone like him worthy of their attention, bother to dig up his name, ask his whereabouts of every acquaintance whose path he might have crossed lately, and then send a helicopter into the air after him—a search helicopter in the hours between midnight and dawn—without harmful intent. And was there any chance they had sent the bird up alone?

No, no, Jarvis thought. The Sunglasses, they did not operate so. Others from the fleet would be headed his way, he knew. Closing in at that very moment, launched off their pads or turned from patrols elsewhere on the peninsula, all of them summoned over their radios by the helicopter that had picked him up. And while no proof had ever been given to him, he'd heard talk among the employees that they carried electronic eyes that could penetrate the darkness, guide them straight to him in the night, make an image of a man by reading the heat that came off his body.

Cooperation. No harm.

Jarvis again considered those words with a black and stinging sort of amusement—and all in an instant had an idea. Perhaps it wasn't so bad that they expected him to give up trying to scram with a simple, trusting smile on his face. Jarvis Lenard's mother hadn't raised any fools, no she hadn't. But if the Sunglasses were expecting to find one tonight, he would be right glad to oblige and give them a peek at what they wanted.

A peek and nothing more, though.

His hand on the shift, Jarvis throttled back hard,

cutting the engine with a jolt that nearly sent him overboard. He held onto the wheel, swaying to and fro, afraid the lightweight boat would capsize from its abrupt power-down.

The helicopter, meanwhile, came gliding straight on from behind and pulled to a hover not thirty feet above his head, hanging there almost like a toy dangled on a string, its blades churning the water to make the boat pitch even more violently. A hand over his eyes to shield them from the aircraft's bright light and blasting wind, Jarvis craned his head back and saw two helmeted crewmen behind its bubble window.

"Remain calm, Mr. Lenard, you're doing fine," the voice from inside the chopper called out. *"We're sending down a rescue basket, and will give you instructions on how to exit the boat once it's lowered."*

Bathed in the unremitting brightness of the spots, Jarvis finally had to break into a grin. He could not help himself, ah no, not after having heard that voice speak the word *rescue*. The men up there had gotten a look at a fool out here, surely he'd given it to them . . . but looks could deceive, as the old saying went.

Jarvis saw a hatch open in the belly of the chopper, watched the basket begin to descend at the end of its line, took a very deep breath, and held it.

Then, his lungs filled to capacity with oxygen, he tore his knitted dread bag from his head, cast it into the wind of the blades, and plunged headlong over the side of the boat into the river.

POINT FORTIN, TRINIDAD

Jean Luc watched Tolland Eckers emerge from the field office and knew he was about to receive word that wasn't good. The security man's stiffly erect walk and hiked up shoulders said it all; he seemed to be overcompensating for the urge to hang his head as he approached.

"I've got that update you ordered from Team Gray-wolf, sir," Eckers said, his voice raised above the thrum of the oil pumps. "It's disappointing, but their search operation is still at an early stage."

Jean Luc leaned back against the Range Rover, holding the protective helmet he'd worn for his inspection at his side. Besides the doffed hard hat with its goggle and earmuff attachments, he had on jeans, tan mocs, and an open-collared indigo linen shirt that was perhaps a half shade darker than the strikingly blue eyes that regarded Eckers from under his tanned brow.

"I want the simple details, Toll," he said.

"Would you prefer hearing them now or on the drive back—?"

"Start right here," Jean Luc said. "Just be kind enough to spare me the excuses."

Eckers took a cautious look around from behind his Ray-Bans while a truck rumbled slowly past on the dirt road to their left, ferrying a group of rough-necks toward the wells.

"The man in that boat's been positively identified as our groundskeeper," he said after a moment. "It took a while to confirm this from our photos—bad angle. The bird didn't pull overhead until right at the last minute, and he was wearing a dread bag that made it difficult to see his features." He paused. "A dread bag, that's one of those knitted caps some of the locals wea—"

"I was born and raised on this island," Jean Luc interrupted. "My time away didn't result in severe loss of memory."

Eckers didn't speak. A warm mid-morning breeze ruffled his loose-fitting guayabera shirt.

"I think we were already clear about who was out there," Jean Luc said. "A man doesn't head full-tilt for the open sea at two A.M. without some pressing reason. Not from where he did, and not on a crap motorboat."

Eckers stood there uneasily another moment, then nodded.

"Yes," he said. "Of course."

"We know it was Lenard, and we know he took a dive out of the boat . . . to everybody's surprise but mine," Jean Luc said. "The question is, Toll, can we say what happened to him afterward?"

Eckers shook his head.

"I'm sorry, sir, we can't with absolute certainty," he said. "Our general feeling is that he drowned, though. The current's pretty strong over near the lower tip of the peninsula. There's soft riverbank—a mix of clay and sand—for a stretch that runs several miles up and down the channel from the point where Lenard abandoned the outboard. Vegetation's weeds and cattails, some scrub growth. Our trackers are familiar with this kind of surface geography, and they'd have likely discovered evidence if he made it ashore. Footprints in the mud, bent or snapped rushes, something of that nature—"

Jean Luc cut him off. "I assume the scuba teams are on this."

"Since last night."

"And they've found nothing? No sign of him?"

Eckers hesitated. Jean Luc looked at him, waiting.

"The dread bag was retrieved from the water about a half mile down from where the son of a bitch took his plunge," Eckers said. "That's it."

"The dread bag."

"Right." Eckers inhaled. "Again, the search is in its initial stages. We've got experience with this sort of thing and the resources to back it up."

There was a brief silence. Jean Luc's eyes remained steady on Eckers.

"Lenard's from that village," he said.

Eckers nodded.

"I see what you're thinking," he said. "Those people know their way around the island. And they're protective of their own."

"Aren't they?"

"As far as that first goes, without a doubt," Eckers said. "They've been there for generations. But a lot of them live in poverty or near poverty and won't need much incentive to give up what they know."

Jean Luc watched his face another moment. Then a smile crept across his strong, full-lipped mouth.

"Take me back to Bonasse," he said, and reached behind him to open the Rover's passenger door. "We'll talk more on the way home."

They got in, Eckers behind the wheel, and drove along the dirt vehicle path across the production fields to the Southern Trunk Road. On their left, pump rods moved up and down over the established well-heads in steady rhythmic fashion. On the right, enormous derricks soared above the newer drill sites, their various mechanical systems powered by humming diesel engines and generators. Beyond these were the storage and refinery tank farms, and further to the northeast the delivery terminals on the Gulf of Paria, barely visible now in the bright blue-green reflectiveness of Caribbean morning sunlight and seawater.

Jean Luc sat in the Rover's comfortable air-conditioning and waved a hand toward the fields as they bumped along.

"You know, when I look out at all this, it would be

easy to see two hundred and fifty years of family ac-
complishment," he said. "But it isn't my perspective.
It wasn't my father's, or my grandfather's, or great-
grandfather's. I'm a *now* kind of person. I focus on
each opportunity as it's presented. That's how I was
raised, a sensibility that's been instilled in me. It's
how I run my life and business." He gestured out the
window again. "What I see out there are separate
parts of a whole, individual projects at distinct, ongo-
ing stages of development. I look at a well that's ten,
fifteen years old, ask myself whether it's almost
tapped out, or peaking, or somewhere in between,
and then ask whether its efficiency can be improved.
I see a thumper rolling over a particular location, or
possibly a rig going up, and make a mental note to
have the latest seismological and core sample data on
my desk *toot suite* . . . Can you appreciate where I'm
coming from, and how it relates our current problem,
Toll?"

Eckers made a quick turn to put them on the main
route.

"You're saying not to lump sum it," he said, nodding.

Jean Luc looked across the seat at him and grinned.

"Nicely put," he said. "And right on. Experience is
always helpful, but you can be lulled by past success.
What we need is to reset our priorities, focus on today instead of"—his grin widened—"our master
plan, if you'll pardon my being cute."

Eckers gave another thoughtful nod.

They rode in silence for the next forty miles, crossing the peninsula on the Trunk, a smooth multilane blacktop that dipped inland from the constellation of industrial towns around the petroleum fields and then swung southwest through undisturbed woodlands toward the beaches, sugar plantations, and fishing villages of Cedros.

Just short of an hour after they had left oil country behind, Eckers made the long, curving turn off the road that brought them within sight of the estate grounds and, high on a hill behind a spread of cedar copses, topiary, and ornamental gardens, the grand Colonial mansion with its witch's hat turrets wrapped in balconies of stone.

"I'll reset and reorganize the search," he said, passing through the electronic entry gate. "See that our men—our assigned *specialists*—understand Lenard has to be their first priority."

"As if our world stands or falls on finding him," Jean Luc said. "In the meantime, I'd better massage our partners at Los Rayos. With their having gotten confirmation that the visitor from UpLink will be coming, this episode's bound to have made them uptight."

"Beauchart's given them his reassurances."

"They'll want to hear from me anyway," Jean Luc said. He paused. "Suppose I might as well make a call to Washington while I'm at it."

Eckers glanced at him.

"Are you surprised?" Jean Luc said.

Eckers shrugged a little.

"Some," he said. "I wasn't sure you'd need to do that."

"I don't. Not absolutely. Not *yet*. But there's the history. The connection between our families. Respecting it's another of my ingrained traits." Jean Luc paused again; Eckers's silence betrayed his reservations. "No fear, Toll, I haven't contracted the honesty bug . . . I suppose you could say fair's fair between Drew and myself, though," he said. "If I expect him to play by my rules of the game, I have to respect his."

Eckers looked as if he was about to say something, but then moved on without another word. He went up the drive to where it rimmed the mansion's front court, pulled over to the low curb, and stopped the vehicle.

"Do you want me to stay on the grounds?" he said as Jean Luc got out.

Jean Luc leaned his head back in the door and shook it once.

"That's okay, I'd prefer you get back to the hunt," he said. "And don't forget our chat. Take one thing at a time, Toll. One thing at a time and we'll be fine."

Eckers nodded and became very still, staring out the windshield through his dark lenses again. Jean Luc studied him a moment, withdrew his head from the Rover, pushed the door shut, and turned up the courtyard toward the house.

A moment later Eckers spun away from the curb and started back down the drive to the gate.

SAN JOSE, CALIFORNIA

Tom Ricci knew as he awoke that he was hung over. It was the dry graininess in his eyes, the sour taste on his tongue, the headache and burning stomach. This wasn't his first time, not by far, and he knew.

He stretched out a hand, found the other side of the bed empty, and lay back in the morning light eking through the window blinds. He remembered her drawing them shut while he'd started to undress her, tugging at the cord as he worked on her blouse from behind. The pile of clothing had built up fast. Hers first, then his—they'd made a bet at the bar and he'd won. Ricci had gaps in his recollection of the night before, but that was among the parts that had stuck. There were enough of those, especially of what they'd done when they got back to her place, even if he couldn't recall what their bet had been over.

He remained very still, his head on the pillow, not bothering to look around for her. She was in the kitchenette; he could hear her through its Dutch doors, opening and closing the cabinet, moving things around. Her apartment was small, a studio— hard to get lost in here for very long.

A minute or two passed. Ricci listened to her in the kitchenette, holding out the slim hope that she'd put up some coffee. But he didn't hear the maker gurgling and supposed he'd have caught whiff of a finished pot.

He pulled off his covers, sat up naked on the edge of the bed, felt his brain slosh against his skull. He was slower leaning down to check for his holstered FiveSeven, making sure it was there underneath the bed where he'd left it.

Devon appeared from the kitchen entrance wearing a short robe of some silky black material and carrying a black melamine serving tray in both hands. She collected Melmac and vintage Ray-Bans and body jewelry, bought them through online auctions. With only two closets and a single cupboard over its half-height refrigerator for storage, her apartment became easily cluttered, but she kept the place neat and planned to start looking for a bigger one soon. The sunglasses were professional accessories, she said. For her costumes when she danced. She'd had the strategic piercings done for work *and* play, but keep it quiet from the IRS, she said. Melmac was strictly a hobby, and she liked the black pieces best. Black was her favorite color, and "black velvet" was the hardest shade of Melmac to find, she said.

Ricci supposed he'd learned a few things about her that weren't in the basic course requirements.

She crossed the room to the bed in her bare feet, a

bottle of Drambuie and two crystal cordial glasses on the Melmac tray, their drinks already poured. She set the tray down on the nightstand, picked up the glasses, carried them over to him, and held his out.

Ricci looked at her fingers around the glass. Their nails were long and carefully painted and manicured. She paid a lot of attention to her appearance and he supposed some of that would be for professional reasons, too.

"Hair of the dog," she said.

"Maybe we ought to try those morning-after pills."

Devon kept his glass between them without lowering it, gave him a slight smile over its rim.

"I already took one, just a different kind," she said, and wobbled the glass. "Come on. My arm's getting stiff."

"No," he said.

"I thought we weren't supposed to use that word."

"Who says?"

"You," she replied. "Last night."

Ricci looked at her. The two of them hadn't done a lot of sleeping, and her large blue eyes were a little bloodshot. In the timid light coming through the blinds, with her makeup off, he could see faint dark crescents under them.

By tonight, when she danced under the bright lights, she would have erased or covered up the dark spots, made sure she was looking fresh for her admirers. Keeping up that appearance.

"We've been drinking too much," he said.

She put the Drambuie in his hand, reached for her own glass, and sat close beside him on the bed, her legs crossed yoga-style, the hem of her robe brushing up their bare thighs.

"Here, here," she said.

They clinked and drained their glasses and sat holding them in silence. Ricci felt the warmth of the sweet, powerful liqueur spread through him.

"It'd be good if we went out for a walk," he said. "Got some air, put something solid in our stomachs."

She moved closer to him, put a hand on his shoulder.

"It would be better if we stay right here and mess around," she said.

Ricci glanced at the display of his WristLink wearable. Nice that they hadn't made him turn it in with his Sword tag.

"It's almost noon," he said.

"I'm not due at the club till five o'clock."

"Happy hour."

"Maybe for the regulars." Devon shrugged her shoulders. "We've got all day."

Ricci looked at her. "What about A.J.?"

Devon shifted her body a little but stayed there close against him.

"You didn't have to mention him."

"He might decide he wants to see you."

"That's what answering machines are for," she said. "He never shows up without calling first."

"And you won't care about the phone ringing. Or him leaving messages on the machine."

"I'll turn off the ringer, and you can distract me from the blinking light." She paused. "A.J. doesn't decide who I will or won't fuck."

Ricci looked at her.

"Kind of obvious," he said.

They studied each other awhile. Then Ricci lowered his eyes to his empty glass and smiled a little.

"What's so funny?" she said.

Ricci shrugged.

"I'm not sure," he said. "Maybe something about my sitting here with no clothes on, and talking about us having an affair behind your married boyfriend's back."

Devon massaged his arm with her fingertips.

"Since when does it bother you?" she said.

Ricci shrugged a second time, leaned across her, reached for the open bottle of Drambuie on the nightstand, and refilled their glasses.

"Bottoms up," he said.

They drank and sat quietly on the bed. Then Ricci took the glass from her hand, put it on the tray alongside his own.

When he turned back to her, she had loosened the sash of her robe, let the robe fall partially open around her body.

He looked into her eyes. They were still a little red

and also overbright now from the alcohol. Probably his weren't any different.

He kept his gaze on hers without saying anything, and reached out, and tugged her robe the rest of the way open a bit roughly, and holding it like that moved his eyes down to her breasts, and let them linger there before taking a long look at the rest of her, and then slowly brought them back to her eyes. He was aware all the while of her touch on his leg, her hand probing, taking hold of him as greedily as his eyes had taken in her body.

"We don't have any shame," Ricci said.

"Like you said, we drink too much."

Ricci looked at her, his head swimming.

"That our excuse?"

"If you need one," she said, and then shrugged out of the robe, and fell into his arms.

He kissed her, and she tumbled onto her back with her mouth against his, biting his lower lip, running her nails over his shoulders, and down his back, and down, digging them into his skin.

The smooth silk of the open robe bunched in his fist, his face tightened into what almost might have been a look of pain, Ricci moved over her, a hard thrust that she arched her hips to receive.

"What about our walk?" she said, the words coming out in a broken moan.

"We've got all day," Ricci said.

TWO

IT WAS AFTER MIDNIGHT WHEN THE LINCOLN
Navigator reached the outskirts of Devoción, a tiny
dust spot on the road some forty miles south of the
U.S. border and roughly midway between Mexicali
and the smuggler's hive of Tecate. Unmarked by direction posts, excluded from most maps of the Peninsula for its slumbery irrelevance to tourists, Devoción
was known to locals as the birthplace and original
home territory of the brothers Lucio and Raul
Salazar, two of the three Magi of Tijuana—*Los
Rayos Magos de Tijuana*, in Spanish—so called for
the blessings and protection they had once bestowed
upon their underlings and lesser allies in a wide-

spread theft, money laundering, and narcotics trafficking empire they built from scratch.

Devoción translates directly into English as "devotion," a word defined as a profound, earnest attachment or religious dedication.

The Spanish give it another meaning as well: to be at another's full and absolute disposal.

For the three decades that the Salazars controlled their native stronghold, it was the latter definition that its sparse peasant community might have best understood. Yet while fear was a constant for them, and obedience to the cartel law, they were grateful for the many tangible dividends of their loyalty. It had meant a meager but steady income, food on the table, and good clothes gifted to the children at Christmas. It had meant paved sidewalks for the town's main street, a new church, and even a movie house that screened first-run American films. Disloyalty would bring swift retribution, but the magnanimity of those who governed was never without strings, and the clear-cut threat of knife and gun could be easier to abide than the hypocrisy of corrupt *Federales* and their stacked courtrooms.

This state of affairs had undergone an explosive upheaval when Lucio Salazar and his rival Enrique Quiros were killed on a night of vengeance and rumored double-cross up over the border in San Diego. No one in Devoción seemed to quite know what ignited the bloody violence. But the warfare between their formerly cooperative families had left the Salazars on the losing end of the struggle, and allowed Enrique's successors to extend Quiros dominance into their vacated borderland territories, including the village at the real and symbolic heart of Salazar power.

Afterward, Devoción had quickly settled down to life as usual. Its five hundred or so inhabitants now pledged allegiance to the Quiros family, who, like their predecessors, continued to put bread and butter on their tables in return. Streets were dusty, faces were resigned and suspicious, and the kids bouncing through the alleys at all hours wore clean white Nike sneakers come the holidays. At the south edge of town, the chop shop garage that was a pet operation of the Salazars—whose lawless careers had started out with their driving hot American cars down across sierra country to the ports of San Felipe and La Fonda, where they were crated and shipped overseas—remained as active as when Lucio had taken in multimillion-dollar profits from the cannibalized auto parts racket, perhaps more so since the garage had become a roof for other lucrative areas of criminal distribution.

A competent mechanic was rarely undervalued, and every man who had worked there for Lucio had retained his job.

The Navigator, boosted up north, had been headed to the chop shop for disassembly when things went crazy.

In its driver's seat, his eyes throbbing in his skull, so wide open with fear and apprehension they felt ready to pop from their sockets, Raul Luiza suddenly recognized the tall, broad shape of Devoción's Catholic church up ahead on his left. His hands moist around the steering wheel, he saw the church, saw the enormous cross atop its spire outlined darkly against the yellow moon, and realized with fresh dread that time was running out. *La Iglesia de Jesus Christos*, it was named. The Church of Jesus Christ. But it was the name of Quiros that the villagers had been calling on to answer their prayers for the past couple of years, the same as he'd done in his own way.

Tonight, though, Raul had started the long list of regrets he'd compiled in his mind wishing to Jesus, the Virgin Mother, and all the blessed saints that he'd never heard of it. From there he'd moved on to wishing he'd listened to his old lady for once, hung at Anna's crib like she'd practically begged of him. Had he done that, stayed there with her, they could have stepped out to score some rock, put the kid to bed early, everything would have been different. But he'd ignored her, and instead hustled over to the car dealership, where it all turned bad for him, turned to absolute *shit* in a hurry—

Raul tightened his sweaty, trembling grip on the wheel. He could remember his cousins in Devoción wanting to parade through town with joy when the

Quiros family moved in, remember them chirping like *perequitos* about how those dudes walked a young man's walk, talked a young man's talk, dudes were players who brought some San Diego *street* with them, a big city style that would open doors most people hadn't even dreamed of knocking on when those old-school fat cats the Salazars were on top.

Even in his gaining despair, Raul thought that was kind of funny. In fact, he might have laughed aloud if he hadn't suspected that was something the man in the backseat would want explained . . . and he'd already asked too many questions, following every answer Raul him gave with another.

Now Raul passed the rear of the church as the road swung off to his right along the foot of the low mesa west of town. He took a final glance at the cross staring down from high above him, then turned his attention back to the road even before the church vanished from sight behind the curve of the mesa's slope.

Raul drove on, his tremors growing steadily worse . . . and it wasn't all because of nerves. *Goddamn*, he thought. *Goddamn.* If his stem had been in his pocket, he'd have tried to talk the head case in back into letting him stop on the way down from Chula Vista, take a few pulls. Just a couple on his way down and he would've been okay. Or okay enough to keep his hands steady on the wheel. But the guy had stamped his kit into the sidewalk, dumped his vials and everything else down a sewer after frisking him clean—

"How long until we're at the shop?"

Raul jerked at the sound of the voice behind him.

"I tol' you," he said without glancing over his shoulder. "Wasn't five minutes ago I *tol' you* . . ."

"Tell me again."

Raul took a breath. He'd driven the entire distance from Chula trying to convince himself he'd make it through this jam, find a way to get out of it alive and whole if he could only manage to keep his cool.

"Two, three miles up, we gon' see it," he said. "Be onna left side th' road."

"Describe it to me."

"Jus' a garage, you know."

"Describe it."

Raul shrugged tensely.

"Place made 'a big cement blocks. Sorta square, got no windows. There a parkin' lot goes aroun' it . . ."

"A paved parking lot."

"Uh-huh. Like I say before—"

"I want to hear more about the garage," the guy behind him cut in. "How many entrances does it have for vehicles?"

"Two in front, two onna side."

"The south side?"

"Yeah."

"Means they'd be facing us when we pull up, that right?"

"Yeah, right."

There was a beat of silence. The Navigator's high-beams slid over the road.

"Tell me what else is nearby," the guy in the back-seat said.

"Lotta nothin'."

"Describe 'nothing' to me."

Raul took another breath. This was some kind of scary hombre he'd picked up, not that he'd done it by choice. Wore a black jacket and pants with all kinds of outside pouches and shit, besides having one of them SWAT cop masks, or hoods, or whatever it was called, pulled down around his neck. Except Raul was pretty convinced he wasn't a cop.

"Ain' no houses, no stores, nothin'," he said. Then hesitated, thinking. " 'Cept, you know, the junkyard."

"What kind?"

"Huh?"

"What kind of junk gets dumped there?"

Raul grunted his understanding.

"All kinda parts for cars," he said.

"You're sure."

"Right—"

"You have some reason for not mentioning this yard to me before?"

Raul shook his head. The motherfucker never got

tired of grilling him, asking the same questions over and over in different ways . . .

"Wasn't keepin' no secrets, that what you mean," he said. "Thought you was askin' about *buildings*."

The guy didn't answer. Raul glanced at him in the rearview mirror, saw a look on his face that he'd already noticed more than once. He'd gone perfectly still, his head kind of tilted to the side, his upper lip curled back a little, his eyes far off and at the same time right *there* and honed in . . . the way a cat looked when it was waiting for some rodent to crawl out of a hole so it could pounce and tear it apart. It was like he was reading signs in the air Raul couldn't see, or listening to sounds he couldn't hear, scary as *hell*.

Raul wondered what he was thinking and planning, asked himself if he could have ever seen that face before tonight and somehow forgotten it. It was long, thin, pale. Black hair combed straight back from the forehead, eyes dark as the night outside. Still as could be when that weird, focused-on-his-own-thing look came over him. Not a face anybody could read. Or forget.

The guy was a stranger, Raul concluded. A total stranger.

He lowered his eyes from the mirror, afraid his passenger would notice the close scrutiny.

"Let's get back to Armand Quiros," the guy said

barely a moment later. "What makes you so sure he's going to be at the garage tonight?"

Raul chewed his bottom lip. He'd figured they'd come around to Armand again, wasn't stupid enough to think the guy was finished asking about him. That hadn't stopped Raul from hoping, but you had to expect it, know what was going down here.

"He hands on," he said with reluctance. "Like bein' the one does the payout."

"The payout in drugs."

Raul felt his insides tighten up. "Look, man, I been straight with you alla way. How come we got to run through this again—?"

"You boost a set of wheels, deliver it to Armand's chop shop heaven, he pays with crack," the guy said. "Yes or no?"

Raul continued to hesitate. He was thinking bleakly about the deal he'd had going with Jose, thinking what an unbelievable piece of luck it had looked to be when they met through Raul's sister, who had been seeing Jose for a while before she hooked them up a couple weeks back. Since then they'd pulled some inside jobs that had been worth a bundle . . . especially with their terms being wheels in exchange for crack, like the man in the backseat had put it. With flat cash you couldn't turn it over to double or even triple your profits.

Now Raul took a breath, held it, blew it out his mouth.

"Yeah," he said finally. Even his voice was quivering now. "That how it works."

There was another period of silence, this one longer than the last. Blackness swarming the SUV's windows, no other vehicles in sight, Raul drove on toward what he felt would be certain death, trying to figure how things could have gone downhill for him so fast. That first time at his sister's place, Jose explained he was a salesman at a dealership in some rich gringo suburb, place with a huge fucking showroom and lot, and that he had access to whatever Raul needed to jack a carriage nice and easy—keys to the building, codes for the gate alarm protecting its outdoor lot, electronic car door openers and starters, even dealer temps and registration documents for him to wave around if he got hauled over by cops. Just as sweet, he could tip Raul to the delivery of a new consignment, give him a chance to roll out a few of the vehicles before they were entered into the computerized inventory.

Raul had really gotten his ass stoked when Jose told him about the expensive Navigators that had arrived, two of them, both cherry and loaded right off the double-decker truck. This was just the other day when they arrived with a big shipment, and he'd known he could drive one from the lot, and that nobody would notice it was gone for at least a month, six weeks. It would probably be another month afterward until the dealer and factory sorted out whether it had been delivered to the lot, or hauled to the wrong one by mistake, or disappeared somewhere else along the way from the production line . . . no way the setup could've have been *sweeter*. Taking carriages from the dealership was a slam compared to looking for them on the street, where you had to get lucky and find a target that had been left with its door unlocked, or make sure you knew how to bust its antitheft system if it had one, maybe even a GPS tracker—and that was while having to look over your shoulder for its owner, the five-oh, or just some busy-body asshole solid citizen who couldn't keep his eyes in his head where they belonged. Raul had almost never worried about being pinched since he'd got down with Jose, and wouldn't in his worst nightmares have thought he'd find himself in the spot he was in right now. The thing was here . . . the thing was that the chop shop would show in his headlights soon, *and then* what was he supposed to do?

Raul drove through the night, not the slightest clue in his mind, seeing only the worst in store. He had driven maybe another quarter mile toward their destination before the questions started coming at him again.

"Tell me how many of Quiros's men I can expect," the guy in back said.

Raul clutched the wheel with whitening knuckles. This was a subject they hadn't touched on yet, and it had rated high among his wishes that they would not get to it. It wasn't enough that the *hijo de puta* had set a trap for him at that streetlight, forced him into taking this suicide ride. He had to keep digging him a deeper hole.

"Can't be sure," he said

"Tell me how many," the guy repeated. "And where they'll be."

"Listen, man, please, I don' *know*—"

Raul suddenly felt a cold, circular pressure between his neck and the base of his skull. He stiffened with fear, not needing to look around to know his passenger had jammed the silenced barrel of his .45 semiauto into him.

"Give it up," the guy said.

"I don' wanna die," Raul said.

"Don't be stupid. You already brought me this far along. You think it'll square things with them if you don't tell me?"

"I don' wanna die."

"Then prove you've got an ounce of brains that isn't fried, Raul," the guy said. And then paused a moment. "That's your real name, right?"

"Yeah."

"You wouldn't have lied to me about it."

"No, man, I swear."

The guy nudged his head forward with the gun barrel.

"Understand this," he said. "I start to think you did lie, I can't trust your word on anything else. And that would make you useless to me."

Raul felt his stomach lurch.

"It my name," he said. "*Swear to God* it my name."

A second or two lapsed. Raul felt the weapon easing back from his head.

"All right, Raul, I'm about to pass along some free wisdom," the guy said. "Armand won't care if I hijacked my way into this cart, or you wore white valet gloves letting me through its door. One makes you a foul-up and a loser, the other a sellout. Either way he'll have you capped without even thinking about any second chances."

"An' how 'bout you?" Raul said, fighting down panic. "We get to the garage, *you* gonna give me one?"

"I have a cross-country Greyhound ticket and expense money in my pocket that says so," the guy said. "Ride this out with me, you can hop on a bus, visit some relatives far away from here. Or sell the ticket and buy a whole lot of stuff to fill your crack pipe. No skin off mine whatever you decide."

Raul felt the slow heavy stroke of his heart in the short silence that followed.

"Ain't got no shot at makin' it," he said. "Gonna get myself *hurt*, don't care what you say."

There was another silence that lasted perhaps half a minute. Then the guy in the backseat leaned forward, coming so close Raul could practically feel his lips brush against his ear.

"It's long odds," he said. "But I'm all that stands between you and crapping out."

•   •   •

The Navigator rolled over the snaking, undivided blacktop. In its cargo section, Lathrop glanced out the front windshield, and then through the limo-tinted windows to either side of him. The chop shop was just ahead to the left. A little closer up on the right he saw the junkyard, its orderly rows of scrap metal hills stretching off into the darkness.

He let his Mark 23 pistol sink below Raul's headrest.

"You look jumpy," he said. "Relax."

"Been tryin', man."

"Try harder," Lathrop said. "If Armand's guards smell you're scared, we'll never get past them."

Raul inhaled. "What gonna happen after we in the garage? Happen, you know, to *me*?"

Lathrop shrugged.

"Just worry about bringing us in," he said. "And about making sure I can believe what comes out of your mouth."

Raul shook his head, his nervous, rasping breaths very loud over the smooth hum of the engine.

"Why you got to be doubtin' me like that?" he said with a kind of fearful indignance. "I swore to God, man. Can swear on my mother's *life,* you wan' me to—"

"Save it," Lathrop said. " 'Long as I'm the man with the gun, I figure your word's probably good."

He was of course telling an outright lie of his own.

Lathrop watched the Nav's headlight beams creep

toward the edge of the parking lot, thinking it didn't matter how many times Raul swore up and down to him, or on whom or what he did his swearing. All Lathrop really trusted was what he'd known firsthand about Armand Quiros's operations before tonight. This included the answers to most of the questions he'd asked Raul on the way here, answers he had compared against Raul's responses to get an idea of whether or not he was being purposely deceptive, almost as if he'd been setting the baseline for a polygraph test . . . though it couldn't be forgotten for a minute that the kid was a pathetic, strung-out crackhead. When the squeeze got too tight, he would say anything he thought might help buy him some wiggle room.

Still, Lathrop had learned enough about the garage from his reconnaissance. Learned its location, its size, its outward appearance, and its immediate surroundings. He had also tracked Armand's normal patterns of movement in and around Devoción. Found out how many guards usually traveled with him from San Diego, and the number of lookouts—mostly young men from town—he kept hanging around the garage and its lot. As Raul had said, though, the place was windowless. Since Lathrop hadn't yet learned the trick of seeing through solid walls from Clark Kent, he'd obtained no advance knowledge of its interior layout, or where Armand would sit down to take care of his private business.

Assuming the kid hadn't tried to sucker him, he knew now.

Lathrop peered out through the windshield, saw several parked cars in the lot, and noted the shadowy figures of Quiros's lookouts in the cast of the SUV's lights. There were five, maybe six of them hanging around near the building's corrugated steel roll-up doors.

"Turn on the rearview video," he said.

The kid was shaking his head again.

"That ain't gonna work while I got us in Drive," he said. "They make it for when people *goin' backward,* you know. When they can't see what's behind 'em inna mirror—"

"Go ahead," Lathrop said. "Turn it on."

Raul obliged without further comment, reaching over to push the dashboard LCD's control button. Its cover panel slid up above the screen.

Lathrop thought for a second, still looking out the windows.

"Okay, Raul, listen close," he said. "Here's what you're going to do next . . ."

Raul stopped at the parking lot entrance, his window about halfway down like the man behind him wanted it. Then he waited in silence as a couple of the lookouts outside the garage strode toward the Navigator. He recognized the first to approach as a dude named Pedro.

"*Hola, Papi,* what'chu bring tonight?" the lookout

said, mixing Spanish and English. He was a little older than Raul—around twenty-three or twenty-four. Lived right in town, hung out with Raul and his cousin at the cantina every so often.

"Ain' no Matchbox toy, man." Raul forced a grin.

Pedro grinned back at him, came around to the driver's side, clasped his hand through the window. Tall, skinny, he wore a two-tone gray basketball warmup suit and a bright purple-and-yellow paisley skullcap with a long, flowing neck shade that made him look like some kind of flashy Arab camel herder. There was a small diamond stud in each ear, another in his right nostril. On a band around his arm was a gum-stick MP3 player.

He pressed a button on the audio player, plucked out a stereo earbud, and let it dangle over his shoulder, leaving the other earbud in place.

"Es un machin mas bárbaro," he said, admiring the vehicle's shiny new flank. "This high line merch."

"Sí, Pedro.*"*

"She somethin' *else,* bro."

"Sí, eso es."

Raul rested his left elbow over the upper edge of the window and leaned against the door, struggling to look calm, look *relaxed* like the crazy man in back had put it, while intentionally blocking Pedro's view of the Nav's interior with his upper body.

"Armand still around?" he said.

Pedro nodded over his shoulder at the garage, his

eyes still admiring the vehicle. "Bet she tricked out nice—"

"Armand gonna wan' to see her."

The lookout was in no apparent hurry in spite of Raul's growing insistence. He leaned against the car, propping himself against the driver's door with both hands.

"Like to be havin' a look inside on my own," he said. "*A ver,* how 'bout you let me see . . ."

Raul drew erect. His head ached and his pulse was racing in his ears. He had the vehicle in Reverse, his foot on the brake pedal to keep it from slipping backward and, more important, to keep its rear lights on. According to Crazy Man, they would give off enough brightness for the cargo hatch's built-in video camera to serve some kind of purpose.

But he couldn't just sit here with Pedro getting ready to climb in front with him. If he could have just taken a hit off his pipe before he got here, *one* hit, he'd have been able to handle things without feeling like the walls of his skull were closing in around his brain, mashing his brain to a pulp.

"Que pasa?" he said. "Been drivin' all night, know what I'm sayin? Wanna take care'a my shit."

A moment passed. Another. Raul's head kept throbbing to the accelerated beat of his heart.

Finally Pedro frowned with disappointment, boosted himself off the Nav, and held up his palms in acquiescence.

"Yo, chill, I hear you," he said, looking quickly around at the garage.

Raul saw one of the dark figures outside the vehicle bays reach for a wall-mounted control box next to the automatic door. As the door started to rise, he almost crumpled in his seat with relief.

"You wan', I give you a ride into town when you done," Pedro said, studying Raul curiously. Then his expression sharpened, and he added in a low, confidential whisper, *"El basuco alvidar mis hambres."*

The crack will fill our hunger.

Raul looked at him, momentarly speechless. He'd been struggling to hide the unbearable fear and need at his core, but realized now that the need showing through might have been the best thing he could have wished for. That it was all that had disguised the other.

"Bien," he said at last, and nodded. "I got you covered."

Pedro gave him another soul handshake, his grip lingering a few seconds. "Hey, awright," he said with a grin.

Raul flashed a pretend grin in return. Then he pulled his hand back through the window, shut it, and reached for the shifter.

On his belly in the Nav's cargo section, his balaclava pulled up so that only his eyes were visible through its narrow opening, Lathrop looked between its two front seats at the video display. He'd thought he might have seen someone's outline at its left-hand border . . . a dim, fuzzy human silhouette flitting into the image, such as it was. But that had been several seconds ago. Now he saw only the faint red glow of the vehicle's taillights tinting the blacktop.

His gaze steady on the screen, Lathrop heard Raul and the lookout conclude their exchange. *I got you covered. Hey, awright.* It had been dicey having the kid lower his window more than a little—Lathrop knew he'd have been discovered in an instant had Pedro stuck his head in. But if Raul had kept the window any higher up, it would have invited suspicion, given the appearance he had something to conceal.

Lathrop had weighed his choices, and what he saw now seemed to confirm he'd made the right one. The lookout had stepped away from the vehicle, stuffing his hands into the pockets of his warm-ups.

Raul had managed to get by him.

Now he raised his window, shifted into Drive, and rolled across the lot toward the garage.

That instantly killed the video, but Lathrop hadn't expected it to be of any real use until they got inside. The rearview camera was a crummy excuse for a spy eye, meant to help an Average Joe driver avoid backing over toddlers, pissing dogs, and low stationary obstacles in his mirror's blind spots . . . not pick out roving Quiros stooges in a dark nowhere like this. A crummy, inadequate option with a range that extended fifteen feet at best. Still, Lathrop had gotten a sense of what he could expect from the thing.

As the Navigator began to move, he slipped his free hand under his partially unbuttoned tac jacket and withdrew a shoulder-slung MP7 compact assault gun he'd carried tucked away against his side at the ready, keeping the other hand around the .45's checkered rubber grip. He had prepared carefully for tonight's work and knew they were pieces he could count on.

Lathrop would have liked to know if anybody was out in the dark circling the wagon, though. For the first time in longer than he could remember, he wouldn't have minded having a second pair of eyes to cover the very dangerous blind spots in his own sight. But he had gotten along with less than he wanted before, and there had been three million dollars' worth of incentive for him to do it again tonight.

Just ahead now, the garage's vehicle bay was opening wide for the Nav. Lathrop pressed his chest almost flat against the carpet. He hadn't seen or heard Pedro indicate he wanted the door retracted, yet the lookout had somehow given the okay to somebody before his prolonged handshake with Raul.

Lathrop wondered if his quick glance around could have been it, decided that explanation didn't wash. The garage was about a hundred feet away, and it was too dark a night for that look to have been seen clearly by anyone out front. So what *was* the signal?

He pictured the MP3 player on the lookout's arm, asked himself if maybe it wasn't what it seemed. A hands-free radio unit could be easily modified to look like an audio player and equipped with an ear/bone microphone that would pick up the wearer's words from vibrations in his skull. If that were the case, Pedro would have barely needed to move his lips to give his order.

It occurred to Lathrop that Enrique Quiros, who'd packaged the family business in his tech savvy and Stanford degrees, would have appreciated exactly that kind of touch. And though his cousin and former underboss Armand had a reputation as a throwback player with more muscle than brains, it might indicate that at least some of Enrique's modern standards of criminality were being carried on two years after he'd been erased from the world.

Lathrop put that thought aside as the Navigator reached the garage, cool white fluorescent light rinsing over it from the open bay entrance. Raul stopped just outside it, his foot on the brake.

About thirty seconds passed. Lathrop scooched forward, raised his chin slightly to look out the windshield, saw two men stepping over to the Nav from inside the garage. Lean, dark, curly haired, they looked enough alike to be brothers. One of them wore a black-and-silver rugby pullover shirt, a handgun bulging a little under the shirt, his neck zipper lowered to showcase the tats on his chest. The other

had on a flamingo pink button-down with short
sleeves, its untucked tails hanging loosely over the
belt holster clipped to his jeans. He also had a lot of
ink on his arms. Neither man wore a vest or had
taken very much trouble to conceal his weapon. Plac-
ing strut over smarts.

They came closer, Rugby Shirt stepping over to
the driver's door, Flamingo Pink hooking toward its
right side.

Lathrop recalled the scouting he'd done, placed
this matched set among Armand's traveling en-
tourage of bodyguards. He had never seen Armand
go anywhere without five or six armed men around
him and didn't suppose it was any different tonight.
There would be more of them around . . . the only
question was where. He couldn't see out the vehicle's
side windows without bringing his head up, but a
glance at the rear video display told him its image
had been improved by the garage's fluorescents—
although the low line of sight still restricted what he
could observe.

Getting his elbows underneath him, propping himself up a bit, he adjusted his pistol in his right hand,
then checked again that the MP7 was within fast and
easy reach under his other arm.

He knew he'd have to move at any moment.

There was nothing left for him to do now but stay
ready for when it arrived.

•   •   •

Raul brought his window partly down again, leaving it raised a little higher than before.

"Here it is." He looked out at Rugby Shirt. "Got what I promised."

Lathrop heard the strained edge in Raul's voice, noticed his fingers were back around the steering wheel, fidgeting with the wheel.

The guard stood there and didn't say anything. His eyes slid over the Navigator, inspecting it in the out-spill of light from the wide bay entrance. Then they came level with the kid's face.

Lathrop drew a breath. The mingled garage smells of car exhaust, valve oil, and gasoline vapor reached him along with the night air . . . that and a metallic clanging beyond the door. There would be other bays besides the one that had been opened to admit the Nav. Some probably with mechanics in them, working to dismantle the latest stolen vehicles delivered by Armand's crack-addicted worker ants.

Raul continued to sit there facing the guard, waiting to be let inside.

"Wha's goin' on?" he said, angling his chin toward the bay entrance. "Thought Armand know I got here."

Rugby Shirt's eyes held firmly on Raul.

"No este tu irrespetuoso," he said.

Do not be disrespectful.

The kid dragged the back of his hand across his mouth. When he clenched it around the steering wheel again, Lathrop noticed it was glistening with streaks of wiped-off perspiration.

"Didn't mean anythin'," he said. "Jus' want to be bringin' in this *coche,* do what I gotta do."

Rugby Shirt stood by the vehicle, quiet and intent, his lips pressed together. Beside the passenger door, his partner was equally impassive.

Lathrop saw Raul shift in his seat with apprehension, got the sense he was starting to unravel under their combined scrutiny.

The waiting silence continued about ten seconds longer, Lathrop down on his stomach in the Nav, his finger curled around the trigger of his .45. He wasn't inclined to act before the time was right, but it would force his hand if either of the guards decided to lean in closer to the windows.

Then Rugby Shirt nodded his head toward the garage, rapping the vehicle's broad flank with his palm.

"Muy bien, es de el jefe agrado," he said.

Very well, it will be to the boss's liking.

Lathrop listened, understanding the guard's Spanish, thinking the look in his eyes didn't at all match his words. He'd caught on that something was up with Raul. Anybody who wasn't blind or deaf would have caught on. And while it was possible he would attribute the kid's twitchiness to his being strung out on rock, Lathrop was not about to stake his life on it.

Still, Rugby Shirt had decided to let the Nav

through the entrance. Whatever his reasons. It moved slowly forward, both guards walking along to either side of it, escorting it into the bay.

Lathrop braced himself. The Nav's heavily tinted glass had screened him from sight out in the darkness, but it would be another story under the garage's bright overhead fixtures.

Now Raul pulled the Nav through the door and shifted into Reverse, leaving the engine on as he'd done out in the lot. Beside his door, Rugby Shirt nodded his head toward the rear of the garage. When Lathrop had questioned the kid back on the mesa road, he'd said that was where Armand's private office was located, its door facing the bay entrance and work area, a large two-way mirror on the wall beside the door looking out over everything.

Lathrop glanced at the rear video screen and saw two sets of legs move into the right side of the picture, coming around from what he assumed was the next bay over. Then a third pair appeared behind the Nav on the left. All of them were in drab green mechanic's pants, Lathrop's view of them cut off above the knees by the camera. If these men were armed, he had no way to tell.

A few seconds went by. Then another pair of chopped-off-at-the-knees legs entered the left border of the picture and came up to join the group behind the vehicle. These were in ordinary brown chino trousers rather than grease monkey work pants.

Lathrop was guessing they belonged to a third bodyguard. He also guessed at least twice as many more were elsewhere in and around the building—the chop shop had its regulars in addition to Armand's personal crew. And he couldn't allow himself to forget the lookouts. They were local punks, sure. Amateurs. But amateurs that he had to believe would be carrying hardware.

He waited a second or two more.

Behind the wheel, Raul had kept the Nav in Reverse, his foot on its brake. He seemed to be hanging onto the last frayed threads of his self-control well enough to stick to the plan. Lathrop had wanted him to keep the pedal down, stay put as long as possible, figuring that some of the guards would be drawn around the vehicle. The closer they got, the better it would be. When the time came, Lathrop would prompt the kid to release the brake and start the Nav rolling backward, throwing whoever was around it off balance, and giving Lathrop a bare moment of surprise he could work to his favor.

Now Rugby Shirt turned all the way around to face the office door, stepping toward it, waving for the kid to get out of the vehicle. Lathrop was convinced he looked more suspicious than impatient.

"Mira, viene aquí!" he said, instructing Raul to follow him over to the office.

Raul hesitated.

Lathrop tapped the kid's backseat, his cue to release the brake.

Raul sat there, unresponsive, his foot leaden on the pedal. He took several breaths through his mouth. It was the same sort of harsh, nervous breathing Lathrop had noticed when they'd approached the chop shop, only with a shallow rapidity that made it sound like he was gasping for air.

Out in the garage Rugby Shirt paused, turned around, waved the kid out of the Nav again.

Lathrop saw the pair of chinos inch closer in the rearview video screen.

Then Raul grabbed the shifter and threw the Nav into Park, reaching for his door handle with his other hand, jerking himself toward the door, starting to push it open, getting set to bolt out into the garage.

The kid's rope had finally snapped; he'd lost it. Lathrop wasn't waiting to find out what he had in mind.

With a quick, fluid movement, he pushed up onto his knees, swung his .45 up above Raul's shoulder in a two-handed grip, and fired three rounds through the windshield.

Rugby Shirt could not have been prepared for what hit him. He would have had only an instant to see Lathrop spring into a double-handed shooter's crouch in the Navigator's cargo section, and was unlikely to have heard the muffled pops of the sound-suppressed gunshots before his developing suspicions came together.

The bullets penetrated the windshield with a loud, sleety explosion of broken glass, meeting his flesh and muscle across the rib cage. He wobbled around on loose legs and smashed backward against a pegboard wall to his left, clawing for a handhold, groping blindly at its cluttered array of power tools in a vain attempt to stay on his feet. Several of them crashed off their hooks as he slid down to the floor of the garage, leaving the board and whatever tools remained hanging from it speckled with red.

Lathrop saw this at the outermost corner of his vision while switching his attention toward the right side of the windshield, moving his SMG around in the same direction. Flamingo Pink had drawn his own weapon from its holster, a big, long-barreled semiautomatic handgun.

The gun a dark rising blur in his fist, he took hurried aim at the Navigator and triggered off a couple of shots.

His speed and accuracy were better than Lathrop expected. The first slug punched into the Nav's hood just below its folded wipers. The next struck the right side of the windshield a millisecond afterward, partially dissolving it, spewing glass *into* the vehicle this time.

In the front seat Raul released a panicky scream and ducked under the steering wheel to avoid a storm of jagged, blown-out shards. He dove facedown across the seat and put his hands over his head as the broken glass showered over him, leaving his door ajar, abandoning his decision to cut and run, looking for cover inside the vehicle now.

Lathrop couldn't afford to let the kid's wild thrashing around become a distraction. He focused narrowly on Flamingo Pink, inhaled, and held the breath to steady his aim like a trained sniper. Then he squeezed the trigger of his .45 to take the guard out with a single clean shot to his heart.

An instant later the guard collapsed in a scattery mist of blood, the front of his shirt billowing out where he'd been hit, his pistol slipping from his fingers.

Of the gunnies Lathrop had been able to see from the Navigator's rear section, that left the man in chinos as an immediate concern.

Raul was another. The kid was out of control. Bleeding from lacerations on his hands, bits and pieces of the shattered windshield pouring from his hair and clothes, he had frantically reached out to shut the door that he'd intended to open moments ago, still hollering at the top of his lungs, repeating a single Spanish phrase as if it were stuck on his tongue: *Lo siento, lo siento!* He was sorry, sorry, sorry.

Lathrop had no idea whether he was screaming at him, Armand's men, or whoever opted to listen amid the surrounding bedlam. Maybe he was apologizing to all of them, and hoping God might have some forgiveness and mercy for him, too. But it didn't really matter. The kid was useless to anybody within earshot.

In fact he'd become a liability from Lathrop's perspective.

His gun extended in one hand, Lathrop grabbed for the door handle to his left and hurled himself out of the Navigator, landing on the balls of his feet, hunkering there on the driver's side. He was aware Chinos would be somewhere close, maybe still behind him—

He looked back over his shoulder just in time to see the guard jogging around from the right side of the cargo hatch, his weapon held level with his hip in one hand. Lathrop could tell at a glance it was an Uzi mini or some close knockoff.

He thrust himself toward the front end of the Nav, snatched at the outer handle of Raul's unlatched door, and gave it a hard tug to overcome the kid's desperate opposition from inside. Pulling the door wide open, he scuffled behind it and squatted down low in the angle between its hinges and the driver's-side panel, pressing against the vehicle so that he was almost wedged against its wheel well.

The move would give him cover from Chinos. That was the plus. The bad part was that it meant he'd had to turn his back to the one-way mirror fronting Armand's office, leaving him vulnerable from behind.

It also meant Raul had been left suddenly and

completely exposed to Chinos, but he had ceased to be Lathrop's concern.

The kid jerked upright in his seat as the door was torn from his hand and flung outward, his lips frozen in a breathless grimace of terror, his throat clamping shut around his screams. Then he turned his head to see the guard hasten around the cargo hatch to his side of the vehicle, advancing behind his tiny assault weapon. His eyes bright staring circles, aware his prospects of survival had radically dwindled all in a second, Raul forced his vocal cords to respond to his commands and started shouting out the door in Spanish again, adding vehement denials to his repetitive declarations of regret, insisting that not only was he sorry but things weren't his fault here. *Lo siento, no es mi culpa.*

Chinos gave him just an instant's notice, scarcely pausing to meet his gaze with his own through the open door. His eyes did not offer the barest hint of whether he considered him a threat, an opportune target of revenge, or both at once. They communicated nothing, nothing whatsoever as they brushed against Raul's and his compact submachine gun unleashed a burst of fire that ripped into Raul at almost point-blank range, snuffing the life out of him even before his body spilled limp-limbed and shuddering against the steering column.

Crouched on his haunches behind the door, aware of that mirror at his back, Lathrop did not miss his

chance to exploit the moment Chinos had wasted taking out Raul. Shoving his pistol into its holster, he
grabbed the foregrip of his MP7, braced its extended
rifle stock against his shoulder, and pushed its bore
around the edge of the door.

Chinos was quick to catch sight of it. He whirled
toward the door seemingly on reflex and rattled off
an arcing volley, smashing the driver's side window
from its frame . . . a reaction that might have done
even more damage if Lathrop hadn't gotten the jump
on him by a slender hair, drawing an accurate bead,
catching him in his midsection with a tight salvo. The
guard pivoted drunkenly on his feet, his gun hand
convulsing to trigger an ineffectual spray of ammunition at the walls and ceiling, his other hand clutching
his stomach, blood dribbling between his fingers
from multiple bullet wounds.

Lathrop was up from his crouch before he
dropped, his MP7 poised.

He looked from side to side. Two of the three
mechs that had approached the Nav's tail section
were gone, but it was hard to tell where. The bays
over to his right were occupied by cars, vans, pick-
ups, and SUVs in various stages of being stripped.
Some of the vehicles were on hoists, the heavy-duty
kind that were built into the floor. There was an open
service pit in the bay closest to Lathrop, a large
Cadillac sedan pulled almost up to it. A small crew of
grease monkeys stood among the different vehicles,

staring at him, looking scared stiff. A couple of them might have been the same men whose legs had entered the rearview video image. Or not. Next to the open bay entrance behind the Nav, another mech had sunk down into a corner and was cowering there with his hands on his head in submission. Lathrop figured him for one of the first three. His friends could have cleared out through the door—or not.

Lathrop reached a hand into his jacket, flashed the special agent badge around his neck, motioned toward the entrance with his subgun.

"DEA!" he said. "*Vaya,* go!"

His face streaked with perspiration, the mech nodded and slowly rose off the floor.

Lathrop snapped the gun toward his head to hustle him along. *"Ahora!"*

The mech nodded more vigorously, sprang the rest of the way up to his feet, turned, and fled the garage.

Lathrop saw him bowl into a cluster of lookouts still lingering in the lot outside the entrance, then push past them to disappear in the night. They all seemed like versions of Pedro with their head wraps or Under Armour skullcaps, their basketball warm-ups, their hoodies and low-waisted baggy pants. And the conspicuously identical gumstick MP3s on their arms.

They looked at him. He looked at them. The thing about the loose-fitting ghetto wear was that it could be a bluff or conceal a small arsenal.

Lathrop fired a burst out the door, his aim intentionally high, displaying his shield so they could see it, hopeful they would get the message that he was giving them a pass. He had not forgotten about the one-way mirror behind him—and whoever might be behind it. Any time he spent worrying about this bunch was too long.

They took his warning and scattered from the lights of the garage, losing themselves on the mechanic's heels.

Lathrop thought about the mirror at his unprotected back and started to turn.

That was when he heard the rev of an engine inside the garage to his right. He glanced toward the sound, saw that the mechs who'd been staring from over by the vehicles were heading for the entrance . . . all except one, and he'd gotten into the Caddy sedan. Almost simultaneously the office door crashed open and a tight knot of three or four men in street clothes broke from it. They held submachine guns of the same sort Chinos had carried and were assembled around another man who could barely be seen through their flanking bodies.

Several of them were rattling fire at Lathrop as they moved toward the auto bays in hurried unison.

He took cover behind the Nav, glanced over at the sedan he'd assumed was their escape vehicle, and realized that assumption was wrong. The gunmen had reached the space between the Caddy and service pit and veered toward the pit instead of the idling sedan. A couple of them paused at its edge, still firing at him. The rest separated from the others, backed toward the pit, and then followed the man they were escorting down into it.

No sooner had the last of them dropped over its side than the Caddy throbbed into gear, screeched a half dozen feet forward, and just as abruptly came to a halt right over the pit.

Lathrop knew that first man into it had been Armand Quiros. He'd caught a glimpse of him when the group left the office and gotten a slightly longer look as he descended the rail or ladder on the side of the pit. But it was really simpler than that. Armand's office plus Armand's bodyguards equaled Armand.

What Lathrop wondered about for a brief instant was Armand racing into that hole. Why would he box himself in while a charged-up getaway car was waiting for him? *If* that was really what he'd done. A man like Armand would be prepared for somebody to make a move on him sooner or later. Whether it was the competition or a takedown by the law, he would anticipate more than a solitary attacker . . . Lathrop had in fact banked on his turn-tail worker ants sharing that same belief. Armand would expect his enemies to be waiting along the mesa road toward Devoción and probably to the south of town as well. In his mind a frontal escape from the garage would leave him open to being followed or caught in a net of barriers, and that meant he would want a less obvious exit through the pit. Want to be sure there was another car ready on the other side of it.

Lathrop ejected his subgun's half-empty magazine, got a fresh forty-round clip from a pouch on his trousers, and jammed it into the weapon with the heel of his palm. Then he reached under his jacket and produced one of three cylindrical flashbangs he'd brought with him in a nylon web belt rig. About a minute had gone by since Armand emerged from his office, too long, giving him more than enough time to rabbit. But the guy who'd driven the Caddy into position had drawn a nine-mil from inside his jumpsuit and was taking shots at him out his lowered window—no mechanic, that ace, it didn't matter how he was dressed—and there was gunfire coming from underneath the Caddy, a shooter in the pit. Lathrop saw him poking his head out of it like an infantryman in a foxhole, his weapon in one hand, no way he could grip it with both of them. The pit had to be eight or nine feet deep and he'd need to cling to the rail with his other hand to fire over its top.

Staying low behind the Nav, Lathrop shuffled left around its rear fender and then forward along its flank, past the still-open driver's door where the body of Raul was thrown back against the steering column. His MP7 on its sling at his side, he leaned around the front of the vehicle and pulled the arming pin from the steel grenade canister with his fist clenched around its flyoff lever. Then he tossed the canister across the garage floor with an easy underhand lob and saw the released lever twirl away as it rolled under the Caddy and into the pit.

The grenade detonated before he could count out two full seconds, the walls of the pit muffling its blast of light and sound in the garage above. Lathrop sprang to his feet and darted toward the Caddy, his gun spitting as thin white smoke came up from the pit to ribbon out between its wheels. He could see the guy in the mech suit through the driver's side window, sprawled back in the front seat with the nine slipped from his fingers, looking disoriented from the concussion.

Lathrop pressed the snout of his MP7 between his dazed eyes, shot him, and pushed his corpse toward the passenger door. Then he leaned in and put the Caddy into reverse to get it rolling backward. As it moved off the service pit, he tossed a second flash-bang down inside.

He gave the smoke a moment to clear, rushed to the edge of the pit, thumbed on the slimline tac light mounted to his weapon. Almost directly below him at its bottom the shooter had fallen in a heap and was struggling up onto his hands and knees. Lathrop ripped into him with a volley and sprayed more fire through what was left of the smoke to take out the other men sprawled around him. Grabbing the rail's handhold, he swung a leg over the side of the pit and dropped into it.

There was plenty of light from glowing tube fixtures on the walls of the little space, rendering the flashlight inessential. Lathrop looked around, took a quick count of the bloodied men on the floor. He'd killed most of them. A couple of them stirred, trying to gather themselves. One was slouched back against the wall spitting up blood and mucous.

Lathrop finished off the survivors and cut his eyes over to a door on his left. It was plain steel with a push bar and had been shoved wide open. On the other side was a lighted, cement-walled underground passage that ran out of the pit. There was a man kneeling in the doorway, blinking and groaning, his stooped form blocking the narrow passage. Armand Quiros was moving unsteadily forward just beyond him.

Lathrop plunged toward the entrance, triggering his weapon at the back of the kneeling man's head as he ran through. Armand staggered on a few feet before he caught up, grabbed him by the back of his shirt, and drove him face-first against the wall.

"Que desa?" Armand said. "What you fucking *want* from me?"

Lathrop shoved his gun barrel between Armand's ear and the hinge of his jaw, pressing his face into the wall.

"One good woman," he said.

THREE

"CAN YOU BELIEVE THAT AIRPORT DOWN there?" Annie said from her window seat.

Belted in for landing, Nimec hadn't noticed the view. A stickler for punctuality, he was checking the time on his WristLink.

"Mhmm," he said. He'd taken an aisle seat aboard their Continental Airbus flight out of San Francisco, which, according to the analog watch display he'd selected, was right on the mark for its scheduled noon arrival.

Annie turned to him.

"Dear me, such enthusiasm," she said. "How will I ever manage to keep up?"

Nimec felt like a killjoy. He supposed Annie would agree that he ought to.

"It's nice," he said a touch guiltily, looking past her out the window. "I think it's a very nice airport."

"Pete, when you told me Los Rayos was a bona fide destination for international passenger flights, I wasn't sure what to expect," she said. "But this just knocks me out . . . I've been to cities back home with fields that aren't anywhere close to its size."

Nimec scanned the rows of interconnected terminal buildings and warehouses, the sometimes parallel, sometimes converging bands of service roads and runways below. An airport, and a largish one, yup. Nice, nice, very impressive, and yet he couldn't muster too much excitement. Still, he should have figured it was the sort of thing Annie would bc keen on. Between her dad having been a pilot, and all those years she'd spent with the Air Force and NASA, she'd been around planes and runways forever. Earned a license to fly when she was, what, seventeen or eighteen? Whatever the minimum legal age might have been in Kansas. Hard to fathom, but she was a special case. He'd been different. The opposite, really—a slow starter. The highest Nimec had gotten off the ground before leaving South Philly to enlist in the service was a tenement rooftop, and he supposed the pigeons he'd flown out of the coop up above Boylston Street might have had a broader outlook on the world than he could have formed at the time.

Now he felt the thump of the Airbus's deploying wheels, quietly sat back for its descent, and five minutes afterward was on the taxiway waiting for the call to disembark, along with the handful of other passengers bound for Los Rayos. The rest would presumably fly on to Piarco in the Trinididian capital, the plane's final destination.

Annie leaned down and slid her carry-on from under her seat. It was an old—she proudly called it vintage—Samsonite leather train case her mother had brought to San Jose with her, passing it on to Annie as a functional keepsake.

She snapped open its lid.

"Here," she said, reaching inside. "You might want to stuff this into your computer bag."

Nimec glanced over at her, happily saw that she'd fished out his Seattle Mariners baseball cap.

"Hey, thanks." He snatched the cap from her hand. "Guess I forgot to pack it."

Annie nodded.

"That's how come I remembered," she said, and shut her case with authority.

The cabin intercom crackled out a pleasant thank-you-and-enjoy-your-stay, and then they were shuffling past the air crew and flight attendants into the jetway.

Nimec had expected to be met at the arrivals lounge by Henri Beauchart, the director of resort security, but they were instead received by his subordinate while looking for someone that matched the ex–GIGN chief's description. A slight, dark-haired, olive-complected man who spoke with a faint British accent, he introduced himself as Kalidas Murthy ("Please feel free to call me Kal."), and explained that his boss had gotten unavoidably detained at the last minute.

Nimec found this annoyed him, and got the sense Murthy had picked up on it.

"I offer a sincere apology on Mr. Beauchart's behalf, madam and sir, and convey his desire that you might be his personal guests at dinner tonight," he said, looking straight at Nimec as he addressed them. "Meanwhile, you must be eager to settle into your villa after what I hope was a good trip."

He waved over a skycap to take their suitcases and then guided them through the terminal's entrance, where a driver stood waiting by a gray stretch limo. As he opened the trunk for their bags, Nimec paused in the hot sun to admire the car's gleaming body.

"A Jankel Rolls-Royce," he said. "Pre ninety-eight."

Murthy smiled.

"You know your automobiles."

"Some," Nimec said. "This one's a classic."

"It's been refitted with the latest modifications and vehicle technology," Murthy said with a nod. "You should enjoy chatting with Mr. Beauchart, who is quite an afficionado, and can better discuss its features . . . but come, I see your luggage is in the boot."

They climbed into the limousine's rear, Annie first, then Nimec, Murthy following to take the jump seat opposite them.

"I hope you won't mind my pointing out a scenic highlight or two as we go along," he said, another smile flashing across his dark Asiatic face.

Nimec leaned back without response. Although his irritation at being stood up by Beauchart had faded under the bright tropical sun, he wasn't really in the mood for sightseeing. But what could he say? He was going to be here awhile and wanted to be courteous.

"Above all else, our planners have made it simple to orient oneself on the island," Murthy was explaining. "This road leads north from the airport, as the signs generally indicate, and will take us beyond our commercial shipping facilities into the resort areas. The area to our south, over a third of the island, is an environmental preserve and wildlife refuge . . . forty miles of mangrove forest, coastal plain, and tidal waterways explicitly prohibited from development by the national government's land use charter."

"Does that mean no guests allowed?" Annie said. She smiled. "I like to explore."

"Their safety requires that access be restricted . . . a decision that ownership left to our security team. But we understand its appeal to nature lovers, and have worked with the recreational staff so that they can conduct guided boat and walking tours," Murthy said. "It may interest you to know there are active sugarcane fields and fruit groves at the jungle's fringes. These belong to local growers descended from freed African slaves who have an economic reliance on the crops. Their claims to the land are also protected by law." He paused a moment. "The villagers of Umbria tend to be reserved and mistrustful of outsiders, but in recent years a significant number have come to Los Rayos seeking employment opportunities, and their initial opposition to sharing the island with us has eased."

Listening to him, Annie seemed intensely fascinated.

Nimec, meanwhile, had studied the interior of the Rolls with a more measured sort of interest before he turned to look out at what clearly had to be the island's main harbor—a bustling complement to the airport. As they drove by, he could see four long quays and a great many smaller docks reaching out over the water. There were ramps, bridges, floating cranes, storage and handling areas with enormous freight containers stacked like building blocks, a lighthouse tower at the channel entrance, and all kinds of barges and ferries coming and going, or in the process of being loaded or offloaded by dock personnel.

The heavy activity surprised Nimec a little at first, although after a moment's consideration he guessed it shouldn't have. A resort the size of Los Rayos would have supplies flowing in continuously, and generate a high volume of waste that he assumed accounted for much of what was hauled off on the ships. Some of the produce grown by those local villagers Murthy had brought up might also leave the island by way of the harbor. Seemed pretty likely, in fact.

Though tempted to ask him about it, Nimec decided the timing wasn't right. He'd been thinking about Megan's mysterious e-mail informant, and felt it would be best to sit on his questions about the harbor traffic for a while.

He watched in silence as they left the docks behind and began driving past some of the island's far more attractive visitor spots.

As threatened, Murthy called attention to them like an enthusiastic tour bus operator.

He pointed out a golf course that came up on the left side of the road, elaborating that it was one of two eighteen-hole championship greens available to guests. He pointed out tennis courts and horseback riding paths, casinos and nightclubs, cabanas and oceanside swimming pools. And he pointed out beach after sweeping beach as the road striped up along the ocean shore.

Nimec gazed out at the shiny white sand and emerald water, quietly succumbing to the serene beauty of the place . . . and the funny thing was that the deeper this almost hypnotic calm settled in, the more he realized how hard he'd been trying to resist it.

"Look, Pete." Annie tapped his arm to get his attention, then motioned to her right. "That's fantastic!"

Out beyond the shore, a tanned, toned couple attached to colorful kiteboard sails was riding the wind with happy abandon.

"I thought about giving that a shot once," Nimec said. "Had to be fifteen years ago, before I got too busy." He shrugged. "The job, you know."

Annie had kept her hand on him.

"We should do it together," she said, rubbing his shoulder. "It's really a kick . . . a lesson or two should be enough for you to get your wings."

His forehead creased with surprise. "You've done it *before*?"

"Sure," she said. "In Florida. When we'd have downtime at Canaveral, I'd try to find ways for my training groups to unwind."

Nimec grunted, still looking out at the airborne couple. Then he saw something else against the blue sky, much higher and further off, a sleek flying object that reflected bright sparkles of sunlight as it needled south toward the harbor and airport.

"That an Augusta one-oh-nine?" he asked, turning to Murthy.

For a moment the security man's expression almost seemed startled. "You have an eye for both air *and* ground vehicles."

"I've seen a few of those choppers . . . UpLink's designed avionics for some of the custom Stingray versions," Nimec said. "The body's pretty recognizable. With how its nose is so sharp, and that frame kind of flaring out between the doors and tail boom."

Murthy produced another smile.

"We have a fleet of four in constant operational readiness," he said. "At least one patrols our airspace round the clock and, your alert eye aside, their fly patterns are charted out to be inconspicuous." He paused. "The goal at Los Rayos is to make our guests feel secure without their being conscious of security, if my meaning is clear. These are men and women who run nations, global business empires. They come here to escape and relax. To temporarily step free of the lifestyle constraints that go hand-in-hand with their positions, and at the same time have confidence they and their families are well protected. To create this environment requires a delicate balance. Our vigilance must be constant and multilayered. It also must be unobtrusive or the island will seem to them like an armed camp."

Nimec tugged his ear. He'd noticed that the chopper had sped out of sight.

"I can see how it'd be a challenge," he said. "The Augs . . . how've you got them configured?"

"Variously." Murthy said. "Here again, I'm not one for technical specifications. I know they are fast and mobile, but will defer to Mr. Beauchart's thorough expertise for the rest." He looked at Nimec, his smile grown bigger than ever. "I'm increasingly certain you and he will find no lack of conversation at dinner tonight."

Nimec guessed that was Murthy's politely professional way of suggesting they move on to other subjects, and couldn't blame him. It would be up to his boss to decide which of their trade secrets to share, the details of how their choppers were loaded among them.

Whatever Murthy's reason or reasons, Nimec didn't want to be pushy.

He fell silent, and after a minute or two realized Annie had taken easy hold of his hand on the seat between them, her fingertips so light against his palm it kind of tickled. She really seemed to be enjoying herself as they viewed the passing sights, and that made him glad.

Then the Rolls turned onto a drive branching off from the seaside road, and slowed, and Murthy pointed ahead at what he announced was the villa that had been reserved for them.

Annie's fingers squeezed Nimec's hand more tightly. There beyond a courtyard lined with palmettos was an expansive, Spanish-looking structure—all railed balconies, wide columns, arched windows, and sunwashed adobe under a red tile roof. Nimec saw a swimming pool at the end of a fieldstone path on one side of the place, and spread across the grounds, spacious gardens with bright exotic flowers and thick green hedges.

"This location is rather secluded, as we thought

you might prefer," Murthy was saying. "We hope you won't hesitate to let us know if anything fails to meet your satisfaction."

Nimec looked over at Annie, saw the barely contained excitement on her face, and then turned back to Murthy.

"I think it'll be perfect," he said.

WASHINGTON, D.C.

Andrew Reed Baxter had dreaded checking his morning voice mail. Three days in Palm Springs had notched the term *long weekend* into a depressing context for him and he'd known there would be a carryover before leaving for the office . . . shit, one stiff hand after another, how much cash had he lost? He didn't need a certified accountant to tell him it was a whole fucking lot—no wonder his reflux was giving him a terrible time this morning. It was doubling down on those soft counts that had killed him, screw those variations; he should have just played his usual game. Next time he'd remember that before deciding to take anybody's so-called expert advice about systems and strategies, stick to what he knew and watch the dealer go bust.

Next time, for damned sure, he'd bring his winning game to the table.

Baxter sat with the phone's handset cradled between his neck and shoulder, listening to the *beep-beep-beep* of the stutter dial tone that indicated he had messages. Then he reluctantly keyed the access number and spoke his password, bringing his antacid mints out of a desk drawer, peeling open the foil wrap with his thumb.

His ex-wife's screeching message was the first to come up.

Shit, shit, Baxter thought, and popped a couple of the peppermint antacid tablets into his mouth.

She was, predictably, calling to remind him the alimony check was late. With her it always started out with a complaint about the alimony. Then the rest of the litany would follow. Alicia's school in New York City had contacted her. The tuition was overdue, why hadn't it been paid? Forty-four thousand dollars a year to keep the kid on an LD track; Baxter knew he should have insisted on being the one to decide where to send her. Failing that, he should have had his lawyer insist on rolling the cost of Alicia's education into his child support, let her mother have to budget it from the blanket payments. Maybe then she'd have found a special ed program that didn't bleed him dry. He'd heard there was a boarding school right next door in Virginia that cost half what he was laying out—why not that one? Everybody knew who ran things down there in New York. Fucking kike moneygrubbers. They didn't nail you to the cross, they hung you from it by your purse strings.

Baxter listened about halfway through her message and then pressed the keypad button to skip to the next one. No break from his misery here; it was old man Bennett—"King Hughie"—on a harangue of his own about the new investment deal Sedco's partners in that Kazakhstan project were negotiating with Beijing. The Chinese, he reminded Baxter, were set to import twenty million tons of oil a year from that Caspian pipeline; how much more were they going to gobble up? Western Europe was already starting to get paranoid about their out-of-control acquisitiveness and consumption, even rumbling about economic sanctions if they didn't curb their appetite. And then there were Dan Parker's opponents in the senate race batting the issue around on the Sunday news shows, wondering aloud where the hell he'd been when the Chinks made their move to buy up those stakes. King Hughie didn't intend to see Sedco's reputation, or his favorite son's election campaign, besmirched with charges that he'd glad-handed former Soviet pawns to the detriment of America's traditional allies. He wanted to call a special meeting of the company's directors and major shareholders, insisting they would have to put on the brakes or else.

If King Hughie only knew the reality of what was happening in his own boardroom, Baxter thought. The old man could still bark with the loudest of them, but he wasn't the watchdog he used to be.

Baxter crunched down his antacids, put a couple more onto his palm, and tossed them into the chute. His eye had been on the Caribbean operation, what he'd gotten going there over the past year. But he knew Parker had been involved with behind-the-scenes talks to rebuff the Chinese proposal and convince the Kazakhstanis it wasn't in their long-term interest to feed another hungry giant on their borders. They were accustomed to handling things quietly in that part of the world and Parker hadn't wanted to throw pie in the faces of his working contacts . . . though the general public wouldn't appreciate these subtleties, would just see Parker having to defend himself over and over against accusations they barely understood. And Baxter hoped he went ahead and knocked himself out. Whenever he heard some politician or other talk about the wisdom and sound judgment of the average American voter, he'd wonder how the son of a bitch didn't bust a gut in midspiel. Man for man, woman for woman, the average American voter was a half step from brain-dead.

Baxter jabbed at the keypad button again to cut off King Hughie's inflamed rant. It was followed by a series of relatively innocuous messages—a PR assistant with questions about Sedco's latest corporate media packet, the president of a greenie advocacy group who wanted to discuss the impact of offshore wells on the Louisiana crawfish population, those contractors he'd hired to renovate his Chesapeake beach house letting him know they'd prepared a final estimate. Baxter paid the least possible attention to them, thinking emptily about that last night at the casino . . . actually the last *hand* he'd played on the last night. He'd been at the no limit table, three hundred grand's worth of chips in the circle, holding a soft fifteen—an Ace and a four—with the dealer showing five up. His instincts had been to stand pat, but instead he asked for the hit and caught a deuce.

The dealer had stood on a soft seventeen, and that was that for Baxter. He'd been beaten, and badly, according to house rules. Three hundred thou to their coffers, added to the six hundred thousand they'd taken from him earlier in the weekend . . . a loss of almost a *million* dollars.

The realization slapped him hard.

Baxter had headed for the elevator almost as his cards were being swept off the table, weak in his knees, a little faint, afraid he might be physically sick right there in the casino's gambling room. This was yesterday, Sunday, just hours before his flight back to D.C. The previous night he had taken an even bigger loss, but it hadn't seemed that discouraging when he got back to his room. Not once he'd phoned out for that blonde, a couple bottles of wine, and a tin of expensive Petrossian caviar. By morning he had cleared out the negativity and was full of restored optimism, sure he would be able to recoup, or better yet head home a triumphant winner. And he still believed he would have if he'd done a gut check and stuck to his customary game.

Next time, Baxter promised himself. Next time it would be the tried-and-true, and with any luck a different fucking outcome . . .

He suddenly heard Jean Luc's recorded voice in the earpiece and sat up straight. What was that he'd said?

He punched in the playback code and listened. The time/date stamp told him the call had come in Friday afternoon. Then, again, the terse message:

"We need to talk about the deleted file, Reed. The one that almost crashed our system. Get in touch with me as soon as you can."

Baxter sat behind his desk a moment, unsettled. Those words had shot through his thoughts like bullets, propelled by the level but unmistakable urgency of their tone.

He hit the phone's disconnect button, started to key in the country code for Trinidad from memory, and then reconsidered. Although the office telephone line was supposed to be secure, Baxter wasn't so much the gambler that he'd bet his entire future on it.

Reaching into the inner pocket of his suit jacket for his handheld satphone, he placed the call on it instead.

"Hello?"

"Jean Luc," Baxter said. "It's Andrew."

"Reed, I've been wondering when you'd get in touch."

"I was out of town."

"So your admin informed me," Jean Luc said. "I'd hoped you might check your messages remotely while you were gone."

Baxter cleared his throat.

"I took a long weekend and I'm back," he said. "Tell me what's happening."

"How openly can you speak?"

"We're on a crypted line, but I'm at the office, so take that for what it's worth," Baxter said. "I need to know about the file you mentioned."

Silence.

"There was another attachment," Jean Luc said after a moment. "One that wasn't wiped."

Baxter felt his stomach tighten.

"You didn't know about it?" he said.

"We didn't know of its connection to the original," Jean Luc said. "By the time that became apparent we'd lost it."

"Jesus Christ." Baxter thought about those crates that had arrived at the Florida airport. It had been all over the news. The human remains found in them were unidentifiable . . . but still, he didn't need something like this on his head right now.

"Listen to me, Reed," Jean Luc was saying. "There's no cause to be too concerned right now."

"No?"

"Not to where either of us overreacts. We aren't positive what's in the other file. It might not contain anything that could cause further damage. Very likely, it doesn't. And in any event, it's bound to turn up. We've got our top men working to trace it."

The tightness across Baxter's middle became a hot coil of pain.

"Goddamn it, Jean, I warned you," he snapped. "How long ago? Months? Years? Hire those fucking jungle bunnies and situations like this are inevitable."

Another silence ensued. It dangled across the thousands of miles between them.

Baxter wished he hadn't let his temper get the better of him.

"Jean, look, I apologize. It's early and I'm feeling a little raw—"

"Never mind."

"You sure? I shouldn't have jumped down your throat."

"Don't worry about it."

"Okay, good . . . I'd hate to think you clammed up because you'd gone PC on me," Baxter said with a strained chuckle. His chair creaked as he leaned forward to reach for his antacids. "The file you're tracing, does it have a name?"

"We all have names," Jean Luc said. Whatever that meant. His tone remained oddly chill; Baxter guessed he was still a little annoyed. "This one's called Jarvis Lenard. He's a groundskeeper from the village."

Which in Baxter's mind meant trouble, no doubt about it, considering how those people stuck together. This time, though, he didn't allow himself to get frazzled.

"Eckers is on the job?"

"I told you we were going with our best."

"That you did." Baxter put a mint in his mouth, decided to add another. *Clearly* Jean was miffed. "Look, I'll take it on faith you've got this covered, and figure you'll keep me posted on any new developments. What do you say?"

"I think that's a sound option," Jean Luc said. "And while I'm offering advice, here's another piece . . . wherever you've been, it's not healthy for you. Take it from a friend, Reed. Next time you decide to get away for a few days, consider going someplace that gives more than it takes."

Baxter frowned, not sure how to reply. But then the click in his ear rendered that moot.

Jean Luc had hung up at his end of the line.

SOUTHWESTERN TRINIDAD

In his study at the Bonasse estate, Jean Luc held the telephone's cradled receiver in his fist a moment, then slowly relaxed his grip and stood from behind his desk. Probably he'd gotten angrier at Reed than his comments warranted; the man was what he was. The penultimate WASP, inescapably cloistered and ignorant despite his Ivy League edu-

cation, a hopeless product of his genealogy and upbringing who couldn't see past the tip of his patri-
cian nose.

Expelling a long breath, he went across the wain-
scoted room to the side table on which the cubical
walnut-and-glass display case had rested for as long
as he could remember . . . his first look at it, in fact,
had come while he was perched on his father's shoulders. Even older than the case, the antique table dated
from the early colonial period and had a blend of sty-
listic influences in its design—the curved, graceful
elegance of its legs showing the hand of a Basque ar-
tisan, its ebony marble surface distinctly French in its
proud Old World solidness.

Here on the islands things had always mixed together, until their origins almost couldn't be sorted out.

With its clear top lid, clear glass front and side
panes, and mirrored back, the case allowed the flintlock pistol it contained to be viewed from many an-
gles. It was a striking weapon, passed down through
the generations of his family from male heir to male
heir . . . Jean Luc's was a strongly patriarchal bunch,
one in which women had often been seen as property,
acquired to serve the needs of the men whose beds
they readied with their hands and warmed with their
bodies.

He looked down at the pistol nestled there in its
fitted dark blue velvet riser, carefully preserved for
almost two and a half centuries. The chased and en-

graved gold cartouches along its long nine-inch barrel, the cocking mechanism shaped like a gape-jawed
serpent or dragon, the grinning gold demon's head
on the pommel—these had not dulled in the slightest
with the years, surpassing in durability the lineage of
the man who had first possessed it, and given it to his
fourth great-grandfather as a seal of alliance.

On occasion when Jean Luc studied the weapon,
he would find himself overtaken with visions of
wooden pirate ships with broad sails and skull-and-
crossbone banners, of naval battles with dueling cannons. Now it took him several minutes to become
aware that his eyes had moved from the gun to center
on his own reflection in the mirrored backing.

Reed was what he was, yes. In all his effete, de-
generate weakness.

And he . . . he himself was passing. Always had
been passing.

Jean Luc Morpaign did not want to look too deeply
into his heart to ask which of them carried the greater
freight of shame, or was the uglier within.

TERRITORIAL TRINIDAD

Hidden in the reeds, he watched the fowl from perhaps a yard away, grateful the thick, lazy air was without any hint of a breeze to carry his scent toward it.

He recognized it as a female whistler, plump with

a wide black beak, long neck, reddish breast, dabs of white around her middle, and dark rump and tail feathers. When the tide had gone out and dusk lifted the afternoon heat, he had seen her venture a short distance from her nest among the mangrove roots, wading through the weeds to the brackish water on stilt legs, standing there in position and occasionally bobbing for small fish, crabs, and insects.

He stood perfectly still and watched, his bare brown feet in the cloying mud, his fingers clenched around a heavy wooden stick that measured about four feet from end to end. He had fashioned the stick from a tree limb, snapping it off a large drooping bough and cleaning the rough bark of spindly branches and leaves with a flat, sharp-edged stone. His shell windbreaker had been folded and knotted into a kind of improvised waterproof sling sack for holding the food supplies that he meant to bring back to his shelter. He wore this against his side, its sleeves tied together at the elasticized wrist openings to form a strap that looped around his neck. Right now it was lightly filled with the plants and such he'd gathered for tonight's supper. There were young cattails and bulrushes he had uprooted from the mud, stripped of their tough, fibrous leaves, and cut down to their edible shoot stems with the same stone tool that had yielded his heavy stick. There were patches of green moss and leathery rock tripe he had soaked in the channel to cleanse them of the toxins that might otherwise wrack him with explosions of vomiting and streaming diarrhea. There were some clusters of wild berries, and even cockle leaves from the thorny clumps that grew in the drier soil inland. The leaf stalks, though bitter on the tongue, were said to ward off the fevers and skin infections with which a man could be stricken in the marshes, and would be more palatable once he peeled away their rinds.

He had survived on slim pickings before, though this particular assortment of food was a lower mark than he could remember.

In the deep poverty of his childhood, the mainstay of his diet had been pap, a thin, simple porridge of stale bread or cornmeal boiled in water. At breakfast his grandma, who had raised him and his two younger sisters since the death of their mother, would sweeten it with honey, or brown sugar, or the pulp of guava or pawpaw or coconut. When the family came together for their evening meal, the pap would be heartened with turnips and carrots and boiled bits of fish or chicken and their broths, and seasoned with the herbs grown in the tiny plot of a garden beside the single-room shack they all occupied. As he approached his teenage years and took on a variety of jobs for the well-to-do—quick to learn how to bring in a wage, he'd worked as a repairman, groundsman, whatever he could do with his hands—they had been able to improve their housing conditions and expand on the staples of their daily meals. And though

Grandma Tressie had passed on long ago, he had continued sharing a portion of his income with his sisters after he went to live and work at Los Rayos, setting aside their money for his regular visits to the village.

Whether or not he had made his final visit . . . *that* was the difficult question, right and true.

Now he saw the whistler make a sudden jab at something she must have spotted in the shallows, her bill coming up quickly, a lump sliding down the sinuous tube of her neck. She would stay only a short time, not journeying too far from the nest she had built in the tangle of mangrove roots on the riverbank behind her, ready to defend her newly hatched ducklings against raiders. The best chance to steal up on her would be as she dabbled for food, dividing her attention between the shapes that flitted past her keen eyes below the water's surface and the sounds that came from the direction of the nest. Should he fail to take her by surprise, the likelihood was that the bird still would not allow herself to be sundered from her young. She would fight to protect them from him, as from any threat, rather than attempt to flee.

This would make his task easier if no less regretful, for Jarvis Lenard hated to kill any living, breathing creature.

He moved toward her, threading a silent path through the eight-foot-tall reed stalks. Jarvis was a Spiritual Baptist by upbringing who, while not a churchgoer, considered himself a man of deep Christian faith. He had, though, sometimes joined friends and relatives at *nyabinghis,* ceremonies of music, religious philosophy, and politics organized by the mainland's Rastafarian community—drawn to these at first by the reggae, the lovely girls with whom he would laugh and dance, and, in his younger years, the free and easy abundance of ganja. At these gatherings the Rastas had introduced him to their ideas about *livity*, a natural way that forbade the eating of flesh, eggs, or dairy in favor of a vegetarian diet, and it had taken hold in his mind and soul. He had come to believe that it was against God's will, even parasitic, to sustain his own body with the meat of animals the Almighty had brought onto the earth, or with anything that carried their lifeblood inside it.

But Jarvis Lenard was a practical, reasoning man as well as a spiritual one. Already today the helicopters had made three passes of the wetlands and bordering jungle—just an hour ago one of them had flown above the wall of trees outside his shelter, blowing a tempest of foliage through its entrance— and their attempts to close in on him would not end when a heavy curtain of darkness fell over the island and they could put their nightseeker equipment into play. The sky would be patrolled day and night, as would the ground. And the village would be watched, and searched, and watched some more, and searched again with sinister, devious eyes.

Jarvis was unsure how long it would be before he might get to a safe place, or even where such a place might be. In the meantime he would need to hide for what could be days, perhaps weeks, and could not be falling short of food. It would hardly be enough for him to scrounge lichen and berries and the pulp of cattails. However much it troubled him, he would have to resign himself to killing if he meant to keep his strength.

He moved on the fowl with two hurried strides and, as he raised his stick with both hands, saw it snap its head up from the water to look around at him. Its display of aggressive defiance was instantaneous—a shrill cry, a puffing out of feathers, a spreading and flapping of wings. Jarvis took another step forward and brought the stick down on it with a hard swing, trying for the long neck or head. But the whistler partially eluded him with a shrieking, fluttering hop and was instead struck on its right flank at the base of the wing. It fell onto its opposite side and slushed about in the marsh, the one broken wing dangling with shoots of bone sticking up through the skin at its base, the other thrashing like a paddle in the water, flinging up clumps of mud.

Jarvis Lenard clubbed the body again, felt the crack of ribs transmitted to his fingers through his stick, saw bright blood splash from underneath its plumage. The crippled bird dragged on its side with its good wing still paddling and scooping mud, and Jarvis stood over it with his stick up over his head for the deathblow. But then his teeth clenched at its dying cries and he knew he could not take a chance that it would not finish the job. The creature had suffered enough.

He lowered the stick across his chest and, gripping it at either end, bent to press it down against the base if the whistler's skull. Then he put one knee heavily on the stick to hold it firm, snatched the bird's legs into his fists, and pulled back with a hard jerk to break the neck apart from the spine as he had seen Grandma Tressie do to the live chickens she would occasionally bring home from market.

The bird quivered as if with a surge of voltage and kept beating its one unbroken wing into the muck for almost a full thirty seconds before its nervous system shut down and the twitches stopped.

Jarvis took his knee off the stick and rose, lifting the warm carcass, standing there a little while as some of the blood and water dripped off. He felt tired, desperate, and sorrowful.

"I beg your forgiveness, little mother, and am deeply obliged for yer sacrifice," he said. His arm and voice shook. "Doan't know if yah would care why I done as I 'ave—an' need yet do—but there are those who must be held accountable fer what's goin' on t'ruout this island, and my intention's ta stick around and see justice done fer a fact."

Jarvis waited another moment, silent and thoughtful, drops of blood and water spilling from the limp bird in his hand. Then he put it in his makeshift sack and turned toward the mangrove thicket where he had spotted its nest.

Without their mother to feed and protect them, the hatchlings would face either starvation or eventual discovery by predators.

He could do no less in his guilt and gratitude than give them the mercy of a faster end.

SAN FRANCISCO BAY AREA, CALIFORNIA

It was half past noon when they met as planned at the Valley Fair Mall on the border of San Jose and Santa Clara.

Megan Breen had exchanged a Louis Vuitton Suhali handbag that she'd purchased the week before, her eye having discriminated a flaw in the stitching of an inner zipper compartment once she got it home. At the price she paid for the bag, this seemed a shameless crime.

Julia Gordian had come for an advertised sale at the aromatherapy and herbal cosmetics boutique. She liked using the tea tree antioxidant facial scrub, lavender and ylang oil body lotion, and rosewater skin restoration gel with "bio-intrinsic essences," whatever *that* meant. All she really knew was that the products made her feel fresh and clean out of the shower and didn't contain too many artificial ingredients, or so their labels said.

Now Megan sat keeping an eye on their shopping bags and other personal articles at the table they had pulled up to in the mall's big, sunshiny food court after doing their errands. In front of her were two cranberry scones, a paper cup of dark Italian roast coffee, and a stack of napkins. The coffee was piping hot and tasted good and had been served with one of those cardboard sleeves that slid around the cup so you didn't have to double it.

She sipped and looked around for Julia, whom she'd last seen getting in line behind her for a garden salad. Then she located her in the crowd of shoppers, leading with a plastic tray as she pushed toward the table. On it was a flat mini-pizza box and some paper plates.

"Sorry it took me a while." Julia said, putting down the tray. "Hot stuff."

She sat opposite Megan. Her black hair cut short and deliberately mussed, she wore avocado-and-cream striped lowrise bellbottoms, a black midriff blouse, and white lace-up Keds sneakers. The blouse was loose and sleeveless with a flared lapel and some kind of complicated sash tied above her exposed navel. On the right lapel was a silver marcasite brooch shaped like a gecko. On her left shoulder was a small dark blue tattoo composed of a pair of stylized kanji ideographs: *Ji*, which means "oneself," and *Yuu*, which roughly translates into the word "reason" or "meaning."

Together they form the traditional Japanese symbol for liberty and freedom.

"Changed your mind about that salad, I see," Megan said.

Julia got comfortable at the table, flapped open her pizza box, and pointed inside. The pie was cut into four slices and topped with a huge pile of onions, peppers, mushrooms, and sausages.

"Wrong," she said. "I just decided it would look better on runny mozzarella, hot tomato sauce, and crust. A nice, thick carbohydrate-ridden crust."

Megan looked into the box.

"No arugula?" she said, straight-faced.

"Or sprouts." Julia smiled. "Those little pieces of spiced ground pork stuffed into intestinal lining do more to zest it up."

Megan cocked an eyebrow with amusement. She had come from the office in a charcoal gray blazer with the Chanel logo on its penny-colored buttons, a matching skirt, an ice blue blouse, and gray mid-heel dress shoes.

"I can't believe you intend to consume that whole pie," she said.

Julia shrugged. She reached for a napkin, put it in her palm, took a wedge of pizza out of the box, put it on the napkin, and bent it slightly along the middle to form a sort of runoff channel for the excess grease. Careful not to lose any of the topping, she tipped the slice down to let the grease drip onto the foiled cardboard liner that had been underneath it. Then she pushed the pizza box toward Megan.

"Mangiare bene," she said. "Take one."

Megan shook her head.

"I already bought these scones."

"Eat 'em afterward." Julia pushed the box closer to her. "Go on, be a lioness."

Megan smiled.

"No, thanks, really," she said. "I have a conference at three o'clock and would rather not belch my way through it."

Julia gave another shrug. "Your loss," she said, starting in on the pizza.

Megan carefully broke a piece off her scone and looked over her business suit for stray crumbs. At the table to her right, a plump woman shopper and her tyke-ish, buddingly overweight daughter had reached the conclusion of their fast-food pit stop. As the little girl started gathering their crumpled waxed wrappers, empty paper cups, and used napkins into the tray between them, Mom admonished her to leave it, somebody who worked in the mall would clean up. Megan saw them stroll away out the corner of her eye, wondering if the kid also caught heat for scrubbing her teeth before bedtime.

"Things moving along okay with your exhibition?" she said to Julia.

"They'd better be." Julia shrugged. "I've got a week to go before the opening, thirty pieces left to hang, and a thousand rapidly multiplying butterflies in my stomach."

Megan took a bite of the scone.

"Still plan on sticking to watercolors?"

"Mostly," Julia said. "I've decided to take your advice and go with a limited mixed media presentation."

"So you included the batiks."

"That abstract series you like, yeah," Julia said. "I brought a few to the gallery yesterday, and have the rest set to go for tonight, which should just leave me needing to drive over my oils."

"Those two great big canvases."

"Right."

"Think they'll fit into the Celica?"

Julia shook her head.

"Not unless I plan on strapping them to the roof." She paused and briefly lowered her glance. "It almost makes me wish I hadn't gotten rid of the old SUV . . . but, hey, you're followed, kidnapped, and almost murdered by professional assassins, you wonder if maybe you ought to appease the gods and trade in the vehicle you were driving that day."

Megan had seen Julia's eyes flick downward as she spoke. It was the same, or nearly the same, whenever she mentioned what happened to her. She would leave it out there, the remembered terror thinly wound in defensive humor, making it difficult to know how to pick up on it, or whether that was even something she wanted.

Julia would talk about it one of these days, Megan thought. Eventually she would need to talk about it in an open way. But the timing was hers to decide.

Megan ate another piece of her scone. A couple of high-school-age boys with McDonald's bags sat down at the table vacated by the round and purposefully untidy mother and daughter. They swept the rubbish and dirty tray that had been left behind to one side of the table, took a bunch of hamburgers from their bags, and plowed into them with enthusiasm.

"I'd be glad to help with the paintings," Megan said. "Far as your transportation problem, though, my car's smaller than yours."

Julia made a swishing don't-worry-about-it gesture.

"Dad's got me covered," she said. "He's coming over tomorrow in the Land Rover."

Megan scrunched her forehead. "Roger?" she said.

"He would be my one-and-only father, right." Julia gave her a puzzled look. "Why the funny face?"

"I didn't know I made one."

"That's because you couldn't see it from here," Julia said, and tapped her side of the tabletop.

Megan lifted her coffee to her mouth, sipped. "Guess I was wondering about your handsome curator friend," she said.

Julia frowned slightly.

"Richard is an *assistant* curator," she said. "One among several at the museum."

"Uh-oh. This already sounds ominous."

Julia sighed.

"We're over," she said.

"Over?"

"And done," Julia said. "I broke things off last weekend."

"Wasn't that your first date with him?"

"Second, if you feel the need to count," Julia said, chewing her pizza. "Take it from a divorced woman, Meg. It's better to recognize a dead-end street before turning into it, because those U-turns can be absolute murder."

"Do tell."

"You really want to hear about it?"

"I would."

Julia looked at her, expelled another sigh.

"Last Saturday night, Richard asks me out to dinner, my choice of restaurants," she said. "I suggest Emilio's, you know it?"

"Sure," Megan said. "That Italian place in Santa Clara with the courtyard in back. Very romantic."

"Which is the reason I picked it . . . that and the cuisine," Julia said. "Easy question, okay? What's Italian cooking supposed to be except this"—she gave the pizza in her hand a demonstrative little shake—"or some kind of pasta dish? Fettuccine, ravioli, lasagna. Maybe veal scallopini. A basket of homemade bread or rolls on the side, a cannoli for desert, nothing too creative. Am I reaching some unreasonable level of expectation yet?"

"Not to me."

"Bam!" Julia said, doing a fair impression of Emeril Lagasse. "In Richard's world, asking a date to choose a restaurant doesn't necessarily mean she's also entitled to choose her own dish. Most especially not if it contains repulsive, unfashionable *carbs*."

"Uh-oh." Megan had to grin. "He's one of those?"

"Hold the bun," Julia said with a nod. "You know how I am, Meg. The reigning Miss Individuality. If he says so right off, no sweat, I find another restaurant. I've got nothing against him believing a certain diet works, but don't foist it on me with a lecture about unburned calories."

Megan was shaking her head. "Did he happen to notice you're in pretty fantastic shape?" she said.

"Not the way he might've if he hadn't blown his chances that night, let me tell you." Julia frowned. "I walked out on him, Meg. Left him right there at the table and hailed a cab home."

Megan's eyes widened with surprise and amusement. "No."

"Yes," Julia said. "He kept insisting I eat the lobster or grilled fish. And he talked over me—*overruled* me—when I tried making my preference of Ziti al pomodoro clear to the waiter." A frown. "That was the last unbearable, embarrassing straw. I've only answered his phone calls once since, and that was to tell him to forget my number."

Megan threw her head back and laughed. "God," she said. "And I thought *my* history with men was a road littered with wreckage."

Julia looked at her.

"Goes to show there's always a person waiting to outdo you," she said, laughing a little, too.

They ate quietly. Megan worked away at her scone as Julia got through eating her slice and then reached into the pizza box for another.

"Enough about my life," Julia said after a bit. "What's with yours these days?"

Megan shrugged, sipped.

"Work," she said.

"No play?"

"No time." Megan sighed. "It's taken everything out of me just trying to settle into the new position. And lately our projects with Sedco have developed some speed bumps. The Caribbean fiber deal sticks out . . . Do you know about it?"

"Some," Julia said. "I heard my father mention it once or twice when Dan Parker was still on their board. He's like a member of our family. Almost a god-uncle to me."

Megan nodded her awareness. "There's a guy that replaced him on the board of directors, A. R. Baxter—that's Andrew Reed, great-great-grandson of the famous privateer—FYI. He's constantly wanting to reevaluate and clarify points of contractual agreement. He's a stubborn pain, and it makes for long, hard days of meeting with our own lawyers and executives."

"Is Baxter the reason for your conference this afternoon?"

Megan shook her head.

"That's a different can of worms," she said. "I felt we needed another huddle to work out a plan for making nice with the Pentagon."

Julia looked at her. "Because of what Tom Ricci did in New York," she said.

Megan nodded, sipped away at her coffee. Again, the subject of the abduction hung unaddressed between them. Ricci had assembled the Sword task force that had tracked Julia to the cabin in Big Sur. He had pressed the search and gotten her out himself and left the man who'd led the hostage-takers dead. But Ricci alone knew exactly how that man died. Ricci alone was in the room with him, behind a locked door, in the minutes before he died. And what Megan wanted to say now, and didn't, was that whatever occurred behind that door had seemed in some indeterminate way to spiral out into what took place those many months later in New York City.

"Tom's name is bound to come up, sure," she said instead, trying with her even tone to reduce his importance as an issue, make it sound as if he wasn't at the very center of things. "We'll have to decide what to do about him when Pete gets back from the islands."

"Has anybody been in touch with him since he was suspended? Anybody from UpLink, that is."

Megan regarded Julia for a few seconds, struck by the too-light, almost singsong quality of her voice right then, thinking maybe more than one of them here wanted to downplay the matter.

"Pete's tried calling him," she said. "Not with any success, though. At least these past few weeks."

"He doesn't answer his phone?"

"Doesn't answer, doesn't return messages, won't give us a clue what's going on with him."

Julia tilted her head curiously.

"That seems kind of odd," she said.

"Come on." Megan couldn't hide her skepticism. "Tom Ricci being incommunicative?"

Julia was looking at her.

"I mean Pete not going to see him where he lives," she said. "I'd always heard they were tight."

The expression on Megan's face went from skeptical to just plain blank. She was unsure why that hadn't entered into her thought processes. But it hadn't. She didn't know what to say, and found herself glad to see Julia reaching for slice number three, apparently satisfied to let the whole thing ride. Besides, a quick glance at her watch told her it was almost time to get going.

She drank some more coffee, ate some more scone, examined herself for crumbs again, discovered a few tiny specks on her skirt, and was brushing them off when she noticed that one of the burger-munching teenagers at the nearby table had turned to watch her, his attention glued to her hand as it moved over the lap of her skirt.

She drilled a cold stare into him and he snapped his eyes away.

"Did you get a load of *him*?" she said, looking aghast at Julia.

Julia chewed a mouthful of pizza, swallowed.

"That's amore," she said.

Megan made a face. "What?" she said. "Getting ogled by a high school kid with acne on his cheeks?"

Julia shrugged.

"At least he didn't hold the bun," she said with a sly grin.

Devon's nightly set at Club Forreál would begin with a shadow dance.

A minute or two before she made her entrance, the DJ would key up something with a heavy beat and a smooth walking bass, and the lights would pulse in rhythm over and around the empty stage. Then she would step from the wings in a slight, clingy bikini top and sarong that gave her an illusion of nakedness in silhouette.

She was limber and acrobatic getting into her dance. As the men around the stage watched her slink out in front of the screen, they would realize she wasn't all skin, and that would build on the tease while her movements became more explicitly sexual. The stage was large, with a couple of runways, and she was skillful at using every inch of it.

Most nights Devon's set went two songs. The opening song would be the longer of them, giving her a chance to warm up the crowd with her bit behind the screen, and then come out and strip off her bikini top while dancing in the swell of lights and music. She called that her first reveal. At the pole Devon would work her flesh hard, sliding, pumping, swinging her body.

The second number in her set would have a quickened tempo, and midway through she would peel away the sarong.

Club Forreál had booze on its menu. This meant the house dancers could go topless but not nude. Under California law, nightclubs that entertained with full nudity were restricted to serving nonalcoholic drinks. The men who came to watch Devon and the other girls weren't happy about it, but the alcohol loosened them up for a good time, and Devon, when she writhed free of her sarong, would leave little to the imagination in a G-string that was almost invisible, and that made for an easy tradeoff.

At his table in the third row from the stage, Tom Ricci finished his Chivas and water, caught the eye of his waitress, and made a pouring gesture over the glass, holding his thumb and forefinger apart to indicate he wanted his next one heavier on the scotch.

She smiled her understanding and waggled toward the bar in her racer shorts.

Ricci turned to watch Devon emerge from behind the screen.

He had seen her dance perhaps twice since the night they had met here, when her name was still Carolina to him. Carolina was her professional alias. It was posted on the schedule outside the club's entrance, and above her gallery photos on its elaborate Web site, and announced from the DJ booth as the music got cranked for her set. It was also the name that customers used when they tapped the maître d's shoulder to request a private dance with her. Ricci had once asked how she had chosen it, and she'd told him it was borrowed from the state where she had grown up. She did not specify whether that was North or South Carolina, and he hadn't pursued the subject. Their involvement was a fair give-and-take that sometimes relieved the emptiness inside each of them. But she gave away nothing extra, and neither did Ricci.

Now the waitress came over with his fresh drink. Ricci paid, tipped, noticed her lingering by the table. He raised the glass to his lips and swallowed. The scotch was warm in his mouth and then going down his throat. She'd done okay with the proportions, he thought, and nodded.

She smiled at him and left and he turned back toward the stage and watched Devon heat up her set.

The sarong in which she was costumed tonight was a dash of metallic fabric with black and blue horizontal bands and long, shiny fringes that would flap over her left thigh. In her bellybutton was a silver serpent pin, its tiny jewel-eyed head dangling downward. Ricci guessed between sixty and a hundred other men had their eyes on her as she slowly untied and shed the wrap. That didn't bother him much. The woman up there in the colored lights almost could have been anybody. She seemed unsolid, a projected image. Only in glimpses could Ricci see Devon in her. Something she did on stage would remind him of something she had done when they were in bed together—a toss of her head, a contortion of her waist, a wanton curl of her lips—and Ricci would wonder whether it had been practiced even during their sex, and if it came from the inside out or the outside in.

Mostly that was the extent of his feelings as he watched. A curiosity rather than jealousy or possessiveness. It was an emotional remove not so different from what he felt toward Devon when they were together. The stage just seemed to frame and accentuate things for him.

He sat and drank more of his scotch.

Club Forreál was a garish island of neon and stucco outside Santa Clara on Highway 101, El Camino Real. *For real*, Ricci thought, and found himself having to smile a little at that. He had the sense that nothing in the place was what it seemed. Or if it was, that it wasn't what he ought to be going out of his way to seek. He neither liked nor disliked watching Devon perform, and she seemed to pretty well match his indifference. He had no idea whether she had noticed him at his table, but he hadn't intended to make a secret of it, or surprise her for any reason. He wasn't even sure why he'd come. He'd simply gotten into his car and driven here intending to sit awhile, and it was all the same to him if she knew about it or didn't. Either way, he would probably leave before she was ready to head out with him.

It was a working night for Devon, and the place was packed; she would want to stay on shift for several hours yet.

Ricci wondered if A.J. ever popped in without letting her know beforehand. He held onto the thought a minute, tried to picture what A.J. looked like, and glanced randomly at some of the men around him, their faces turned toward the stage, staring at Devon as they were swept by the crayon colors of the disco strobes. Any one of them might be A.J. All Ricci knew about him was that he had a wife and kids and a high credit line and, Devon had once casually mentioned, a boat that he liked to launch out of Monterey. It was a waste of time trying to figure out who was the strongest candidate, but so was a lot else.

Ricci played the game with himself awhile longer, grew tired of it, and drank. Then he heard a loud squall of laughter from a nearby table and turned to see what had provoked it. There were four men at the table. They were young, maybe in their early twenties. A look of hang-jawed arousal on his features, one of them had pushed himself back from the table's edge and was getting a chair dance from a blonde who had finished her set right before Devon. His friends seemed boisterously amused and elated by the whole thing.

Ricci watched her bump and grind between his outspread legs, bare-breasted, wearing only a red sequined thong and high heels. Here again the law would have something to say about how far she could go. But while it prohibited physical contact between performer and client, and house rules declared they could come no closer to each other than six inches, nobody was holding a tape measure between the blonde and the guy at the table, and she seemed more than open to some occasional rubbing up against him.

The good money for dancers at Club Forreál was in chairs. Elsewhere in a room its owners called the VIP Lounge, the better money was in couches. Their maroon velvet cushions lined two of its walls, and the men who sat on them could get a private dance that was supposed to have the same restrictions on touching as the dances in the main hall. But the doors of the VIP Lounge were kept closed, and watched from the main room by security guards on the lookout for vice cops, and the girls inside the

lounge, who would start out a couch dance straddling a customer's lap, would bend the hell out of
both legal and house regulations if the price was
right.

Devon had told Ricci she preferred doing chairs to
couches. They didn't bring in nearly the same cash
but let her stay within eyeshot of the bouncers at the
front entrance, who would step in when guys got too
touchy. She had told him she followed the six-inches-
of-separation rule to the letter in the main room and,
on the rare instances she worked the VIP, gave the
rule just enough slack for her customer to feel "nice"
about his experience. She had said that she could
identify the ones who would be trouble and was careful to steer away from them. She claimed to likewise
recognize the ones who were okay, and she looked at
every situation from the perspective of whether it
would let her stay in control.

Ricci hadn't been certain if she honestly believed
that. He knew the power of female sexuality but also
understood the power of men with money. And he always gave an edge to the men when they kept their
clothes on and paid women not to for their pleasure.

Once he had asked Devon exactly what she meant
by control, and by a customer feeling nice, and she
had remained quiet for a long while.

"Do you really want to know?" she'd said at last.

He'd told her he did.

"I'll come down as low as they want, for as long as

they want," she'd said, her hesitation suddenly gone. "But their hands stay off me."

Three rows from where Devon was deftly bending herself around a pole, Ricci took a deep breath and lowered his empty glass to the tabletop. He felt a kind of soft grayness settling over his thoughts and guessed he was a little drunk. Not too drunk to drive, but he could see how that might be a biased opinion. If he went for another refill, he might have to dispute it himself.

He stood up and pushed in his chair. Devon was almost through with her set and he'd decided to leave before she got off stage. He didn't want to know if she'd spotted him. He didn't want to know if A.J. was in the house. He didn't want to see her go one-on-one with any of the customers who'd watched her dance, or make her feel as if she shouldn't because he was here. He wanted nothing except to leave.

He turned and strode between the tables in the main room, and past the cashier's counter, and then past the hulking bouncers in black pants and T-shirts at the door, giving them a nod as he walked outside.

The night was cool and breezy with mist that carried the salt smell of the bay across the parking lot. Ricci stood on the neon-splashed sidewalk before the entrance and took it in for a moment. He felt steady enough on his feet and told himself he'd be okay behind the wheel.

He stepped off the sidewalk into the parking lot

and went around back toward his Jetta. The lot was illuminated by high overhead sodiums, but the club's rear wall largely blocked his aisle from the glow of the lights. Though he had a decent recollection of where he'd left the car in the solid row of vehicles, he had to pause and search the darkness for a minute or two to locate it.

Ricci finally saw it about a dozen cars up ahead and moved on.

That was when he noticed a shadowy figure crossing the lot from its perimeter fence opposite the club. The man cut through several aisles of vehicles, momentarily slipped out of sight between two cars, and then emerged into Ricci's aisle three or four yards in front of him. He wore a raincoat—a trench—belted at the waist and flowing well down below his knees.

Ricci's guard raised itself a notch. You were alone in a dark place and saw somebody appear out of nowhere, you would be a fool in general not to be alert. He had met some dangerous people in his time at UpLink. And before that, and after—if his life as it was proved to be after.

And there was the coat. And the smooth, almost gliding way the man moved in it.

Ricci couldn't dismiss the association they brought to mind.

He suddenly felt the absence of his weapon under his sport jacket. His suspension had not up until now cost him his carry permit, but the bouncers who wanded everybody who passed through the club's door didn't worry about permits, they worried about men with too much testosterone and alcohol in their bloodstreams acting like they were in some Dodge City saloon, and thinking they would get into it over the dance hall girls. Coming here tonight, he'd had to leave his apartment without his FiveSeven.

Ricci walked a little further through the aisle, stopped. The man approached to within a couple of feet of him and did the same, hands in the pockets of his coat.

They studied one another with quiet recognition in the darkness and fog.

"Lathrop," Ricci said.

"Surprise, surprise."

Ricci stood there watching him. Lathrop's hands being out of sight in his coat pockets made him more acutely conscious of his own lack of a weapon.

"How'd you find me here?"

"Doesn't matter." A shrug. "I've managed to find you in all kinds of places."

"Super," Ricci said. "Now lose me."

Lathrop was quiet, seeming to notice where Ricci's gaze had fallen, his lips parting in a kind of smile.

"You think I came to take you out," he said.

Ricci shrugged.

"I don't know why you came," he said. "Wouldn't waste my time worrying about it."

Lathrop slowly slid his hands out of his pockets and let them drop to his sides.

"This better?" he said.

Ricci just looked at him and shrugged again.

"Seems to me," Lathrop said, "you could use a cup of strong coffee."

Ricci remained silent. The breeze had picked up strength and he could feel the drifting mist on his cheeks.

"What the hell do you want?" he said after a while.

"My car's back near the fence." Lathrop nodded slightly in that direction. "Let's go for a ride."

"No, thanks."

"We need to talk."

"No," Ricci said, edging past Lathrop and up the aisle.

"Ricci," Lathrop said in a calm voice. "Not so fast."

He kept walking.

"You owe me, remember?" Lathrop said from behind him. Again calmly, softly. "Big time."

Ricci took another couple of steps forward, slowed, and finally halted. He stood there for almost a full minute, his back to Lathrop in the deserted parking lot. Then he turned around to look at him.

"Damn you," he said. "God damn you."

Lathrop smiled his enigmatic smile.

"I'll buy the coffee," he said, his long coat ruffling around him as he led the way off into the deeper shadows.

FOUR

THE WATERFRONT AT ALVISO WAS NOT MUCH
more than a drainage slough for the Guadalupe River,
but then the Guadalupe itself amounted to little more
than a glorified creek as it snailed through downtown
SanJo, and then out of the city to deposit its sewage
overflow between Alviso's dirt levees and reeded
banks before wearily petering off into San Francisco
Bay.

From where Lathrop had parked at the end of Gold
Street, Ricci could see nothing in the fog and distance besides some aircraft warning lights on the
power transmission towers across the slough. Pale
beacons under the best conditions, they gave the illu-

sion of flickering on and off now as the high, slow mist dragging past them over the marshes began to gradually mix with light rain.

Behind the wheel of his Dodge coupe, Lathrop reached into the 7-Eleven bag he'd stuffed into a molded plastic storage compartment on his right side, produced a Styrofoam coffee cup, and handed it across the seat to Ricci. Then he got out a second cup for himself, peeled open the sip hole on the plastic lid, and raised it to his lips.

The two men sat quietly, as they had throughout the entire ride on the freeway to the extreme northern edge of San Jose, their silence uninterrupted even when Lathrop had pulled up to the gas station convenience store for their coffees.

"So here we are," Lathrop said. "Like a couple of old friends."

Ricci drank from his cup.

"No," he said.

Lathrop shrugged.

"Here we are, anyway," he said.

They sat looking out across the ugly mud flats. Lathrop had driven from the club with his wipers set on intermittent, and now that they'd been turned off, the windshield was smeary with an accumulation of moisture.

"Too bad about what happened to you," Lathrop said. "Enforced leave . . . I might have figured."

Ricci's remote stare didn't move from the windshield. "How do you know they're calling it that?" he said.

Lathrop shrugged again.

"They can call it anything they want, doesn't matter," he said. "Somebody phones the switchboard operator at UpLink to ask for you these past few weeks, she connects him or her to your voice mail. Somebody asks the operator why you aren't returning messages, her answer's that you're on leave of absence. Somebody asks how long you'll be gone, she just says indefinitely."

Ricci sat watching the inconstant tower lights through the haze. "Could be that's my own choice," he said.

Lathrop shook his head.

"There are newspaper stories about an incident at that chemical factory outside Manhattan, and UpLink security being involved, and how the Feds are crying foul because they didn't get invited to the party," he said. "Knowing you called the party, it's easy to dope out the rest."

Ricci still hadn't turned from the windshield.

"Tell me what you want," he said.

"I heard you the first time in that parking lot," Lathrop said.

"Then get to it," Ricci said.

Lathrop nodded.

"In a minute," he said. "First we need to finish up with New York."

Ricci didn't say anything.

"I tipped you about the Dragonfly laser," Lathrop said. "I know what was supposed to go down at the plant. There wouldn't be an available grave plot in the city today if it was up to the people who want your head on a pole, and they'd have swallowed that a lot easier than you doing what you did. It's all about control for them, and they hate losing their hold on it to a guy like you."

"Good that you're so sure," Ricci said.

"Don't let yourself believe anything else," Lathrop said. "I'd love to hear them talk about it behind closed doors. Seriously, Ricci. I would love it."

They were both quiet for a while as the mist and drizzle began intensifying to a steadier rainfall against the windshield. Lathrop leaned back in his seat and drank some coffee.

"Quick story about an acquaintance of mine," he said. "Special agent, counter drugs, deep cover. Doesn't matter which agency and I probably couldn't remember it to tell you. But what I do remember is he wasn't interested in the rule book. Didn't follow the rule book. Too many other guys did and it got them killed or burned. Because the players on the other side were smarter and meaner and knew how to turn the rules against them."

He paused, sipped.

Ricci kept staring out toward the glints of distant light on the electrical towers.

"This guy any good?" he said.

"From what I know he got the job done," Lathrop said, and shrugged. "If he rubbed his bosses wrong, they left him alone. The main thing for them was he delivered for a long time. And that meant they could stay posed for the television cameras behind piles of seized dope and guns." Lathrop fell silent a moment. "Doesn't matter who the bosses are, it's the same. They don't have to get their hands dirty. They don't deal with the snarling dogs. They never get bullet holes in their foreheads, or have their dead bodies dumped in weed fields with their privates stuffed down their throats. From where they sit in their pressed suits and white shirts, everything's risk free, and that's exactly how they want it to stay. Gives them a chance to act like winners every once in a while without ever taking the hurt when they lose."

"Tell me the rest about your friend."

"Acquaintance," Lathrop said. "Like the two of us."

Ricci grunted but didn't comment.

"I hear a federal judge took exception to him giving a Big Willie drug dealer rough treatment, made some noise about looking into how he'd handled some other investigations," Lathrop said. "His bosses started to worry about what might turn up, wanted the problem taken care of before stories started leaking to the press, and cut him loose. Erased his name from their employee records, wiped out every mention of him in their case files."

"Just like that?"

Lathrop snapped his fingers.

"Got it," he said.

Ricci grunted. "Where'd that leave him?" he said.

Lathrop shrugged.

"Far as who or what?" he said. "He didn't go away, he was going down. There were some things about his tactics that would have gotten the kind of publicity nobody up the line appreciates. Things he did that wouldn't jibe with what your ordinary citizen hears is right and good at his Sunday morning church sermons."

"And how about after he went away?" Ricci said. "He keep on playing by his own rules?"

Lathrop shook his head.

"My guess is this guy would tell you that'd be too simple," he said. "He would have stepped off the board. Made up his own game, shoved its rule book in his back pocket, and left everybody else guessing. Their guesses get too close to suit his interests, I could see how he'd change the game on them. Or maybe even play a bunch of different games on different boards. All at the same time just to keep things jumping."

Ricci looked around at Lathrop.

"This one of them?" he said.

Lathrop shrugged again and said nothing more for a long while.

"Remember the night we first crossed paths?" he said finally. "The Quiros and Salazar clans mixing it up in Balboa Park. Enrique and Lucio getting popped. You after information I'd got on Enrique Quiros."

Ricci kept looking into his face. "You're the person who brought me there," he said. "Always figured it was the same thing for them, but that maybe they didn't know it."

Again Lathrop's veiled expression showed neither confirmation nor denial.

"Lucio was an old school handler, used muscle and guts to keep his syndicate together," he said. "When he died, it was over for them. But Enrique's style was different. He had the personality of a pocket calculator, ran his business like any other corporation. His branch got clipped, the power just shifted over to another office. Juan Quiros, one of Enrique's cousins, took charge, pretty much oversees operations from out in Modesto these days. Without Salazar's competition, the Quiros bunch marked their territory all up and down the coast."

"And?"

"There's a girl, Marissa Vasquez," Lathrop said. "She's twenty years old, a college student. Sort of kid every father would want for a daughter. Her dad happens to be Esteban Vasquez, ever hear of him?"

"No."

"He's Enrique and Lucio rolled into one . . . the

badges would call him an up-and-comer and they'd be wrong. Been on the scene for years giving cash subs to pot growers across the Rio Grande, uses his construction companies in Frisco as laundering fronts for his return on investments. Until lately, Vasquez kept his trade away from his own neighborhood, but that's changed, maybe because he saw some openings after Balboa Park. Ecstasy, meth, smack—Vasquez has couriers moving stuff right through Quiros turf." Lathrop flicked his eyes up to Ricci's. "Quiros had Marissa kidnapped to get him to back off."

Ricci held his gaze.

"Haven't heard anything about that, either," he said.

Lathrop nodded.

"You wouldn't have," he said. "Guys like Esteban try to avoid bringing their troubles to the cops."

"So he came to you," Ricci said.

"Right."

"And you came to me."

"Right."

"Why?"

Their eyes remained locked. Lathrop raised his coffee cup and drank from it very slowly.

"Esteban Vasquez wants me to find his daughter," he said. "I want your help."

Ricci sat there, his face very still.

"I don't do favors for drug dealers," he said.

"We'd be in it for ourselves," Lathrop said. "Working freelance."

"Whatever word you use, my answer won't change," Ricci said. "It was my kid, I'd find a different place to run my business."

Lathrop shook his head. "You aren't Vasquez. If he gives in to the competition, it'll make him look weak. They'll devour him wherever he tries to migrate."

"Then he'd get what he deserves."

"And how about the girl?" Lathrop said. "The way these flesh eaters work there's no guarantee Vazquez gets her back alive no matter what he does."

Ricci was quiet a second.

"Might be true," he said. "Still doesn't make it my problem."

Lathrop shifted around to look out the rain-streaked windshield, rested back in his seat.

"You ever been to the Sierra Nevada? Out there in the canyons along the mountains between Fresno and Yosemite?"

Ricci shook his head.

"Marissa Vasquez was baited by a slick operator name of Manuel Aguilera," Lathrop said. "Didn't know he was connected. He romanced her and set her up to be taken and now she's somewhere in all that nothing with about eight to ten *cholos* in guerrilla outfits imported from down around Ciudad Juárez."

A long silence spent itself between them. It was

pouring outside now, raindrops dashing against the windows, beating erratically on the roof of the car.

"How do you know?" Ricci said.

"Where they brought her?"

"Where they brought her, how they did it, everything."

Lathrop made a low sound in his throat.

"Got it from another Quiros relative. I crashed his party down in Baja three, four nights ago," he said. "He's tight with Juan and Aguilera and hooked them up. Pretty much told me everything."

Ricci flashed a glance at him. "He give you any details about the abduction besides what you told me?"

Lathrop shrugged.

"Some," he said. And paused. "Won't be doing any more talking, though."

Ricci watched the raindrops splash the windshield, slither down over it to further distort the red warning lights on the high towers across the slough. The coffee had succeeded in sharpening his thoughts, but while he was mostly sober now the feeling of inner grayness had persisted.

"I could find Marissa Vasquez on my own," Lathrop said. "But the banditos would be a problem at ten-to-one odds."

"Ten-to-two doesn't sound much better," Ricci said.

"It does if we're the two and have each other's back," Lathrop said.

Ricci was silent staring out the windshield. The cup had cooled in his hand.

"We pull this thing off, Esteban's reward would be hefty," Lathrop said. "Three mil split right down the middle."

Ricci was silent.

"And," Lathrop went on, "we'd be saving a damsel in distress."

Ricci held his silence, his eyes peering into the rainswept night. Then he turned to Lathrop.

"Play your games with me, you won't have to worry about those mercs," he said.

Lathrop smiled a little, put his cup into the holder beside him, reached for the key in his ignition.

"Anything else I need to be warned about?" he said.

Ricci shook his head.

"Then I'll bring you back to your car before its spark plugs get soaked," Lathrop said, and cranked up the Dodge's engine.

Roger Gordian seemed pleased with himself as he pulled the Rover to a halt in front of his daughter's garage. He also seemed braced for what was coming from her, and would be very determined to head it off.

"Mission accomplished," he said, and shifted into Park. "The paintings have been hung. You're back home safe and sound. And we managed to beat the rain."

Julia sat quietly in the passenger seat watching him tick off his successes on his fingertips.

"But not the drizzle and fog," she said.

Gordian poked a finger at the control panel on his dashboard.

"That's why I've got fog lamps," he said.

On motion sensors, Julia's exterior garage and porch lights had instantly begun shining down over her lawn as they turned in from the road. She regarded her father in their brightness now, impressed by how well he'd learned to use the warm and cuddly senior routine to his charming advantage since retirement. But the look of dead-set resolution in his steel gray eyes was no different than ever. It didn't matter if he was laying the foundation for a backyard dog pen, talking about the Dream of global freedom through communications on which he had built Up-Link International, or anticipating an invitation he'd already made up his mind to decline.

Gordian's problem tonight was that he and Julia were two of a kind when it came to persistence—and he knew it.

She waited beside him for a moment, parked there with the mist draping over the Rover's windshield, and isolated droplets of moisture splatting onto its hood and roof from the branches of an old sequoia overhanging her driveway.

"You really shouldn't drive in weather like this, Dad," she said, getting it over with. "It's already after eleven. The smart thing would be for you to stay overnight."

Gordian went from poking at his dash console to tapping his steering wheel column.

"I'll be fine," he said. "Thanks, anyway."

She looked at him.

"You can fix us hot chocolates," she said. "I've got about four kinds of Ghirardelli's. And a fresh quart of milk and some whipped cream in the fridge."

He smiled.

"*I* can fix them?"

"Nobody does it better."

"I'm proud to see my daughter's as kind and generous as she is talented," he replied, still smiling. "Seriously, hon, I appreciate the offer. But I'll be home inside an hour."

Which meant his return trip might total almost *two hours,* assuming the rain didn't intensify to the extent that it slowed up road conditions, she thought. It had taken them about forty five minutes to get back here to Pescadero from the gallery in Boulder Creek, and a lot of it had been country driving on some of the darkest stretches of Highway 9. Tack on their ride out to the gallery, and it would mean some four hours behind the wheel for him tonight if he headed off into the Palo Alto hills.

"Okay, here's where the deal really gets sweet," she said. "I'll let my adorable canines sleep in the guest room with you. Jack, Jill, Viv, too. So what do you say?"

Gordian suddenly burst out laughing. Julia took that as a good sign considering she'd been braced for his I-flew-fighter-jets-through-enemy-flack-and-can-handle-a-drive-on-the-freeway argument.

"A man's got to beware of having all his wishes come true at once," he said. "Any other attempts to buy influence before we say good night?"

Julia gave him a level glance.

"There's something serious I've meant to discuss with you," she said. "And if that's not persuasive enough, I might threaten to call Mom and ask her to decide the issue."

Gordian looked at her and cleared his throat. It was over and they both knew it.

"Do you mean it about wanting to talk?" he said.

Julia nodded sincerely. There *were* some thoughts that had been bearing heavily on her since she'd gotten together with Megan that afternoon, although she'd wondered whether to keep them to herself. But so much for that.

"I'll phone Ashley and get those hot chocolates on the burner," Gordian said, and reached for his door handle.

Thirty minutes later, they were sitting over their cocoa mugs in Julia's kitchen breakfast nook, cornered by three relentlessly staring greyhounds. The rain was falling in sheets outside.

Gordian looked from Jack, a brindle male, to the two females—Jill, a teal blue, and Vivian the blond bombshell. All of them were stretched out on the floor, their heads cranked toward the table, ears perked, penny-colored eyes fixed on his steaming drink.

"Don't they know dogs can be deathly allergic to chocolate . . . or are your constant reminders just for *my* benefit?"

Julia shrugged. "Ex-racers don't know anything besides being starved for food and attention," she said. "They'd crunch their insatiable jaws down on our cups if I gave them half a chance."

Gordian sipped from his mug and listened to the rain pounding against the windows.

"It's coming down in buckets," he said.

Julia nodded.

"Lucky thing I didn't give you a tough time about staying the night," he said.

She smiled at him. "Not *too*."

Gordian was quiet awhile, his face turning serious.

"That talk you mentioned . . ."

Julia noticed his hesitation, reached out to pat the back of his hand.

"Don't look so concerned," she said. "I'm fine."

He kept his eyes on her, visibly relieved.

"Oh," he said. "I was . . . well, you know . . ."

"You worry sometimes."

Gordian nodded.

"I never doubt that you can take care of yourself," he said. "But since the divorce . . . and then after what happened last year . . ."

"I know, Dad," she said. "And I appreciate it."

He looked at her.

"And you honestly are okay?"

"Aside from being pregnant by an axe murderer named Jason, yes."

Gordian's eyes widened for the briefest of moments. Then he raised his cup to his lips.

"As long as this Jason respects his elders and earns a decent wage, you two have my blessing," he said.

Julia smiled, spooned some whipped cream into her mouth off the top of her hot chocolate.

"What I wanted to ask isn't about me," she said after a bit. "It's about Tom Ricci."

Gordian looked surprised.

"Oh," he said.

"You all right with that or should it be none of my business?"

"Why not?" Gordian shrugged. "You just caught me unprepared." Another shrug. "I don't know exactly what I expected, but guess it was something else."

Julia lowered the spoon to the table and sat with her hands wrapped around her cup.

"I met Megan Breen for lunch today and his name sort of came up in conversation," she said, unsure why she'd elected to omit the fact that she was the one who *brought* it up. "I knew he'd been suspended, and was wondering if anything was ever made final." She paused. "Meg told me there hadn't been a decision."

Gordian nodded.

"That's my understanding," he said. "It will be her call when it's made. And Pete Nimec's, I'd imagine."

"You don't have any part in it?"

Gordian shook his head.

"One of the biggest things I decided the day I stepped down as UpLink's CEO was to place my un-qualified trust in Megan. She's too competent to be a figurehead and shouldn't have to contend with a meddling old know-it-all getting into her abundant red hair." He scratched under his chin. "Besides, that would defeat the whole aim of retirement, don't you agree?"

"Yes," Julia said. And hesitated briefly again. "Nine times out of ten."

Gordian crooked an eyebrow at her. "You think the Ricci situation ought to be an exception to the rule?"

"I'm not sure," she said. "It's hard to be objective considering I owe the man my life."

Gordian didn't answer. He sipped his hot choco-late and seemed to listen awhile to the whisk of rain on the windows.

"I understand how you feel," he said at last. "I'd have to be cold and ungrateful not to feel that way myself. But we need to put personal feelings aside here. No doubt, Tom Ricci has proven he's capable of being the best at what he does. On the other hand he's shown a contempt of authority that makes him a serious wild card. From an organizational perspective, his . . . I don't know what to call it except *insubordination* . . . has brought on a world of trouble."

Julia inhaled, held the breath a moment, then blew it out to disperse the thin filaments of steam curling from her drink.

"I've been thinking about when you, Megan, and Pete cooked up a name for UpLink security all those years ago," she said. "Sword, you decided to call it. And I felt that sounded so hokey and pompous, remember?"

Gordian nodded, smiling a little.

"I remember," he said. "You've never been shy about your opinions."

Julia gave him smile of her own.

"Or you about your opinion of my opinions," she said. "I can still see the annoyed look on your face. And hear you explaining that the name was a sort of play on words. That it referred to the legend of the Gordian knot, and how Alexander the Great was supposed to have solved the problem of untwisting it with one swift hack of his sword, and how *that* perfectly described the approach your people would take to solving problems. Realistic, direct, practical, determined . . . those were the exact words you used."

Gordian looked straight into her eyes.

"We don't forget much," he said.

"No," Julia said. "We hardly forget anything."

Gordian nodded, and for a while the only sound was the rattling of rain on the windows.

"If your point is that the actions Ricci took are somehow in keeping with the premise behind Sword's formation, I don't think I'm able to bite," he said then. "It's based on taking that premise to a reckless extreme. And it's judging those actions by results that could very well have been calamitously different."

"That's what I keep hearing, but where's the proof?" Julia said. "Think about it a minute, Dad. Somebody infects you with a germ hatched in a lab, almost kills you. A year later this head case has me kidnapped. And then another psychopath with a mission tries to wipe out New York. What situations could be *more* extreme? How do you deal with any of them without taking risks? Tom Ricci's always been ready and he's come up a major stud every time."

Gordian looked at her again. "A major stud?"

"Blame them." Julia nodded at the dogs. "You live in a house full of animals, you start thinking in animalistic terms."

Gordian's brow had crinkled with amusement.

"If you say so," he said.

They spent a few minutes quietly drinking their hot chocolates. Then, his cup emptied, Gordian pushed it slightly to the side, leaned forward, and massaged the back of his neck.

"You make a better case for Ricci than I could," he said. "Unfortunately his attitude doesn't help. Because of him UpLink's under pressure from all sides, and from what I hear he's dropped out of contact. If he wants trust, he's got to show some. In somebody. How can Megan and Pete go to the mat for him, buy him a chance, when he won't give himself one?"

Julia considered that and realized she didn't have an answer. She sighed, finished her own drink, and glanced at the clock on the wall.

"It's after midnight," she said, and stretched. "Suppose the dogs ought to be getting in their Z's."

Gordian nodded.

"A little sleep wouldn't hurt us, either," he said.

A moment later Julia rose, pushed in her chair, and gathered their cups and spoons onto a tray. She was carrying it between three wet, sniffing black noses toward the sink when she turned back to face her father.

"Do we do anything for him?" she said.

Gordian looked at her from the table, smiled gently.

"We're thinking about it," he said.

LOS RAYOS DEL SOL, TERRITORIAL TRINIDAD

Pete Nimec hadn't been able to fall asleep and that puzzled him. It should have been easy, he thought.

Certainly easier than staying awake. He ought to be dead tired after everything he'd done in the past forty-eight hours or thereabouts, starting with having to pick up his mother-in-law at the airport, then practically turning right back around in the car with Annie to catch their flight to the Caribbean, followed by the trip itself, and the dinner invite by Henri Beauchart that had barely given them time to settle into their villa before drawing them out again. And all that rushing only accounted for *last* night, the first they'd spent here at Los Rayos. Up with the sun today, Nimec and Annie had climbed onto a pair of silver Vespas they'd discovered along with a Mustang soft-top in their villa's attached garage—the transportation provided without fanfare by their hosts— and then zipped off to see about getting him signed up for kiteboarding instruction at a beachfront water sports shop Annie had highlighted in her resort guide.

The shop owner was a jaunty bronze-skinned titan from Australia named Blake. As advertised, he offered a beginner's course and a full assortment of gear rentals. Prominent on the wall behind his counter was a certificate that declared him an "official skyriding instructor" but failed to particularly impress or encourage Nimec. How, he'd wondered, did somebody become an official skyrider, instructor or otherwise? What standards were applied to earning a cert? And by whom?

182 Tom Clancy's Power Plays

Nimec hadn't had the foggiest notion. On the other hand, Blake was enthusiastic enough and seemed to know his stuff. And Annie was determined to get Nimec airborne. Urged on by her along their way to the beach, he'd acquiesced to possibly scheduling a session toward the middle of the week, but as it developed Blake was booked solid—except for a slot which had opened that morning due to a sudden cancellation.

Not quite feeling ready, Nimec had started to decline.

Before he could, Annie accepted on his behalf.

Minutes later, Nimec had been rushed into a dressing room and suited up in a board shirt and shorts, water booties, a buoyancy vest, and an impact helmet with a molded foam liner that made it hard for him to hear his own grumbled complaints. A couple of hours and several dry runs over the sand after that, he was floating on his back in the warm ocean shallows with a harness around him, his feet in the straps of a plane board, and his hands on the control bar of the rig that connected him to a bright red-and-white foil hovering in the air overhead. And then the kite had scooped wind, and Nimec had been pulled to his feet by the tautened lines, and the next thing he'd known he was airborne, swept into an updraft, looking some fifteen or twenty feet down at Blake the Bronze astride the jet ski they'd ridden from shore.

Blake had shouted a few words from below and behind him that sounded like: *"You're blowing away!"*

Asked about it when their session was over, however, he had only recalled praising Nimec for "doing
great."

Whatever he'd said, it had proven to be a lasting
thrill for Nimec. Between the six or seven dunks he
took—each of which had brought Blake to his rescue
on the fleet little jet ski—he had spent about half an
hour soaring above the flat blue water in defiance of
gravity. Nimec would remember his periods of flight
seeming longer, and the heights he'd reached feeling
higher, than they actually were. He would remember
having an incredible, dizzying sense of mental and
physical lightness. Perhaps most of all, he would remember looking back toward Annie on the beach,
where she had stood watching him ride the wind, re-
peatedly raising her arms high above her head to
wave from the edge of the lapping surf. Though he
hadn't been able to see her face from his distance,
Nimec had known she was smiling at him, *felt* her
smiling at him, and taken an undeclarably boyish
pride in having evoked that smile.

Back at the villa that afternoon they'd decided to
scrub up, change their clothes, and then grab some
lunch at a restaurant. As Annie prepared to run her
shower, Nimec had found himself looking quietly out
a large bay window at the exotic flowers planted one
story down in the courtyard, cruising along in a care-
free and contented mood that had seemed almost foreign to him.

"You know," she'd said, poking her head through the half-open bathroom door, "that seat in the shower stall makes kind of a handy perch."

Nimec had turned to look at her, noticed the swimsuit she'd worn to the beach dangling from a hook on the door. Then he'd noticed that faint sort of blush she would get above her cheekbones.

"Handy," he'd repeated.

Annie nodded.

"Bet it would be sturdy enough for two," she'd said. "The shower seat, I mean."

Nimec had looked at her.

"I know what you mean, Annie," he'd said. "And I'm getting lots of ideas."

The color on her cheeks had spread and deepened.

"Me too," she'd said. "Want to try some of them out together?"

Nimec had nodded that he did, and pulled shut the louvers, and they had spent a long, leisurely while trying out quite a few of their ideas, and coming up with some new ones besides, before finally driving off for a much heartier meal than either had anticipated.

Now, at half past eleven that night, Nimec was in the chair by the bedroom window again, his robe belted around him, wondering what had happened to the blissful guy with his face who'd sat in that spot not too many hours earlier. He'd tried referencing the various thoughts and events that had brought about his calmly untroubled state of mind, but they hadn't helped him settle back into it. And, most irritatingly, he just couldn't get any shut-eye.

Filled with tension, Nimec had briefly considered a stroll through the villa's sculpted gardens, then decided against it—walking without a clear sense of purpose and destination never relaxed him. He thought about taking a swim in the big tiled pool across the grounds, but bumped the notion for similar reasons. The reality was he felt derelict. A splash under the full moon would only compound that feeling and frustrate him with more self-disapproval.

Nimec shifted restlessly, thinking he could use something to help him unwind. Roaming about downstairs yesterday on a minor expedition of discovery, he'd stumbled upon what he supposed was called an entertainment room, with a high-def flat-screen television and a wet bar. The bar had a refrigerator that he'd found stocked with beer, wine, and soft drinks. A beer would go down nicely, he concluded. If all the amenities went to type, there might be satellite TV feeds from the States. The difference in time zones between Trinidad and California made catching a West Coast baseball game a distinct possibility . . . some late innings, at least. Maybe the Mariners were pounding Oakland tonight. Or better yet, Anaheim. Though, given the injuries they always got from plowing into bases, walls, and opposing players like fools, Nimec figured it might be best leaving the Angels alone to pound on themselves.

He stood in the darknened room, turned from the window, and carried his chair over to the little table nook from which he'd taken it. Then, as he was starting toward the door, he saw Annie sitting up in bed.

Nimec looked at her with mild surprise in the moonlight coming through the parted blinds.

"Didn't know you were awake," he said.

She shrugged, leaning against a mound of pillows, her shoulders bare, the covers pulled just above her breasts.

"I haven't been for very long," she said in a quiet voice. "You?"

"Awhile," he said.

Annie was watching him.

"I kind of guessed," she said. "Can you tell me why?"

Nimec hesitated, produced a breath.

"You know," he said.

"Work," she said.

He nodded.

"I've been having a great time here, enjoying every minute of it," he said. And paused. "I love you, Annie."

She watched him another moment and suddenly chuckled.

"Something funny?" he said.

"Remembering our shower this afternoon," she said, "I was left with the distinct impression that you might like me some."

Nimec massaged his chin, feeling a little stupid.

"Is it still Ricci?" Annie said.

"No," he said. "I promised myself I'd put that away for a while, and I did."

"So it's about Megan's tipster."

He nodded.

"I'm supposed to be finding out about it," he said. "And I feel I'm losing time."

Annie was silent.

"What is it you want to do?" she said.

Nimec rubbed his chin thoughtfully again.

"I want to head over to that main shipping harbor we passed on the way in from the airport," he said. "And I want to have a look around."

Annie was silent again, her eyes steady on him.

"Go," she said. "Do what you have to."

Nimec stood there near the foot of the bed for perhaps a full minute.

"You sure you're okay with me leaving?" he said at last.

Annie looked at him from where she sat against the headboard, then gave him the slowest of nods.

"As long as you always make sure to come back," she said.

Out in the garage, Nimec opened the front door of his Mustang loaner, but stopped himself before climbing inside. He'd recalled something Beauchart had told him over their dishes of curry duck and roti at the previous night's dinner reception.

A thin, hatchet-faced man with a broad expanse of forehead and smoothly combed gray hair, the one-time GIGN chief had, as advance-billed, matched Nimec's fondness for vintage cars and shown a keen interest in discussing them. He'd also been quick to talk shop about how the expensive vehicles in his fleet were adapted for extreme high security usage.

"The Jankel Rolls you sent to pick us up almost had me fooled," Nimec had said. "I wouldn't have known it was armored except for the weight of its door. Then I noticed the flashers, and the extra buttons on the rear consoles, and those speaker covers for the P.A. And I guessed it had a full package."

Beauchart had nodded.

"For me, retrofitting the older model passenger cars is an enjoyable challenge," he'd said. "As an enthusiast I don't want to compromise their luxury and style. Even so, I insist they meet or surpass NATO Level Seven standards of protection."

"Hard to improve on armor that can stop AP rounds and take the brunt of a mine or grenade blast."

Again Beauchart had nodded.

"I admit to being a compulsive tinkerer," he'd said. "All the work is done at our own armoring plant on the mainland. And with an open-ended budget, which is far too great a temptation." Beauchart had smiled. "The first question I'll ask myself about a vehicle is, 'Would I be at ease having a Forbes Top Ten business leader ride in it?' Then I ask, 'What about the American president?' Last, I ask, 'What about the bloody *pope*?'" Beauchart's smile had grown wider. "If there's any hedging in my mind, I'll order added upgrades that cost a small fortune . . . and will be unnoticeable to the casual eye."

He had eagerly compared notes about specific shielding materials, and Nimec had found his preferences not unlike UpLink's standard high-sec configuration, a multilayered system of ballistic laminate inserts and flexible nylon floor armor, coupled with steel panels and anti-explosive engine, radiator, and fuel tank wraps. Beauchart had also gone on to mention loading his VIP sedans with options such as automatic fire controls, run-flat tires, hidden ram bumpers . . . and real-time satellite tracking units with remote door lock and ignition disconnects.

Now Nimec couldn't help but look at the Mustang and wonder. A sports convertible was too light to be armored without having its balance thrown dangerously out of whack. But there wasn't much of a trick to putting in GPS acquisition hardware its driver couldn't see. Assuming for a moment that was somebody's goal. Even if it was just hidden for aesthetic reasons.

Was he too suspicious? Could be, he decided. But what was the harm in playing it safe?

Nimec turned to the Vespa. Less likely that it would have a built-in tracking device. The object of installing one on this island would not be to locate a

stolen vehicle, which couldn't go further than the island's shores without being loaded onto a boat, but to
get a bead on a person who'd been snatched when
driving or getting into or out of it. In the case of a
grab taking place while somebody was out with the
little scooter, the abductor would want to ditch it as
fast as he could and then make a getaway with his
victim, eliminating any use in having a tracker
aboard.

Or so Nimec figured his good hosts would figure.
Unless, of course, their goal was to keep tabs specifi-
cally on *him,* which would leave his feet as his only
safe mode of transportation. Except that the harbor
was miles away . . . twenty or thirty miles, he
guessed.

A bit much for that midnight stroll of his.

Nimec sighed. In the absence of any other ideas, it
looked like the scooter was his best bet.

He got on, pressed its electric starter, and sped
from the villa's grounds into the tropical night.

Just under two hours later Nimec was looking out at
the harbor with a pair of high-magnification Gen 4
night vision binocs, the Vespa leaning on its kick-
stand where he'd stopped it in the roadside darkness.
He had been wishing that nothing out of the ordinary
would turn up. When you saw a single unusual sighting or occurrence, it was often a strong hint that other
oddball things were happening *out* of sight—once

these affairs got going, there hardly ever seemed to be a simple explanation. The further you went beneath the surface, the more you seemed to find that begged closer inspection. And like bugs and rodents lurking under the floorboards, they tended to be the sort of discoveries you would rather not have made.

Right now Nimec wasn't optimistic about tonight's foray being an exception to that unhappy rule. When he thought about it, though, it had really started with those e-mail messages to Megan. He'd viewed Rayos del Sol with a probing eye from the moment of his arrival yesterday, already one layer deep into a mystery. What he was doing here at the waterfront was just following through. Burrowing down to the next level, you might say.

From the little he'd seen thus far, Nimec got the sense he might be in for some nasty business.

He stood in the shadows amid a grove of tall royal palms and gazed steadily through the lenses of his binoculars. They represented five thousand dollars' worth of sophisticated viewing power, their filmless, auto-gated electron plates channeling and amplifying the ambient light through thousands of fiberoptic tubes to give their image greater clarity than any previous generation of night vision device had afforded . . . and there was plenty of light available, between what was emanating from the harbor's terminals and berthing areas and the full moon and stars shimmering in the sky.

Maybe, Nimec thought, they would show him something in the next few minutes that would justify their expense and put his peculiar observations into an explainable context. Something out on the quays across the road, or in the open water beyond the inlet channel and lighthouse, where he'd seen the feeder barges and immense box boat converge. At any rate he *hoped* some sort of evidence would reveal itself to him, in complete defiance of all his presuppositions. Then his suspicions might quiet down for a time, and he could return to the villa, and slip into bed with Annie. Possibly they could even pick up where they had left off that afternoon, get back to the pleasureful exertions of trying to make the baby they'd decided to have. It could happen—why not? But instinct and prior experience told him that babymaking would have to wait.

Nimec drew his focus in from the vessels he'd been tracking to the nearby waterfront. He hadn't had a whole lot to notice there since the last of the three feeders had been pulled away by tugs, and that continued to be the case. The crane operators and other shipyard workers who had lowered numerous forty-foot containers onto the barges had come down from the loading bridge. The heavy-load forklifts and straddle carriers that had hauled the containers to the bridge had mostly rolled back to a storage terminal across the yard, and then parked among the stacks of forty-footers still awaiting transport to off-island or interior destinations. A handful of long-shoreman had remained on the quay to supervise the movement of trucks toward the terminal, but the occasional directions they were giving through their bullhorns had a perfunctory sound now that the shipment had departed.

Though Nimec's knowledge of dockside transport practices was limited at best, he believed what he'd seen in the yard to this point was probably S.O.P. Had that been all he'd seen, in fact, he very well might have shot away on his scooter over an hour ago.

It was the deepwater rendezvous that had gotten him wondering. Or what happened *during* the rendezvous, to be entirely accurate.

Nimec decided it might be time to check on the freighters again, and was shifting his glasses with that in mind when he heard the unmistakable *whap* of helicopter blades slicing the air. The noise was coming from a moderate distance to his right, and seemed generated by more than a single chopper.

Eager for a look, he angled his binocs up at the sky just as a pair of birds appeared above the dark wall of trees marking the northern edge of the island's wilderness area. They were clipping along in tandem at an altitude of less than five hundred feet, heading northward almost perpendicular to the shoreline. As they reached the harbor, their flight path took a sharp westerly turn away from shore, coincidentally or not toward the anchored box boat and its feeders.

Nimec studied them through his eyepieces moments before they angled seaward. Like the helicopter he had seen the day before, they were Aug 109's . . . and now, staring at their magnified images in shades of green, he could definitively tell they were examples of the Stingray patrol variant he'd mentioned to Murthy, conforming to specs that had become thoroughly familiar to him when UpLink had outfitted an entire fleet for U.S. Coast Guard antiterrorism and drug interdiction units. Both had multiple-tube rocket pods under their flared "wings," FLIR housings for heat-seeking search equipment above their noses, and open port and starboard gunner posts behind the pilot cabin. The pintle guns themselves, he noted, appeared to be Ma Deuces or some lighter weight .50-calibers. Formidable weaponry for safeguarding paradise.

Nimec sighed thoughtfully. What had Murthy said while driving from the airport? *The goal at Los Rayos is to make our guests feel secure without their being conscious of security, if my meaning is clear.*

It couldn't have been clearer, Nimec reflected. But he didn't have to reach further back in his memory than that afternoon and evening for instances on which the security net around the island had been evident to his trained eye. This was his third helicopter sighting, his last one having occurred as he'd piggy-backed to shore on Blake the Bronze's jet ski after his kiteboarding lesson. And later on, when he and

Annie were at the beachfront café where they'd gone
out for Creole food, he had paid close attention to a
Land Rover with black-tinted glass windows that had
gone cruising past the parking area, and discerned
that it was not only armored but armed . . . or ready
for armaments. There were well-camouflaged firing
ports on its side, and the rooftop hatch had been set
above its rear seat rather than in front, indicating to
him that it was likely equipped with interior machine
gun mounts.

Nimec grunted to himself, lowered his binoculars.
The Stingrays having tailed off over the water, he
wanted to resume monitoring the cargo vessels. They
were, he'd estimated, somewhere between a quarter
and a third of a mile from his position, almost at the
limit of his viewing range. The box boat's enormous
bulk was visible in silhouette to his naked eye—
probably a thousand feet from stem to stern, with
four towering jib booms lined along one side of the
deck. It had dwarfed the three- or four-hundred-foot-
long feeders as they'd approached it soon after leaving the quay.

Nimec had watched them begin the process of
transferring their containers, a feeder barge pulling
up under each boom, the larger vessel dropping its
cables, the barge crews securing the containers to
their lifting slings, the crane teams hoisting them
from the feeders onto the box boat's sizable payload
areas. There again, he'd considered none of it excep-

tional. Even the late hour at which the job got started had seemed normal to him, since commercial harbors commonly operated round-the-clock and had longshoremen working in rotations.

It had been the running of what might have been fuel supply lines from the huge container vessel to the barges midway through their freight transfer that had perplexed Nimec. Hardly anything to make him cry out from the hilltops about demons and goblins spreading wickedness under the full moon, true, but it still struck him as a little conspicuous. Once the hoses were reeled out from hatches in the hull of the box boat and connected to their opposite numbers on the sides of the feeders, he'd heard a sort of dim, mechanical pumping sound echo over the water in the post-midnight silence. And though he couldn't claim to know what it sounded like when boats fueled up, Nimec had been around enough airports and landing strips to immediately compare it to the rhythmic pulsations of a jet having its tanks refilled.

His problem with this was that feeder ships didn't *need* fuel. Or shouldn't need it. They didn't have any means of onboard propulsion. Meaning no engines. Granted he was far from a maritime expert, but to his understanding it was why they were attached to tugboats. And say for argument's sake he was mistaken . . . Nimec had never heard of a container vessel that could double as a tanker and carry fuel for ship-to-ship resupply.

He'd been anything but done pondering that apparent anomaly when a couple of closely related ones had started to crop up in a hurry minutes ago. As the unladen feeders disengaged from the box boat, they proceeded to move on *past* it rather than make a return trip to the harbor. And watching the water, carefully following their progress, Nimec had seen them go outside the effective range of his G4 lenses and disappear into the dark horizon.

But the tugboats hadn't. To Nimec's utter bafflement. On the contrary, they were growing larger in his binoculars at that very moment, plying through the channel, returning to port without the barges.

Try as he might, he couldn't make sense of that. And the more he thought about it, the more it threw him.

Plain and simple, it defied logic.

Nimec frowned. Speaking of returning to port, he was sure Annie would be worried about him by now. He'd seen things here that had added all kinds of questions to those he'd had before, and knew it would absolutely pay to get some of them answered before he went ahead with his snooping.

Reluctant as he was to do so—or part of him was, anyway—he needed to call it a night.

Still frowning slightly, Nimec brought the binocs down from his eyes and climbed onto the Vespa, suspecting he'd have a great deal to occupy his thoughts on his way back to the villa.

• • •

Its bark-colored housing placed just below the crown of fanning leaves at treetop level, the thermal imaging camera that had picked up Nimec where he'd stood was one of a great many like it carefully hidden at outdoor and indoor locations throughout Rayos del Sol— under four ounces in weight and small enough to sit on a man's palm, with a lens that could be covered by the fleshy part of his thumb. Its chip-based microbolometer sensor technology operated coolly, efficiently, and unnoticeably on an internal low-voltage power supply that required infrequent recharges and allowed it to transmit a continuous gray-scale digital feed across the island using a network of compact microwave amplifiers. From the central observation post where the video feed was initially received and processed, it could be relayed to both fixed and mobile secondary monitoring stations via secure wireless internet at a speed almost indistinguishable from real time—blink twice and it would measure the difference between a captured event and its detection by human observers.

While considerably more than a single pair of eyes had been watching Nimec watch the harbor, the key witness as he mounted his scooter now was seated over two miles north of him in the rear lounge of a Daimler stretch limousine parked outside the flamboyantly decorated and lighted Bonne Chance Casino. Here at the heart of the resort's entertainment complex, this long-bodied vehicle was not ostentation but camouflage. The Bonne Chance's wealthy amusement seekers could afford to toy with luck and saw no crime in putting their status and success on display. The Daimler, then, shone only like a diamond in cluster, blending into rather than standing out from the sparkling field of luxury cars in the valet lot.

Skilled at blending in under any and all conditions required of him, Tolland Eckers much preferred the comfortable back of a limo to hiding with his belly down in South American mud and weeds, or with his throat and eyes burned by the freezing cold in rocky Tora Bora, or with the Rhub' al-Khali's hot desert grit caking his nostrils. He had roughed it around the globe for almost two decades in service to the Agency; service to Jean Luc Morpaign was a less taxing and dangerous way to earn a living. And, really, it hadn't compromised his patriotism. Eckers more or less accurately reported his income on his federal returns, paid state taxes on his two hundred-acre property in Pottawattamie County, Iowa, and voted Republican by absentee ballot in every election. To say he'd committed acts that were in betrayal of American interests would be to make naive assumptions about how business worked at the highest levels—Jean Luc was only pissing in a pond where other, bigger fish had already taken their turns.

"Alpha One, this is Gray Base," a voice said in Eckers's headset. *"Do you want us to stay tight on our man?"*

Eckers considered that a moment, studying the picture on his screen as the guest from San Jose mounted his Vespa.

"Let's not ease up too much," he said. "I want him covered till he's returned to the nest."

"Yes, sir. That's the standing order."

"I know the order, Gray Base."

"Yes, sir . . ."

"I said *make sure*. Don't get lazy about this or I'll have your ass."

"I'll oversee the check myself, sir."

"You do that," Eckers said. "And report in to me afterward."

"Yes, s—"

Eckers reached for his headset's belt control and lowered the volume, needing to think without distraction. When Jean Luc had told him of Nimec's impending visit weeks ago, he'd known he had a potentially serious problem on his hands. But he could strike the word "potentially" tonight. The situation had heated up sooner than expected—although so far as he was concerned, putting out flash fires was simply part of his job. The question for him was whether to contact Jean Luc right away or wait for the morning. Probably he'd hold off on a decision till it was confirmed that their Mr. Nimec had gone back to the villa and was finished poking around for now. Whatever he settled upon, however, Eckers knew it was six of one, half dozen of the other. Jean Luc's options were narrow. Nimec was a top professional and would have access to a limitless variety of resources at UpLink. There was no telling how much he'd already added up, or who he could contact to help him figure it out. He wouldn't waste time, though. He certainly hadn't this far. And he'd seen enough of significance so Jean Luc would understand it was no use to just wait around hoping for the best.

Eckers sat there in silent contemplation, his face bathed in the IR monitor's bluish-gray radiance, his eyes staring at the now-static image of the roadside opposite the harbor. He could call Jean Luc tonight, he could call him tomorrow morning, but either way was already planning beyond that. He'd dealt with fires before, doused every sort imaginable, and could tell this latest one would need to have water poured on it quickly if he was to keep it from spreading out of hand . . .

And if every last trace of it was going to be washed away, which was precisely what Eckers intended.

Jarvis Lenard cowered at the rear of the shallow cave, his head bent under the irregular furrows of its ceiling, his knees pulled up to his chest, his back flush against cold, damp stone. He scarcely dared move a muscle. The search team was close by; he could hear them through the screen of brush with which he'd covered his hideout's entrance, their passage making a flurry of unaccustomed sounds in the forest. And minutes earlier, he had done more than hear them. Having left the cave to empty his bladder, Jarvis had caught a glimpse of them within a half dozen yards of where he'd stood watering the ground. It had cut off his flow midstream, but a small discomfort that had been compared to the unpitying hurts Jarvis was firmly convinced his hunters would dole out if he was captured. He'd been far more willing to tolerate the pressing fullness inside him—and if he couldn't manage that, to foul himself from top to bottom, or suffer any other indignity his mind could conceive— than to have been cost dear by one extra moment out there.

It was the hack of machetes that had alerted him to their approach—and none too soon. Barefoot over the meager puddle he'd created, Jarvis had peered toward the noise and distinguished their outlines in the soft film of moonlight that had sifted its way down through the jungle's leafy roof. He'd counted five of them in single file, black-clad, rifles at their hips, their curved blades slicing a path through the tangled, twisted masses of vines and branches hindering their progress. They wore goggles Jarvis knew would allow their eyes to see in pitch darkness, and the lead man had been holding what almost looked like a video camera in front of him—but camcorder Jarvis didn't believe it was, oh no, at least not the type that someone would bring on a vacation to capture the smiling faces of his wife and children. Its handle was like the grip of a pistol, and its enormous lens about equaled the size of its entire body, and there was a wide viewing screen in back that cast a strange bluish-gray light upon the features of the spotter who carried it, giving him the look of a ghostly apparition. Jarvis had noticed these things—the glow especially—and come to realize that the device was a heat-reader akin to those aboard the helicopters scouring the island for him. The friend who had told him of the nightbirds, an aircraft cleaner he'd linked up with at Los Rayos's employee compound, had described this machinery one night when rum had turned his mouth to chattering, and Jarvis hadn't forgotten his words: *Their picture's all gray an' not green, an' the lenses can do more'n pierce the black'a night. They can see the natural aura'a heat that come off the skin'a everyt'ing alive, see the vapor that leave yah mout' when ya breath, even see the shape'a yer ass on a chair yah been warmin' a full quarter hour after yah 'ave lifted yerself off it.*

Jarvis Lenard had stood with his heart pounding against his ribs as the spotter paused ahead of the others in line behind him, and swept the heat-reader first from side to side, and then up toward the treetops. Last, he'd bent and aimed its lens toward the ground . . . and that was when Jarvis had taken the opportunity to flee, scampering back to the cave entrance before the man could straighten, or resume moving forward with his team. Still hanging out of his pants, he'd dropped onto his stomach, wriggled in under his brush cover, hurried to replace whatever foliage he'd disturbed, and scampered through the claustrophobic, rough-walled tube of rock, which narrowed like a periwinkle shell toward the back to end in a tight, angling notch where he'd finally hunkered down in dread.

Squatted on his heels in that little sideways cut now, Jarvis took a deep breath, another, and then a third, making an effort to slow his racing heartbeat. But his throat had tightened with fear, and only thin snatches of air seemed to reach his lungs, and the hard throbbing in his rib cage did not ease up. He continued to pull in breath after breath, regardless, understanding he must try to be calm . . . must try mightily to remain still and silent if he was to have any chance of avoiding capture, however easier it might be said than done. From what he could hear, his stalkers had gotten to within a few paces of the cave entrance and stopped again. To its left, as it seemed to him. Had they come this far into the woods because they had picked up his trail? Or was it plain, fickle chance that had brought them here?

Jarvis Lenard could not know. Yet he *did* know that the side of the cave where they had now made their second halt was the same side he'd chosen for taking care of his business, and that the spot of a puddle he'd left there could madly enough do him in. For it had struck him that a device able to read a man's lingering body heat on a seat cushion would also detect the warmth of his freshly released urine. And if it were to meet the notice of those who sought him, acting like to a beacon, glowing on the face of that viewscreen as though the pecker that had peed it had been flooded with radioactivity . . .

Jarvis had a moment when he was gripped by a suicidal urge to laugh aloud at that thought—or rather cough out an anxiety-fraught mockery of laughter. But he managed to suppress it, refusing to yield to crazed hysteria. The Sunglasses might take him, yes, they might. He was determined not to serve himself up to them on a platter, though.

Two or three minutes went by with the slowness of as many hours. Jarvis could still hear shuffling footsteps outside. And the chop of machete blades. He had no way to see past the vegetation he'd piled in front of the cave entrance to keep it from sight, but sadly the opposite wouldn't be true of the instrument in the spotter's hand. Its lens did not see objects for what they were, not really. Instead it would sense only the heat that escaped them. Leaves and branches would give off no warmth, or very little compared to what was coming from Jarvis, and would be a poor excuse for a barrier. To his understanding, incomplete as it might be, a man's body heat would appear to burn a white-hot hole through the fold of brush on that evil device's monitor.

Same as my piss would seem to be burnin' like an atomic spill, Jarvis thought with a humor that was far more subdued—but no less grim—than the spasm of crazed mirth that had just come so close to pushing him around the corner into lunacy.

If there was anything that might work to his favor and protect him from the searching electronic eye, he supposed it was his having scurried away to hide in the notch, with its wall of thick, solid rock separating it from the forward length of the cave. The question then would be whether the eye was keen enough to penetrate that wall should it be turned in its direction, although Jarvis would be glad never to learn the answer . . . as if what he wanted mattered at all.

He lowered his head between his knees and took another series of breaths to quiet his nerves. For the present he could only wait like a hunted animal in its burrow, hoping it was only a fluke that had brought these bloodhounds close, and that they would pass as suddenly as they'd appeared without sniffing out any trace of him.

Waiting. Hoping. Words for the desperate, true, Jarvis thought.

He would gladly take them on himself.

A scared, desperate man, he would take them on without argument, and take as well the uncertainty that was their constant companion, if it meant he could elude his pursuers yet another night, and stay free to worry about the next day when it came.

SAN FRANCISCO BAY AREA, CALIFORNIA

Julia Gordian broke out of her nightmare with a start, her eyes snapping open in the darkness, her mouth gasping in air, her right hand going to her throat. Her other arm jerked up at her side with a stiff, violent movement that tossed her blanket partway off the bed.

She'd been awakened by the trailing end of a moan that she instantly realized had come from her own lips.

Shaking hard, Julia drew herself to a sitting position. Then she let her fingers slide from her neck, covered her face with both hands, and stayed like that for several minutes. When she at last raised her head from her palms, they were left wet with perspiration and tears.

She took a while longer to collect herself and then reached down for her blanket, thinking the sounds that had torn out of her must have been pretty awful, wondering if they'd been loud enough for her father to hear them. Probably not, she decided; the guest room was on the other side of the house. And though he wouldn't have admitted it, Dad seemed tired from standing on a ladder with those heavy abstracts. And then the drive, and her laying the rest of that stuff on him. With even a shred of luck he'd still be sound asleep.

Julia wiped her stinging eyes. That other stuff, she thought. Just something incidental she'd wanted to mention. Uh-huh, sure.

Let her go. Let her go now. Let her go, it's finished . . .

She took in another breath. The words from her dream clung to her. Those words, and the fearful sensation of the combat knife against her throat, held to her throat in the Killer's grip. And then the images returned: Tom Ricci standing in the entrance to that room in Big Sur, the door he'd kicked open flung back from the splintered jamb.

Let her go, it's finished . . . You do her, I do you, what's the point?

Ricci again. His eyes on the Killer over the out-thrust gun in his hands, the gun targeted on the Killer's heart.

In Julia's nightmare, the Killer had been as faceless as he'd been nameless. Wait, maybe not exactly. His features had been constantly *changing*. One moment they'd been average, even bland. Then atrociously cruel and monstrous. Like in her actual recollections of those black days, she couldn't quite fix on them.

A year now of trying to remember the Killer's face, and she couldn't do it.

But Tom Ricci's—

His face, eyes, voice—they would return with absolute clarity in her memory and dreams.

You can make it on your own now. Go. It'll be all right.

Those words . . . he'd spoken those words to her

after persuading the Killer to lower his knife from her throat and slice the ropes that had bound her wrists and ankles to her chair, a straight-backed wooden chair on which she'd been forced to sit until she lost most of her circulation. When Julia lifted her arms, they'd been cramped and stiff as boards. Her legs were worse, so numb at first she had been unable to feel them. And then the painful tingles as she stood up and blood began flowing to them. Trying to take her first step toward Ricci, she had almost toppled over.

And Ricci had steadied her with one hand. Keeping his gun on the Killer with the other, or so she assumed. That was one of the blanks her mind *had* filled in for her, not because she'd had any awareness of it at the time, but because it had to have happened that way.

At the time there was only Ricci for her.

His face, his eyes, his voice . . .

His firm, steadying hand. He'd slipped it around her back, held her erect, kept her from falling as the strength returned to her legs, helping her toward the door.

Guiding her toward freedom with his hand.

You can make it on your own now. Go. It'll be all right.

Julia had hesitated before she stepped out into the hallway. Looking into his eyes, meeting them with hers, wanting to say something. Groping in her mind for something to say, and not quite knowing what in the moment she had available.

A hurried thank-you had seemed woefully, ridiculously inadequate, but it was all that had occurred to her . . .

And only then had it registered with Julia that there was still a gag around her mouth. The scarf, or strip of cloth, or whatever it was, taut between her lips, its knot uncut.

It had left Julia with no chance to say anything, no chance, and she had simply nodded mutely and gone through the opening, the door shutting behind her with a slam, Ricci's team of Sword operatives rushing around her, sweeping her down a flight of stairs—a spiral staircase—and outside into the sunlight, and then finally through the door of a car and away, all of it happening in a blur from the point at which she'd heard the loud slam of that door at her back.

Now, over twelve months later in her darkened bedroom, Julia sat up thinking for a time, letting her dream's intensity fade, as it did for even the worst of dreams, before she gradually let her head sink down to her pillow.

Turning onto her side, she reached across to the empty half of the bed where her husband had once slept, briefly spread her fingers over the cool, unruffled sheet, and then pulled back her hand to gather the covers against her breast.

The tears came on and off before she slept, but Julia had learned to get by with that sort of minor nuisance.

At the herbal boutique today, in fact, she'd picked up a fresh bottle of eyedrops that would wash away the redness before she again had to face the world.

FIVE

NIMEC HELD OFF ON PHONING VINCE SCULL, UP Link's chief risk assessment man and lead crank, until nine o'clock in the morning. With the difference in time zones, this meant it would be five A.M. in San Jose, not exactly regular office hours, but Nimec had punched in Vince's home number and figured he would be up getting ready for work by then. And if he wasn't, Nimec figured he ought to be. And if that was a stretch to justify the early call, Nimec wasn't about to let himself feel too bad. He'd waited to the extent that his patience had allowed, reasoned he'd suffered enough aggravation from Vince over the years to be due a huge credit bonus, and in any event had never known Vince to react any better to consideration versus inconsideration. The guy would invariably find some reason to grouse, so why let it be a factor either way?

"What the hell do you want?" Scull said groggily once Nimec had announced himself.

"We need to talk, Vince."

"Gee-fucking-whiz what a treat," Scull said. "Just when I think I'm rid of you for a couple weeks, you decide to haunt me long distance."

"This is important, Vince."

"It occur to you I might have company and we're maybe in the middle of something?"

"No, Vince. Honest. Can't say it did."

"Yeah, well, up yours, too," Vince said. "Speaking of which, want to hang on while I pay a visit to the throne, or is it okay I carry the phone in and chitchat as things move along?"

"We need to talk right now, Vince."

There was a pause of what Nimec took to be consternation at the other end of the line.

"Have it your way," Scull said. "You hear a grunt come out of me, it's not because I got turned on by your voice."

"Good of you to share that," Nimec said, and without any further holdup went on to outline the observations he'd made at the harbor.

Ten minutes and various undefined rumblings from Scull later, he'd gotten around to the questions that had plagued him since then . . . the first of which concerned the lines he'd seen run between the main container ship and its three feeders.

"I think they were fuel transfer hoses," he said. "And I'm wondering if you've ever heard of cargo ships that double as oil tankers."

"Uh-huh," Scull said. "I have."

"You *have*?"

"Oh, sure. Multitasking's the word these days. What it's all about," Scull said. "Take this pair of shoes I bought, for instance. Put 'em under a bright light and they can dance ballet, tap, and modern jazz on their own. I'm telling you, Petey, you oughtta see the razzle-dazzle show they give on my kitchen table."

Nimec rubbed his eyes with his thumb and forefinger.

"Come on," he said, exasperated. "Be serious."

"Okay, I was full of crap about the ballet part, and the taps lose rhythm after a minute or two," Scull said. "What the fuck you want for fifty bucks at Payless?"

"Damn it, Vince—"

"I'm seriously trying to tell you I've never heard of anything like you mentioned," Scull said. And was quiet a second. "Well, okay, strike that. Think it was in World War Two, the Allies used to dress up fuel tankers heading out to the Pacific as standard freighters. Made 'em lower value targets for the Zeroes. And far as I know they really carried freight on deck."

"Dress them up."

"Is what I said two sentences ago, yeah," Scull said. "There's a problem with your phone connection, Petey-boy, you could always hang up and call back after the birds start to chirp."

Nimec was tugging his chin.

"The Second World War dates back a ways."

"You're implying what's old ain't relevant, I'd have to take that as an insult."

Nimec ignored him. "Question, Vince. You figure it's possible anybody would be doing that now?" he said. "I mean *legitimately* using dual-purpose carriers."

"Anything's possible," Scull said. "Can't be too complicated a trick to overhaul a ship. But you know you're asking me a two-in-one of your own here, right?"

"Yeah."

"So which you want me to check out for openers? Who might be doing it on the up-and-up, or who might have reasons that're on the slippery side?"

"Both," Nimec said. "It's why I asked the way I did."

Scull gave him a somewhat exaggerated harrumph.

"This happen to tie in with Megan's mystery e-mails?"

"I'd say so if knew, Vince."

"But you don't."

"No," Nimec said. "I don't."

"How about theories?"

"Yours would be good as mine."

Again, Scull didn't say anything.

"I wanna be sure I've got one thing straight before I go ahead and do your bidding," he said after a moment. "Those cargo ships . . . you positive they were feeders and not coasters?"

"What's the difference?"

"Coasters wouldn't need tugboats because they've got engines aboard to power 'em," Scull said. "They're usually sorta long and narrow so they can snake through tight spots. Canals, river openings, that kind of shit. I saw a lot of them that year I was in the Polynesian islands scouting out sites for our ground stations. How they get their name is bringing loads along coastal routes."

Nimec remembered what he'd seen beyond the piers.

"The boats last night *had* tugs," Nimec said. And paused. "Until they didn't and still sailed out of the channel."

"Instead of pulling back into the harbor."

"Right."

Scull sighed. "I gotta admit, Petey, that right there confuses me."

"Same here," Nimec said. "And the sooner you can find information that'll *un*confuse us, the better."

The phone became quiet again.

"Still with me, Vince?"

"Yeah, I had some private business that needed doing, want a graphic description?"

"No, thanks."

"Then why don't you hang up and let me roust my top-notch staff from under their quilts," Scull said.

"Think we can keep this in-house?"

"Don't see why not. Cal Bowman, you know him?"

"The name rings a bell."

"He's got a good bunch under him who specialize in what we call maritime works issues. They do reports on coastal processes, traffic forecasts—"

"Great, Vince."

"I'm guessing you're on a 'crypted freq?"

"Yeah. My satphone."

"Keep it handy," Scull said. "I'll call back in a few hours with whatever we can pull together."

Nimec considered that and had to smile.

"Those birds chirping in SanJo yet?"

"Not anywhere near my block, how come?"

"Thought you'd feel it was a little early to be waking people up."

Scull produced an ogreish chortle.

"I give what I get when it comes to distributing the misery," Scull said. "Fuck 'em all, big and small."

"That a Vince Scull original?"

"A collaboration between me, Robin Hood, and Karl Marx," Scull said. "Like it?"

Nimec shrugged. "Sends a clear message."

"On behalf of the three of us, I'm glad you got it loud and clear," Scull said.

And on that delightful note he signed off.

Henri Beauchart had been at the surveillance station well before Eckers arrived at nine A.M., accompanied by three of his adjuncts from Team Graywolf.

It only fed Beauchart's existing unhappiness. He and his own staff had already completed their electronic probe. A simple effort, yes, but hastily called for. And here Eckers would come walking in the door to take control of an operation that was itself something Beauchart detested at his core. Still, what was to be gained from dwelling on his resentments? That would only make him miserable. The time for second thoughts or complaints was long past. His position at Los Rayos had been one thing before Jean Luc Morpaign returned from Paris to handle his deceased father's business affairs, and another thing afterward. The brutal truth was he'd allowed himself to be purchased, gone from preventing and solving crimes to committing them. And he should be accustomed to Tolland Eckers stepping on him these days.

Eckers was Jean Luc's man. Indeed, his spiritual familiar.

Now he approached the U-shaped terminal where

Beauchart sat beside a young, dark-haired woman wearing a conservative blouse and skirt, a red *bindi* dot of Hindu tradition in the center of her forehead.

"Henri," he said. "You have what I wanted?"

Beauchart looked back over his shoulder at the American. His companions had remained a few paces behind him.

"It is all done," he said with a nod toward the woman at his console. "Chandra is one of my best intranet monitoring operators. I've had her bring up this graphic so you can see for yourself how the information was obtained."

Eckers waited.

"The summary log reports and strip charts have been hard-copied, but I'll venture a guess you won't care to review them," Beauchart said, pointing to the screen in front of him. "What you see here will be good enough."

Eckers leaned forward and scanned the screen. Its galaxy view of the resort's network architecture showed a large circle representing the primary host surrounded by smaller circles that depicted its various nodes, with connecting lines to display the inbound and outbound communications routed between their portals. On the perimeters of the orbiting circles were hundreds of tiny colored points, each of which stood for an individual computer in the system.

"My first step was a global query, entering the names of Mr. Nimec and his wife," Chandra explained. "This sought them out of the resort's computer databases and those of any licensed and rented alliance businesses they might have visited on the island." She paused. "Shops, nightclubs and restaurants, tour organizers . . . we require they use certain collaborative software applications to give us different sorts of information. Most of it's statistical. They rarely raise complaints, since the stated reason for this is our desire to learn which attractions and hospitality providers are popular with our guests, and how to improve and better target services for them."

"Tracking their activities being a fringe benefit," Eckers said.

The woman nodded.

"Our partners understandably do object to having some of their programs, or specific program files, interface with our central database . . . There are degrees of overlap in the merchandise and services they provide, and that creates occasional competition between them," she said. "An example of what they like to keep private might be their accounting and inventory figures. Scheduling information is another very pertinent example, as I'm about to show you. The business owners are often insistent about maintaining the confidentiality of this data, which is why we slip trojans into their computers over the intranet. They're self-updating and undetectable to any firewall or spyware-detection program compatible with our system infrastructure. And we have built-in alarms

222 Tom Clancy's Power Plays

should they try to install any other such programs."
Chandra placed a hand over her computer mouse.
"To get back to my global search, it gave us several
immediate hits. But the tracking data we needed
would usually take from several hours to a day before
being transferred between their computer subsets and
our host by the trojans."

"Why's that?" Eckers asked.

"Too routine to red flag other than for a special action," she said. "Then it suddenly becomes important. But an unregulated flow of traffic would overtax
the system's capacity, so we use automatically staggered cycles."

"Like timed stoplights on a busy intersection."

"Yes . . . unless circumstances dictate that we go
into the computers, override the predetermined cycle,
and extract the information packets as I did from
here," Chandra said, and then moved and clicked the
mouse.

Eckers watched closely as she highlighted one of
the orbital subnet circles on the galaxy view and then
zoomed in on a specific point along its circumfer-
ence. It grew large on the screen, a numerical internet
protocol address appearing above it.

Beauchart saw the American's eyes narrow with
curiosity. Again, he had to stamp down on his distaste.

"The computer we've identified belongs to one of
the resort's licensed agents . . . a water sports shop
that also schedules a range of excursions," he said.

"The Nimecs are booked for an outing this afternoon. One that I believe will present the singular opportunity you desire."

Eckers caught his quick, meaningful glance.

"The shop's name?" he said.

Chandra clicked her mouse and it appeared over the IP address.

Eckers read it off the screen, grunted as his interest was further stirred.

"Okay," he said. "Give me a look at the details of what they've got scheduled."

Chandra gave them to him.

They were, as Beauchart had predicted, good enough.

BONASSE, TRINIDAD

Jean Luc winced when his blackline cell phone rang on its docking station first thing in the morning—the caller ID display told him it might only complicate what was set to be a busy day. At the top of his schedule was a ten o'clock meeting in Port of Spain to settle down the apprehensive gentlemen at the Ministry of Energy and Energy Industries. Then it would be across Independence Square to the Finance Building, where he'd no doubt have to apply more verbal palliatives. And then an international call to Reed Baxter, during which he'd be obliged to pass on a filtered and edited version of the gaining worries in the Capitol and tolerate Reed's whining on about his own. So much nervous energy generated on both sides, and he the transoceanic conductor that made it flow smoothly back and forth rather than build to some dysfunctional system overload. Jean Luc hated to think what might happen if he decided to let it go. The whole shebang, everything. And sometimes he felt he could, even would, inherited alliances and duties aside. He had an ample bequest and many interests. He could travel the globe for the rest of his life and never grow tired of its sights and cultures. The past bore on him only to the degree that he allowed it, and by no means would Jean Luc continue shouldering its burdens if he grew convinced they'd add up to his personal ruin.

Now he entered his study in a robe and slippers, thumbing the cellular's talk button and shooting a glance at the antique Boullé clock on his mantel.

"Toll, it's barely eight," he said. "I've got my fingers crossed you're calling with good news."

"I wish I was, sir," Eckers said. "There's been a development that's going to need our attention."

"Involving our elusive islander?"

"Elusive if alive," Eckers qualified. "The perimeter watch has been maintained around the village, but Team Graywolf gave me nothing to indicate a substantive change in that situation when they last reported in. They're convinced he wouldn't have made it out of the southern preserve, and are combing it day and night."

"Then what's this about?"

"The visitor from San Jose," Eckers said, and then paused. "I think this has to be considered highly time-sensitive, sir."

Jean Luc closed his eyes and released a breath.

"Let me hear it," he said.

Eckers did, his summary delivered cool-headedly enough—he was a man whose calm outward demeanor rarely if ever gave a read of his true level of concern. Jean Luc appreciated that, considering what little it took to induce fits of panic in too many of his business and political associates. But Eckers's haste to contact him was itself a measure of the seriousness of what the cameras had apparently picked up at the harbor last night.

"You don't suppose he could've missed the transfer, do you?" Jean Luc said. He was reaching, of course, and could tell from the momentary silence in his earpiece that Eckers knew it.

"We'd have to rule that out," Eckers said. "Our surveillance video's close-up, and digital quality. And I reviewed it in various enhanced modes to eliminate any guesswork." He paused again. "He observed the whole thing, sir. Those were high-magnification surveillance NVG's he was using . . . advanced military grade optics. The ships would have been well within their range at the point of rendezvous, and he was looking directly out at them."

"And I don't suppose we can gain any comfort by telling ourselves he probably doesn't know what he saw."

"He'll know he saw something," Eckers said. "If he didn't realize what it was, he's going to want to find out."

Jean Luc sat behind his desk and stared at the glass-door bookcase against the wall to his right. On its upper shelf were four thick, leather-bound volumes that comprised the family record, notably minus the diary pages of Ysobel Morpaign, wife of Lord Claude, which had remained locked away in a vault for over a hundred years after her suicide. The Morpaigns had always revealed more truths about themselves between the lines than in them, but on occasion Jean Luc would read through their handwritten memoirs and try to decipher the reality of who his ancestors had been compared to how they'd wished to show their faces to the world—in some indescribable way, it helped put his responsibilities in their rightful place. He was the family scion. The keeper of its legacy, obliged to oversee its commercial holdings and carry through its immediate and far-reaching goals. *A now kind of person,* as he'd put it to Eckers. But that was his own outward face. Privately, he dwelled on the past more than he would have cared to acknowledge, and time and again found himself wondering about old Lord Claude, plantation owner, bootlegger, and forerunner of an oil dynasty in Trinidad. Claude, whom Ysobel's sad, secret writings claimed would have ordered his only son thrown into the pitch lake as a newborn infant, his body left to sink down into the tar with the bones of nature's failures and discards, had not letting him live been a wiser expedient. Childless in his marriage, Lord Claude had desperately wanted a male heir. That it had been conceived out of his lust for a black slave woman was something he could abide, just so long as the light-skinned son could pass as his legitimate issue, and its birth mother could be made to disappear forever. And so long as fragile, vulnerable Ysobel, who had assumed her husband's disgrace as her own by blaming it on her infertility, could be manipulated into spending the nine months of a supposed pregnancy in her Spanish homeland to enable the lie.

It was, Jean Luc knew, all dust and cobwebs. Ancient history that shouldn't matter to him, let alone be a kind of closet obsession. And what did his preoccupation with it signify if not a shameful lack of pride in who he was, a hunger for acceptance from elitists and polite society bigots about whom he shouldn't give a good God's damn?

"The visitor," he said now, turning from the bookcase. "He's supposed to be staying at Los Rayos a few more days, that right?"

"It's my understanding, yes."

"Which means he can be expected to do more poking around."

"I'm convinced he will."

"And how do you feel we should handle this problem?"

"Honestly?"

"I rely on you to be honest with me, Toll."

"We know what he's up to. We know his background and capabilities. It makes him a threat that has to be eliminated."

"He's with his wife, isn't he?"

"Right, sir."

"You sound as if you've considered that."

"I have. And it could be to our benefit."

"How so?"

"I recommend we take care of them together," Eckers said. "There are scenarios that will give authorities on the mainland a plausible explanation. And that should also take the legs out of any progressive investigation by his people at home."

"You sincerely believe their suspicions won't be raised?"

"Of course they will. But they can suspect whatever they want. We just have to be careful not to leave them any solid proof."

Jean Luc thought a moment.

"The one hitch in all this might be Beauchart. He's been difficult before—"

"Beauchart's already aware of what I have in mind."

"And he hasn't objected?"

"No," Eckers said. "And if he does, I'll quiet him. It wouldn't be the first time."

Jean Luc held the phone silently to his ear, seized at once by a kind of morbid humor. In a few minutes he would have to get dressed and ready for his meetings—discussions meant to reassure his partners that their illegal oil shipments were being successfully covered up despite a glorified bookkeeper's aborted attempt at snitching them out. But not until he'd started his day with some brief words about double murder.

"And He shall come again with glory to judge the quick and the dead, whose kingdom shall have no end," he mused aloud. "Is that line by any chance familiar to you?"

"No, sir, it isn't."

"It's a quote from the Christian scriptures I memorized a long time ago," Jean Luc said. And shrugged a little in the stillness of the room. "Go ahead, Toll. Do whatever's necessary. Keep us among the quick. Because if I'm going to be judged at all, I'd rather it be that way than the other."

BOCA DEL SIERPE, TERRITORIAL TRINIDAD

It was a quarter to ten when Vince Scull called back. Nimec had hung around the villa's pool all morning, watching Annie take some laps and admiring how graceful and relaxed she looked. He'd learned to swim in the military as part of his combat survival training and, even so many years later, found that being in the water made him revert to the tight discipline the training had instilled.

"Okay, Petey, what am I interrupting?" Scull said.

Nimec shrugged with the satphone to his ear.

"Me getting a kick out of Annie enjoying herself," he said.

"Uh-huh." Scull said. "Don't suppose I should want to go there."

Nimec frowned. At least Vince sounded wide awake now—maybe even excited, the way he did when his juices got flowing.

"Your noggins find out anything?" he said.

"Haven't talked to a single one of them who's heard of combo tanker-freighters. but they're on it," Scull said. "Meanwhile, Bow—I mentioned him, didn't I? Cal Bowman?"

"Yeah, Vince. You did."

"Bow helped me with some groundwork, basic shit just might interest you."

"Let's hear it."

"You told me the feeder ships you saw were maybe three-hundred-footers, right?"

"Be my guess," Nimec said.

"Give or take, it puts them in line with the size of industrial oil barges," Scull said. "They'd be anywhere between two forty and two eighty feet long and carry loads of crude, refined, gasoline, home fuel, asphalt, or all the above and then some. The number of tanks in a barge's hold depends on how many types of product they've got aboard. Might be one, two, four . . . there'd need to be different tank linings for different grades of petroleum."

"And different ways of filling the tanks," Nimec said. "I figure if the feeders were taking oil, it would have to be a lighter type. Put crude in the hoses I saw and it would gum them up like thick molasses."

"Bow said about the same," Scull answered, and then paused for a long while.

"Vince? You still with me?"

"Don't get your bathing trunks in a knot, I need to look at my notes." An audible shuffling of papers over the phone. "Okay, here we go . . . It's twenty-four thousand."

Nimec's forehead creased.

"Must've missed something," he said, sure he hadn't. "What's twenty-four thousand—"

"Barrels, Petey. It's the typical load on one of those barges. Talking equivalents, that comes to one million gallons. You want another example, imagine a convoy of a hundred twenty tanker trucks, because that's how much rolling stock it'd take to move it by ground."

Nimec let that settle in for a minute. He was wearing a short-sleeved Polo shirt and the morning sun was already hot on his bare arms. He reached for the icy glass of Coke on a table beside his lounger, sipped, watched Annie from under the bill of his Seattle Mariners cap. Stroking to the deep end of the pool, she dove like a seal, then executed a kind of acrobatic loop-de-loop that left her long, toned legs briefly sticking straight up out of the water before they submerged with the rest of her. He'd promised they would go snorkeling together that afternoon. A boat would take them out over the coral reef beds for a couple of hours, and there would be exotic fish, and maybe dolphins and sea turtles. Then Annie was hoping they could hit another restaurant on the beach—it had a steel drum calypso band performing at dinner. After dark he'd leave her alone in the villa, head over to the harbor again, do a little undercover work like a character from a spy movie. That was the main thing on his mind right now and he felt lousy about it, but not lousy enough to bump it down on his list of priorities.

Pete Nimec, Man from UpLink, he thought. *Some vacation you're having . . . some great husband you are.*

"Got anything else for me?" he said into the phone.

"You sound testy all of a sudden, Petey," Scull said.

"I'm not," Nimec said. "Anything else?"

"Maybe," Scull said. "Remember what I told you about those disguised tankers in the Big One?"

"Yeah."

"Well, here's some history I found in our computers that's a lot more recent—don't know why it wasn't right in my head, because it should've been," Scull said. "A few years ago, around the time Uncle Saddam had his ass kicked out of Baghdad, two thousand troops from the Thirteenth MEU were assigned to a Brit naval operation to choke off oil smuggling on the Iraqi coast. There's that city there, Umm Qasr, you might've heard of it. The country's biggest port. What the smugglers did was tap crude from the Rumeila pipelines, run it down the al-Faw Peninsula in tanker trucks, then pass it off onto barges at Umm Qasr. Our troops pulled in dozens of non-Iraqi flagged ships moving about five hundred thousand gallons of oil out to sea every night—and, guess what, some of them were converted freighters."

Nimec sat quietly for a moment. Oil. According to his company travel and intelligence briefs the area certainly had a rich supply—it'd accounted for most of Trinidad's export economy for decades. In fact, they had those tar pits in the south where a British outfit built the first well rigs in the Americas, maybe in the world . . . a plantation owner had leased them drilling rights to a pitch lake on his land after his father, or grandfather, or somebody like that, had made a fortune marketing kerosene that had been distilled from it. Nimec believed the family still owned some processing plants, but would have to glance over the briefs again to be sure. In any case, it was oil that had indirectly brought Up-Link here through its wiring deal with Sedco. There were the onshore fields and refineries, and some new deepwater patches. Lots and lots of oil. But oil *smuggling* . . . who would be doing it? Why? Where would it be going? And more to the immediate issue, what were the chances of his having stumbled onto something like that after just an hour or two of compulsive peeping through his five-thousand-dollar binoculars?

Probably much slighter than the odds that he was starting to let his imagination carry him away, Nimec admitted to himself. Still, he'd seen *something* peculiar at the harbor. No getting past it. He could hardly wait to head back tonight for another—and if he could swing it, closer—look around.

"Thanks for getting on this for me, Vince," he said. "Keep in touch, okay? Something turns up, I want to know ASAP."

"Got you," Scull said. "And be sure to send my regards to the missus . . . that's if you wind up seeing her before I do."

Nimec blinked his eyes.

"What's that supposed to mean?' he said.

"Figure it out, honeymooner," Scull said, and terminated their connection.

Nimec let the phone sink from his ear and exhaled, staring at Annie in the pool.

Figure out what Scull meant? It would have been too easy.

The rough part was that he already damned well knew.

NORTHERN CALIFORNIA

The Modesto offices of Golden Triangle Computer Services occupied the entire top floor of a four-year-old medium-rise office building overlooking the downtown arch at 9th and I Streets. Behind the receptionist's and security stations were large double doors with a sky blue satin-finish metal skin and the name of the concern plated across them in liquidy gray- and blue-toned prismatic lettering. This reproduced the decor of Golden Triangle's original headquarters hundreds of miles to the south outside La Jolla, where Enrique Quiros had once run his narco empire surrounded by the sleek, stylish trappings of modern corporate respectability.

Lathrop took a stride or two out of the elevator toward the pretty young secretary sitting near the double doors, gave her a little smile, and waited. Their eyes met in brief, unacknowledged recognition as a dark-suited guard came around from his station, passed a metal detector wand over Lathrop, and then nodded at the secretary. She punched a button on her

switchboard, spoke quietly into her headset's mouthpiece, and the doors swung open, another guard appearing in the entrance to motion Lathrop past him
into the carpeted hallway beyond.

The second man conducted Lathrop through several turns of the office-lined corridor, walking
slightly ahead as if to guide him along, but that was
just a formality. Lathrop knew his way around and it
was no secret to the guards, the woman at the reception desk, or anyone else he passed approaching the
main executive suite.

Juan Quiros was waiting for him inside, his elbows resting on his desk, his thick hands folded in
front of him.

A stocky, bull-necked man with heavy features and
an olive complexion, he seemed as constricted and ill
at ease in a beige Italian designer suit as his prede-
cessor Enrique had been sleek and loose, as out of
place in an office setting as Enrique had been harmo-
niously compatible. Since his rise to ultimate power
in the clan, Juan had acquired an overmanicured look
from evident and increasingly frequent visits to the
salon. His curly black hair had been treated with re-
laxers and imparted with a sprayed-on plastic gloss.
His needle-sharp mustache might have been drawn
with the fine point of a pencil. The eyebrows that had
formed a solid bristly line above his nose before being reshaped by a series of waxings and tweezings
were now neatly separated on his wide forehead,

their high, thin arches giving him an appearance of perpetual surprise. But there was something in his eyes, something baleful and wolfish, the soft touch salon cosmeticians couldn't lift away or mask.

"I thought about having you kicked the hell out of the building," Juan said.

Lathrop glanced at the door to make sure it had been shut behind him by the departing guard.

"Always ready with a pleasant greeting," he said to Juan.

"Pleasant doesn't interest me," Juan said. "I'm not sure you do, either."

Lathrop looked at him.

"That wasn't your attitude when I called," Lathrop said. "You've changed your mind, tell me."

Juan didn't move or answer.

"Go on, tell me," Lathrop said. "I'll walk."

Juan watched him closely, his fingers still linked together.

"What do you want?" he said.

"I hear that question a lot from people," Lathrop said. "The smart ones have learned to ask what I've got, and I figured you were one of them."

Juan's smile showed nothing.

"Okay," he said. "You have edge for me, talk."

"Edge costs," Lathrop said. "Figured you'd know that, too."

Juan's gaze was as empty as his smile. "I don't spend money on thin air," he said sullenly.

"How about on finding out who killed your cousin Armand?" Lathrop said. "And why."

Juan regarded him without visible reaction for a moment.

"Tell you what," he said. "The trade we're in, we make enemies, and Armand was good at that. Maybe I got my own ideas about who would've killed him and am dealing with it."

"Maybe," Lathrop said. "Or maybe you don't have a clue who sent that masked white man came blasting his way into that garage in Devoción. And maybe you'd better for your own health."

Juan took a breath, his full lips parting over rows of white capped teeth. Then he slowly reclined and pulled apart his stubby hands. There were kinks of hair on their backs and on his knuckles that had escaped, or been ignored by the cosmeticians.

Lathrop waited.

"Give it to me," Juan said at last.

"There's more in the package and I don't break it up," Lathrop said. "You pay for all or nothing."

Juan nodded, his eyes suddenly narrow and gleaming.

"We've done business before," he said,. "I know how it goes."

"A minute ago you acted like you didn't."

Juan kept staring at him.

"Give it to me," he said again. "Everything."

Lathrop grinned, waited another moment. Then he stepped closer to the desk and took the seat in front of it.

"The man who killed Armand was hired by Esteban Vasquez to find out where you're keeping his daughter and bring her back to him," he said. "You make it worth my while, I'll arrange to bring you that gringo's head on a stake instead."

Tom Ricci was in the bedroom of his rental condominium zipping the HK G36 into its case when he heard the doorbell. The sound took a moment to sink in, as if it was something new to him. He listened, thinking maybe there had been a mistake. Not many people came to call lately. And to his surprise the bell rang again.

Ricci finished packing away the carbine, propped it in a corner, left the room, and pulled the door shut behind him, listening for the solid click of the latch. Then he went into his entry hall and looked out the peephole.

He straightened up, doubly surprised now. But this time he reacted with a jolt.

He'd recognized Julia Gordian at once.

Ricci stared at the door as confusion took hold of him. His first thought was to turn back around without answering—he had no use for company, and what would she be doing here? They'd only met once or twice before that day in Big Sur and hadn't seen each other after. It didn't make sense and could only mean problems for him.

Ricci stared at the door, not reaching for its knob. She'd have seen his Jetta out front but that didn't mean anything. Let her decide he was asleep, or out for a walk, or whatever. He didn't want or need company, especially this morning. He just wanted her to leave.

He waited.

Another ring. A soft knock on her side of the door.

Ricci swore under his breath. His hand grasped the doorknob, turned it, and pulled the door half-open.

He looked at her for several seconds.

"Hi, Tom," Julia said from the front step. She nodded toward her station wagon in the driveway. "I happened to be driving past your neighborhood this morning and figured I'd stop and say hello."

Ricci was quiet. Julia had her black hair pulled into a loose ponytail that was kind of twisted up and clasped to the back of her head and seemed to be almost but not quite coming apart. There were three small gold rings in her left ear and two in her right and she was wearing black capri pants and flip-flop sandals and a lilac-colored sleeveless blouse with a lot of small yellow polka dots on it. In her hand, the one that hadn't just dropped from the buzzer, was a waxed white paper bag.

Ricci kept the door partially closed between them.

"I never told you where I live," he said.

Julia shrugged. "Are you sure?" she said.

"I'm sure," he said.

"Guess I must have found out from somebody else, then," she said with a smile. "Because I remembered the address while I was passing by. And since you're you, and you're here, and this looks like a *home*, the evidence shows I got it right."

Ricci studied her, his eyes adjusting to the sunlight flooding over the small plot of lawn neatly maintained by the condo development's service staff.

"Look," he said, "I'm kind of busy."

Julia stood there on the front step, shrugging again, her smile becoming a little sheepish.

"I don't want to bother you," she said softly, and held up her bag. "But I brought coffee and muffins . . . and, well, I haven't had a chance . . . that is, much as it's kind of late, I really want to thank you for saving my life."

Ricci regarded her through the entryway awhile longer, hesitated. Then he grunted and pulled open the door.

"I'll need to get going soon," he said.

Julia nodded.

"Actually, that's perfect," she said. "I have a bunch of stuff ahead of me today, too."

She entered, paused inside the door, and glanced around. The living room was medium sized with a pale gray carpet, a small sofa, a plump bustle-backed wing chair, and a television/satellite box setup on a plain black stand. It gave way to an open sort of hall-way that led in turn to a combination kitchen and din-ing area. Everything seemed clean and orderly and comfortable enough in a sterile, impersonal way that reminded Julia of a motel room on check-in.

Ricci closed the door and led her toward the dining room. As she passed the wing chair, Julia noticed a big, packed sporting duffel—or *hunting* duffel, she guessed, since it had a woodland camouflage pattern—pushed against one of its arms.

"Planning to visit the great outdoors?" she asked, and nodded at the duffel. "I like to go camping my-self a couple of times a year . . . y'know, just to clear my mind."

Ricci's glance went to the chair. He seemed a little thrown by her question, as if he hadn't realized what was on it. Then he looked at her.

"Don't need to clear my mind," he said.

His chill tone, coupled with the stony expression on his features, caught Julia unprepared. She mo-mentarily wondered if she'd done the smart thing coming to see him, then decided his reaction was proof enough that she had. Or at least that was how she was determined to take it.

She followed him to the table and set her bag down.

"I brought chocolate chip and macadamia nut muffins, my pick of the month," she said, opening it. "Ever try them?"

Ricci's head moved from side to side in the negative.

"They're from that bakery practically around the corner from here, Michael's Morning Toaster," she said. "Good luck to anybody who tries finding them in Pescadero, which is why I drove all this way to relieve my sicko addiction."

Ricci turned to her.

"We going to need dishes?" he said.

She flapped a hand in the air.

"C'mon, we can rough it," Julia said, and patted the tabletop. "We've got paper cups, napkins, paper plates . . . the bakery guy even tossed in plastic knives and forks. That's, God forbid, in case you're the type who'd actually use them to eat a muffin instead of your bare fingers and teeth."

Ricci stood stock still, quietly watching her. She had reached into the bag and begun to empty it, laying out its contents on the table, carefully peeling the lids off the coffee cups, setting the muffins onto the paper plates.

"You don't need to thank me," he said.

Julia stopped what she was doing and looked up at him, her face abruptly serious.

"Would you prefer I didn't? Or can't I be the one to decide that?"

"I'm saying you don't need to," Ricci said. "I was doing what I got paid to do."

Julia stood there holding a muffin halfway out of the bag in its waxed tissue wrapper.

"All right," she said. "Want to hear my stroke of genius?"

Ricci's piercing blue eyes went to hers. He held them there for a full thirty seconds, and then nodded.

"Let's just enjoy a nice breakfast before we go about our busy days," she said. "I won't spout on to you about my feelings of gratitude, and you won't talk about why you've dropped off the face of the earth when it comes to your friends. And we'll consider it a fair bargain."

A silence. Their gazes held together across the little dining area as the aroma of the hot fresh coffee rose in wafts of steam to permeate it.

Then, slowly, Ricci gave Julia another nod, and approached the table, and pulled out the chair opposite her.

"How's Vivian?" he said after another long spell of silence. "She come around okay from those gunshot wounds?"

Julia reached for her muffin and raised it to her mouth. "Viv goes jogging with me every other morning," she said. "Rain or shine, like it or not."

Ricci's face took on an expression she interpreted as pleased.

"Great dog," he said.

Julia glanced at him, about to take a bite of the muffin.

"Yeah," she said, and smiled. "She sure is."

And with that they got started on their food.

SIX

"GOOD ON YA, LUV. TAKE HOLD A' ME HAND 'ere and I'll getcha right up."

His shoulder-length golden mane sweeping around his tanned face in the onshore breeze, Blake the Bronze leaned over from the pontoon boat Annie had reserved and extended a sculpted arm toward the pier. He wore a pookah shell choker, a yellow tank top, paisley swim trunks with a lot of bright pink and blue in the print, root-beer-colored wraparound Oakley sunglasses with reddish-pink lenses, and flip-flops.

Annie reached out from where she and Nimec stood on the floating gangplank and let him help her onto the boat's flat fiberglass stern platform.

"Okeydoke, mate, you're next!" Blake shouted

over the side at Nimec. "Or don't you need an assist now?"

"Think I can manage on my own," Nimec said.

He grabbed the boat's rail, climbed aboard, and a moment later was standing next to Annie under the twenty-footer's sun canopy. Both were wearing swimsuits and windbreakers, their snorkeling equipment in mesh totes on the deck. Nimec, in addition, had a pair of standard rangefinder binoculars on a strap around his neck. All around them a diversity of pleasure boats were making their way to and from the busy marina, one of them a double-deck cruiser booming hip-hop music from its cabin as it left a nearby slip.

Nimec pulled a face. "Loud," he muttered.

Annie rolled her shoulders to the beat.

"*Paa-aarty!*" she said with a grin, playfully bumping her hip against his.

Nimec looked at her and, before he knew it, had a wet kiss planted on the tip of his nose—an instant frown-killer despite everything on his mind. He had deliberately failed to tell her what he'd hashed over with Vince earlier, and when she asked about it had just offered a few general words about them having to look into some things. No sense getting Annie disturbed over what were really just questions at this stage of the game. It was possible that by the time he and Vince consulted again, Vince might have cleared them up.

He put his arm around her waist and moved toward the middle of the boat, walking easily on the wide, well-balanced deck mounted atop its pontoon hull. Blake, meanwhile, had reeled in the aft mooring line, then started forward to do the same at the bow.

"It's really great of you to take us out," Annie said, turning to him. "I wouldn't have even asked if I'd known we'd be imposing on your day off."

Blake smiled as he unfastened the bowline from its support.

"Don't mention it," he said. "The reefs're in a favorite spot a' mine, and it's a joy sharin' it with a lovely couple like yourselves." He neatly wound the line in his hands and set it down. "Gem of an afternoon like this, it's fair odds I would've gotten my bathers on and headed out to relax on me own."

The Aussie went into the helm station, slid in behind its console, and adjusted the tilt wheel.

"Another bit an' we're off 'n' away, won't be more'n a half hour's ride," he said, and then tipped his head toward the plush lounge chairs to his left. "Settle back if you'd like, friends; the seats're comfy's can be an' you've got acres a' room. And if you lift the top a' that ottoman there in front a' your legs, it'll open into a cooler full up with drinks 'n' sandwiches, though I'd wait on the food till after your dive—cramps, y'know."

Nimec sat with Annie on the cushioned chair, listened to the engine throttle up, and gazed out at the water.

He was thinking he might have enjoyed being a spectator to the aquatic goings-on at a coral reef under different circumstances.

Right now, though, he would rather have been headed out to get a closer look at those feeder ships he'd seen last night.

Wherever on the deep blue sea they might have gone.

"I believe I've covered it all," Tolland Eckers said, and slid his GPS pocket navigator into the pouch on his belt. "If any of you still have questions, or need something clarified, let's hear it before we get moving."

None of the other three men assembled on the beach spoke. They were in a sandy little cove formed between two lumpish masses of black igneous rock, wearing skintight neoprene wetsuits with short trunks, and ankle-high zippered booties. Behind them, at the surfline, their semi-rigid inflatable strike boat sat where it had been delivered ashore, its scalloped Kevlar-reinforced hull painted bright yellow, a custom touch added to give it the appearance of a sport racer. And while the Steyr 9mm TMP compact submachine guns stowed in compartments near the speedcraft's straddle seats could hardly be considered standard sporting equipment, Eckers had stressed that they were only to be used in an extreme pinch.

It was what had been loaded in with them that would be the unlikely weapons of choice.

Eckers looked from one face to the other. This was a team of skilled professionals, men who knew what they were doing. Having already made his critical points, he ordinarily wouldn't have bothered to hammer on them again. But he also would not have led the group out himself under ordinary circumstances. The job they were about to launch was of greater consequence than most, and he decided it could do no harm for them to have a quick final review before kickoff.

"First thing to remember: Nature's given us a window of opportunity. We have more speed than we should need, and water and sky patrols making sure nobody else comes near it," he said. "It's up to us to get in the window when it opens, get the job done, and get out."

Eckers saw nods.

"Second thing: We can assume our targets will be the objects of an exhaustive search, and that they'll be given equally thorough postmortems when they're found," he said. "This must—I stress *must*—pass for an accident under intense scrutiny. I don't expect it to happen, but the moment one of us has to fire a shot is when we'll know something's gone critically wrong, got me?"

Eckers saw more nods around him and left it at that.

"Time's come," he said, and then turned toward their waiting craft.

The Aug Stingray was into its third pass of the overflight zone when its pilot sighted an immense yacht nearing the cordoned off area . . . surprisingly the first boat he'd encountered, but he'd heard reports of several perimeter interceptions on the shared communications channel.

He tapped his copilot's shoulder, pointed to the tuna tower aft of the enclosed bridge.

"Looks as if'n 'twere headin' out t'fetch some big yellers," he said. "Gon' be some bloody disappointed faces on that fishin' tub, don' 'e think?"

The copilot nodded, withholding a frown. *The perils of multinationalism*, he thought. A Frenchman who'd once flown with the DAOS special operations aviation unit in a squadron attached to Henri Beauchart's Group d'Intervention, he often had to strain to decipher his fellow crewman's pronounced Yorkshire accent.

"I'll notify a patrol boat to turn them aside," he said in perfectly enunciated English, and toggled on his radio headset.

Nimec had assumed the pontoon boat would provide a smooth, quiet, and comfortable ride—that was the whole idea behind its low-drag design—but he'd thought it would be kind of weak in the horsepower department. All told, though, it moved at a faster clip than he might have expected, and he guessed Blake the Bronze must have pushed it up to a speed of about forty knots getting them to the reef area.

In the stern with Annie, Nimec was also surprised by the sense of well-being that gradually came to possess him. It didn't quite shut out his thoughts of what he'd observed at the harbor, and he would have felt delinquent if it had. But the pleasures of the ride swung him *away* from those thoughts, removed him from them mentally as he gained physical distance from Los Rayos, to find himself in a seemingly end-less space absent of anything but blue water and sky. Within ten or fifteen minutes after setting out, he'd even ceased to notice other watercraft nearby. And while the faint, recurrent drone of patrolling helicop-ters would occasionally remind him of the island at his rear, its tug at his consciousness lost insistence as the trip went along, the choppers seeming far off and peripheral in their unseen flight patterns.

At one point he'd gotten up to lean quietly out over the rail, the breeze streaming over him, when Annie came over and gently took hold of his arm.

"This is how it's always been for me on an air-plane," she said. "Even before the Air Force or NASA. When I was a teenager flying in my dad's rat-tletrap Beech."

Nimec had looked at her, smiled, gone back to staring out at the water.

They had been standing there together for a few minutes when her fingers tightened around him a bit.

"Pete, honey, look at them!" she said, and gestured excitedly to their rear with her other hand. "Aren't they *beautiful*?"

Nimec had glanced down and seen the scythe-like dorsal fins and curved backs of dolphins breaking the water as a bunch of them raced toward the boat, stayed alongside it for a while, then shot past like light gray torpedoes.

He'd returned his eyes to Annie's face.

"Beautiful," he'd said, his throat inexplicably tight.

Fifteen minutes or so later Blake had cut the engine and come around out of the pilot's station. Turning toward him, Nimec noticed a group of steel deepwater buoys some distance from the bow . . . far enough away, in fact, so that they might have been small red and green apples bobbing on the calm surface. He lifted his binoculars and had a look.

"That where the reef is?" he'd asked, wondering why they would have stopped so short of it.

Blake had shaken his head.

"Attaboy, ace—nice to see you payin' attention even if you're a tick off the mark," he'd said with a throaty laugh. "I suggest you leave the sailin' to me, though. We're sitting right over the coral banks. The water's shallow enough hereabouts, too right. Those warning buoys are to steer you 'round an underwater ledge three quarters, a half mile on . . . you wouldn't want to conk into it when the tide's low, and that'll be soon enough by my figurin'."

Nimec had grunted. Had his question really been that funny? Nothing like somebody having a chuckle at your expense, he'd thought.

But Blake had hardily slapped his back before he could get too annoyed. "C'mon, mate, hand off the binocs, an' let's see if we can't get you an' the missus ready for a dive," said the Aussie.

Upon which he'd gone back across the deck to where they had deposited their equipment bags.

Although Nimec hadn't needed assistance gearing up, Blake was determined to provide it, and it seemed more trouble than it was worth to even consider fending him off . . . a sentiment Annie indicated she shared with a private little wink. As she sat to slip into her fins, clip her snorkel to her diving mask, and fit the mask over her face, Blake bent over her to make some vague added adjustments, then sidled over toward Nimec and did the same for him.

"A few tips I'll have you remember while you're dippin' under," he said, fiddling with the strap of Nimec's mask for no apparent reason. "Twenty feet down, twenty feet from the boat's my rule of thumb. And don't pet the cute little fishies, 'cause it can hurt 'em. And don't go reachin' into any holes or crevices 'cause some wonky creature hidin' inside'm might want to hurt *you*." He paused, looked the two of them over with his hands on his hips, nodded pridefully as if at a job well done. "Summin' up, don't bother anythin' with scales, tentacles, or a jelly bod, or get bit, stung, or snagged on the coral and you'll be jake . . . an' much as I'd like to accompany you lovebirds, I'll be up here keepin' lookout if there should be any problems."

They waited until he was finished talking, got up, and flapped toward the stern in their fins.

Crouching beside Annie on the dive platform, Nimec glanced back over his shoulder at Blake.

"Forgot to ask," he said. "There sharks in these waters?"

Blake grinned from where he stood on the deck.

"Just of the laid-back variety, mate!" he said.

And before Nimec could manage a frown, Annie grabbed his wrist, let out a yip of frisky delight, and rolled into the water, pulling him in with a splash.

Steering his regular course to the yellowfin tuna grounds about thirty kilometers out from his dock at Los Rayos, Greger Fisk, the captain of the sportfisherman charter *Norwegian Wind,* had scarcely taken notice of the helicopters overhead. The least well-off passengers on his luxurious Netherlands-built Heesen were millionaires, and they were looked upon with near scorn by the truly prosperous aboard, who were in turn thought of as a bare step up from crude bourgeoisie by the wealthiest of the resort's guests—sheiks, royals, and business tycoons of celestial power and financial means who would sail their own motor yachts or none at all, in search of prized finned specimens.

In the air for purposes of security, the helicopters were constants in these parts and, like hovering gulls and clouds, had come within range of the captain's awareness only as familiar aspects of the scenery. To be sure, Fisk was used to them. But he had sometimes found it a comfort to see them in his first months captaining a ship based on the island, given that he'd known he must navigate his important and valuable patrons—prize specimens in their separate right— through a dangerous world of terrorists, hijackers, and modern pirates.

The coastal patrol boat with a Los Rayos Security emblem on its prow, however, caught his attention even before it came speeding up on his port side to hail him on its public address system. And unbeknownst to Captain Fisk, his newbie spotter on the radar-equipped tuna-and-marlin tower had reacted to the sudden, deafening alert with a startlement that nearly sent him tumbling down from his high platform to the bridge.

"You are entering a temporarily restricted zone, Norwegian Wind," the voice blared over the cutter's loudspeaker. *"Inform us at once of your destination over intership channel twenty-two B—that is two-two-Bertha—and we will reroute. Over."*

Fisk reached for the radio handset on his helm

console, identified himself, gave the coordinates of the tuna grounds, and then listened to the specifics of the detour with chagrin . . . It would cost him an hour, or even longer. Then he thought about the level of ire it would bring about in his fanatical anglers and almost shuddered. A year or so back, his ship had been just ten miles short of a teeming pod of fish when a British prime minister's vacation yacht had crossed its path, the attendant patrol boat escort forcing him into a circuitous, lengthy, and in Fisk's opinion unnecessary course change that had left his infuriated passengers with limp lines, empty hooks, and many, many vocal complaints.

He pressed his handset's talk button, mindful of past experience. Perhaps today he might succeed in a compromise.

"Captain Fisk, again, coastal patrol. I roger your alternate coordinates," he said. And then took his stab. "Request permission to stand by and wait if that would be shorter, over."

"Negative, Captain. Our action will take a while."

"I'm going to have some very unhappy passengers," Fisk pressed.

"We apologize, Captain. This area's off limits and must be cleared of traffic."

Fisk felt the wind go out of him.

"Can you help me with explanations for when they chew my head off?"

"We've received a Mayday distress call and are

taking appropriate action. That's all I can tell you, Captain. Out."

Fisk expelled a long, defeated breath and set the handset into its clip, wondering how serious the Mayday might be. With so many amateur boaters in the water panicking if they so much as got splashed by a wave, one never knew. Nine times out of ten it was something minor.

Captain Greger Fisk sighed again, girding for his announcement over the ship's intercom, thinking he might as well throw himself overboard afterward and give the patrols a real problem to worry about.

Nimec and Annie swam a few feet from the boat in the warm, placid green water, then floated facedown on the surface and immediately saw the great reef below them.

It was, Nimec thought, spectacular. What he might have described as a sort of forest masquerading as crusted, irregular shelves of rock. The growth of new living coral flared off it in shoots, spurs, and willowy masses of different shapes, all of them covered in seaweed that ribboned out and out in long, drifting strands.

They kept looking down through their face masks a bit, pulling regular breaths into their snorkels. Then they filled their lungs and dove.

Nimec had expected to catch a glimpse of some underwater life, but the reef was *teeming* with creatures everywhere. It was, he thought, almost too much to take in all at once. Schools of tiny silvery-blue fish darting between coral branches that swayed and undulated in the gentle current; some spidery, leggy thing that fled through a nook in the formation in a scattery cloud of sand; a great bugeyed fish with iridescent red scales, blotchy blue spots on its massive head, and what seemed to be dozens of fins spraying from its sides. It at first moved slowly past them, and then put on a sudden, explosive burst of speed to plow away through a dense clump of plant growth.

Then Nimec felt Annie tap his shoulder, looked over at her, nodded.

They went up for air.

The racing boat moved at idle speed like a restrained thoroughbred, its twin 225hp outboards humming in low gear.

Beside his pilot in the forward bow seat, Eckers checked the time with his digital wristwatch, fingered on its compass display for a moment, and then shifted his glance to the GPS marine chart on his handheld. The latter device would have sufficed to give him all the information he wanted, but he was a cautious man, and a comparison check could only back up and refine his situational awareness.

He brought his binoculars up to his eyes, spotted

the target at rest in the clear distance ahead, turned the zoom knob with his thumb, studied it more closely, and nodded to himself.

"Kick it, Harrison," he said at last, glancing over at the pilot. "They're ours."

Nimec had plunged down for his fourth or fifth dive to the reef when he heard the distinctive thrum of an engine somewhere above. It made him curious. He turned to Annie, who was beside him exploring a huge knob of coral that was plastered with starfish and other tentacled, suctiony things. He pointed to his ear, then pointed toward the surface, and up they went to investigate.

On his deck enjoying the fresh air and sunshine, Blake was a touch perplexed when he noticed the yellow racer planing across the water toward him. This was not because crafts of that sort were rare sights in themselves, but because they usually came in pairs or threesomes . . . hard for a crew to stage a race if they didn't have any competition. Course, he thought, these blokes might be on a solo practice run. Made good sense, since they were traveling at a moderate speed, and the environmentalists looked upon contests near the reef formations with sneering disapproval. Did all sorts of bad, said they in their cries for legal restrictions—damaged the coral heads, tore apart the seaweed growth, disturbed and injured the sea life. And who with a right brain and working eyes could dispute it?

Blake watched the racer continue to approach from starboard, the sound of its engines growing louder by the second. Then he thought about his love-birds and glanced to the left, making sure they were still safely on the opposite side of his boat, where he'd last seen them . . . and there he found them surfacing for air within the approximate twenty-foot boundary he'd laid out. Fine couple, they were. And took instruction with no flapping of the lips, which made them all the finer.

He saw Pete wave to him, waved back, noticed him stay on top looking his way, and made the OK sign to let him know everything was all right, betting he'd heard the hum of the racer's outboards and gotten curious. It was easy to hear a noise like that when you were underwater, tough to judge the direction it was coming from because of the way vibrations scattered.

Blake smiled. Maybe old Pete was worried he'd scram off with the boat. It was dotty to even think he'd be concerned about that, sure, and wasn't something that struck Blake in a serious-minded vein . . . or not too much so anyway. Hard to put a finger on it, but there was quite a bit more to that fellow than might seem. Always on the watch, he was. And three or four thoughts deeper into his head than he let on.

Blake turned toward the sled-shaped racing boat

again. It was still coming on apace, and had gotten
near enough for him to tally a crew of four aboard,
men in gray shortie wetsuits. A few minutes later it
had almost pulled abeam and was throttling down.

He moved to the starboard safety rail, watched the
racer slow to a halt in the water several yards away.

"Hello!" hollered the man seated beside the pilot.
He was an American, to tell from his accent. "Em-
barrasses me to say this, but we've gotten ourselves
lost."

Blake stood with his hands on the rail. Well, he
thought, that answered a question or two.

"Sorry to hear it, mate," he said. "You out of Los
Rayos?"

"And trying to find our way back," the man replied
with a nod. "Our GPS unit went on the blink."

Blake gave him a commiserative look. Lord knew
why, but it was just the sort of thing that happened
with tourists.

"Got to love those gizmos . . . It's why I always
bring a good, old-fashioned reliable map for
backup," he said. "No need to fret, 'owever, I could
shout you directions if you'd like. The island's no
more'n forty minutes due east, with a small twist this
way 'n' that." He paused. "You gents set for petrol
an' supplies?"

The man nodded.

"No problems there, thanks," he said. Then he
tilted his head toward his pilot. "Hope I'm not impos-

ing, but it'd be a help if we could have a look at that map of yours."

Blake thought about it a second and then shrugged his broad shoulders.

"No imposition 't all," he said. "Pull yourselves broadside, toss a line across, 'n' we'll bring the two of you aboard—how's that?"

The man offered a big smile.

"Sounds perfect," he said.

"I 'ave a spare chart in this chamber a' horrors somewhere, worst part's findin' it 'midst the rest a' my junk," Blake was saying a few minutes later. He was in his pilot station bent over a storage compartment below the butterfly wheel, the men from the racer's bow seat standing behind him, their craft bound fast to his gunwale. "Soon's I pull it out, I can get the route 'ighlighted with a marker an' you'll be on your way right quick."

"Can't tell you often enough how much we appreciate it," Eckers said. He nodded to his companion, who reached into a belt pouch against his hip.

Blake fumbled in the compartment, moving aside a first aid kit, a pack of facial tissues, a bottle of sunblocker, a box of toothpicks, and a two-year-old program for the Matildas women's soccer team with a feature article on a particularly sexy goalie.

"You blokes keep thankin' me, I might start to believe I'm doin' somethin' that deserves it," he said without turning, his hand still in the box. What on earth was a plastic bag filled with marbles, metal jacks, and a red rubber ball doing in there? One of these days he'd have to tidy up. "By the way, m'name's Blake Davies. Didn't catch either a' yours."

Eckers glanced at the man beside him, saw that he'd taken the blunt wedge of stone from the pouch into his hand, and nodded again.

"They call us Grim and Reaper," he said as the rock was smashed forcefully against the left side of Blake's skull.

Nimec had surfaced to look over at the pontooner several times after Blake flashed the OK sign with his thumb and forefinger. He didn't think much of it when he saw the yellow racer approach, except that maybe the Aussie had run across a couple of his water-loving buddies having their own little jaunt off the island.

On the instance he came up to see lines being cast between the boats, it drew his closer attention.

"Annie," he said. "What do you make of 'em? Those guys who came in that racing boat, that is."

Swimming in place beside Nimec, she watched a couple of them board the pontooner.

"They seem friendly with Blake," she said, and kind of shrugged her shoulders out of the water. "Why?"

"I don't know," Nimec said.

He kept watching the boat. Blake had gone around into his pilot's console, followed by the two men.

"Pete?"

"Yeah."

"Are you thinking something's wrong?"

He took a moment to consider that, lifted his dive mask over his forehead.

"I'm not sure what I'm looking at, and I'd like to be," he said, glancing over at her. "If that makes sense."

Annie read the expression on his face.

"It does," she said. "Should we go back to the boat?"

"Maybe I should," Nimec said.

"You?"

"Right."

"By *yourself*?"

"Right," Nimec said, shooting another look at the boat. "Find out what's up, then come on back."

She shook her head.

"No, Pete. Where you go, I go—"

Annie broke off, the words dying on her tongue, her eyes grown wide with shock and confusion as she saw what was suddenly happening on the boat, happening all in a terrible second—the one man raising something in his hand, bringing it down on Blake's head, then Blake slumping over the console, falling below it onto the deck.

"*Pete!*" she cried, and reached out to grip his arm. "*Pete!*"

Nimec turned to her.

"Annie, stay put," he said.

"What about *you*?"

"I need to swim over there," he said. "It's our best chance."

Annie shook her head again vehemently.

"How, Pete?" she said, clinging to him. "What can you do against them alone?"

He looked at her, unable to think of a reply.

And then the men aboard the pontooner made any answer he could have settled upon irrelevent as they hurried to the side of the boat, pulled guns from under their wetsuit jackets, and pointed them at Nimec and Annie over the safety rail.

"*Over here*," one of them shouted in a voice that carried clearly over the water. "*Both of you. Now.*"

Tolland Eckers faced Nimec and Annie across the pontoon boat's deck, the Steyr 9mm in his right hand leveled on them. He had donned thin black boater's gloves as a precaution against fingerprints.

"It fascinates me how quickly a person's situation can change," he said. "Turn from one thing to another overnight. Or sometimes in the blink of an eye. You never know what might happen next."

Still dripping water, Nimec stood there in the booties he'd worn under his fins before removing them on the dive platform. He lowered his gaze to where Blake lay fallen in a motionless heap, blood oozing from his temple to mat his thick blond hair against the side of his face. Then he shifted his eyes onto those of the man with the semiautomatic.

"What you did to him tells me everything I need to know," he said.

Eckers shrugged.

"Does it?" he said. "The poor fellow was enjoying himself when he slipped and took a nasty fall. What I'd call a piece of bad luck, or couldn't you see?"

Nimec nodded toward the other man, who was now busy loosening the ropes that secured the racer to the pontoon boat's gunwale, his own portable weapon in a sling harness at his side.

"I saw your friend hit him with whatever was in his hand," he said. "Go ahead and call that a fall, or anything you want."

"You know what you know, is that it?"

Nimec didn't answer.

Eckers looked at him and smiled coldly.

"It's your knowing too much that changed your situation," he said. "Changed it in a sudden, drastic way. Turning you from an invited guest to an interloper."

"I have no idea what the hell you're talking about," Nimec said.

"Nothing to what I'm saying, is that it?" Eckers motioned toward Annie with the Steyr. "And you? Also without any ideas about why we're all here? Or do you mean to keep them to yourself like your husband?"

She just stared at him in silence, as if simply trying

to process what was going on. Eckers's companion, meanwhile, had finished unfastening the lines between the boats and come around to stand slightly off to one side of Nimec.

"Whatever I saw, or you think I saw, I didn't tell my wife."

Eckers shrugged a third time.

"Maybe, or maybe not," he said. "Sadly, I won't leave *maybes* swirling around."

Nimec felt his stomach tighten.

"Whatever you intend to do out here, you're out of your mind to think you'll get away with it."

"Because?"

"Because of who I work for," Nimec said. "Because they won't let up on you or the people you work for."

Eckers continued to look at him, his weapon steady in his grip.

"Accidental deaths happen," he said. "Your employers can have suspicions. They can search, and investigate, and they can be left with their nagging doubts. But in the end, if the evidence still points to an accident, none of that will matter."

Nimec was silent. He hadn't wanted to use words like *death* or *kill* or *murder*, had hoped to protect Annie from hearing them. But while he'd done a lousy job of protecting her from anything so far, that might be about to change.

If the evidence still points to an accident, he thought.

But how could it, if both he and Annie had bullet holes in them?

He stood watching as Eckers glanced over at the racing boat.

"Take it out to the ledge," he said to the two men inside it. "Kettering and I will join you shortly."

The man at the wheel nodded, and a moment later the racer's powerful engines roared to life. Then it turned in the water and sped off westward toward the buoys, churning up a long, white wake of foam.

"We're almost finished now," Eckers said, looking back at Nimec. "This may give you small comfort, but I'm a professional and will be"—he hesitated a beat—"as efficient as possible."

Nimec had kept his eyes locked on Eckers's, peripherally aware of the man he'd called Kettering sidling closer. *How did they intend to do it?* He needed to buy some time. Seconds, minutes, whatever he could.

"Except your plan won't work," he said, thinking hard. "You figure you'll ride this boat out to the ledge, or outcrop, or whatever it is. Wait there till the tide goes down, make it look like it crashed and took on water, then head away with your friends. Could be you've even got a Mayday logged somewhere so you're covered on that end." Nimec paused a second, took a deep breath, wishing again that he could have spared Annie from what he needed to say. "But we won't stand around waiting for you to drive us into the rocks," he resumed, then. "Not if we're going to die anyway. We'll try to stop you and you'll have to use that gun of yours to stop us. And the people who come out searching won't stop till they find our bodies. You know that. You need them to find us for this to seem real. And they see bullet holes, there goes your accident."

Eckers's cold smile reappeared, but Nimec believed he saw something in his eyes that conflicted with it.

"Gamma hydrooxybutyrate," he said. "Ever hear of it?"

Nimec looked at him. He hadn't, but he wasn't giving that away.

"It's a drug classified as a sedative and anesthetic," Eckers said. "Short form nomenclature, GHB. Common street names 'soap,' 'scoop,' 'grievous bodily harm,' 'easy lay' . . . although by now the kids who use it for date rape have probably replaced them with a dozen others, our youth culture always being in a hurry to move on."

Nimec watched him silently. Watched his *eyes*. And at the same time remained watchful of Kettering.

"As far as you're concerned, the important things to understand about GHB are that it's odorless, tasteless, and instantaneously induces rapid sleep or coma at elevated doses. And it becomes undetectable soon afterward," Eckers said. "In fact, it's synthesized from a chemical that's normally manufactured in our brains . . . that's present in every one of us . . . and that increases its concentration in a human body as death occurs. Which makes it a forensic pathologist's nightmare, and a defense attorney's dream. Especially in the form my own people have developed."

Silence. Nimec had realized he was almost out of time, his thoughts racing along as he listened.

"Your drug doesn't change anything," he said. "You use it on one of us, you think the other's going to stand and watch? Knowing you can't chance shooting that damned gun of yours? Or you want to convince me you've got designer bullets that evaporate and close their own wounds?"

Eckers looked at him. Again something turned in his eyes. And again Kettering slipped closer to Nimec, easing slightly behind him, almost breathing down his neck.

And then Eckers extended the Steyr further in front of him.

"I don't need both of your bodies to be found," he said. "There's Blake, whose skull will have been pounded by the ocean rocks. And then there's one or the other of you that will be dredged up, it makes no difference whom. Two floaters, a third body lost to the sea, and that will be that."

No, Nimec thought. No, it wouldn't. Because the man holding him at gunpoint *was* professional, and smart enough to figure he'd probably have gotten in touch with somebody at UpLink about his sightings at the harbor, and that UpLink's investigators would be more than suspicious if he was the one who disappeared. That happened, they would know without question what took place out here. They would know, and wouldn't quit till they found a way to prove it.

Which exposed the gunman's bluff. He needed Nimec. Needed his body intact to pull off his scheme.

Leaving Annie—and Annie alone—immediately vulnerable to the gun.

Nimec did not wait so much as another heartbeat to make his move. Glancing quickly around, he spun in a half circle and snatched hold of Kettering's wrist with his right hand, wrenching it up and backward as he jammed his left shoulder against Kettering's chest, driving into him with all the momentum he could summon. Kettering grunted and began to stumble backward, but Nimec held on to his wrist, seeing the hank of cloth bunched in his gloved hand, saturated with the goddamn sleep drug he'd been about to smother him with. Nimec simultaneously jerked the hand up again and twisted it over and around, slapping it over Kettering's face, holding it there over his nose and mouth.

"Stop or I'll kill the bitch!" Eckers yelled, waving his Steyr as he moved forward in a kind of charge. *"You hear me, I said sto—"*

"Down, Annie!" Nimec said, shouting over him. And she did, hurling herself flat to the deck as he whipped Kettering around in front of him, pushing his suddenly limp body between Eckers and himself while reaching for the stock of the submachine gun against Kettering's side, tearing it from its harness, and getting his finger around the trigger to squeeze off a two-round burst.

His chest soaked with blood, Eckers wobbled on his feet a moment, looking straight at Nimec as Kettering sagged and then fully collapsed between them. Then his eyes rolled up in his sockets so that only their whites were visible, and he also dropped to the deck.

Nimec turned, hurried to Annie, knelt beside her.

"You all right?" he said, taking hold of her arm.

She nodded, started to push herself onto her knees, trembling all over.

"C'mon, honey," Nimec said, helping her up. He shot a glance around toward the buoys across the water. "We've got to move fast."

"That's it," said the racer's copilot. He'd heard the report of the Steyr TMP come echoing across the water perhaps a second before. "They've done the woman."

At the wheel in the silence following the gunshots, Harrison lifted his binoculars to his eyes and peered eastward. Having reached the safe passage lane marked by the buoys, yards from where the broken points of the ledge had emerged above the receding tide, he had only to follow orders and wait for Eckers and Kettering to bring the pontooner in their direction. By the time it arrived, enough of the formation would be out of the water for the pleasure boat and its unconscious passengers to be driven into the rocks, a seeming mishap that would claim the lives of both the guide and their prime target. The woman's body would need to be transferred to the racer and disposed of separately, and Harrison assumed the job would fall on him, as it had with that bookkeeper and the hired men who'd come to take him off the island. Carving them up had been unpleasant but not unprecedented—Harrison did whatever was required and accepted his pay, that was all.

His lenses focused on the pontoon boat now, he suddenly straightened and cursed under his breath.

The racer's copilot looked at him. "What's wrong?" he said.

Harrison let the binocs sink down from his face.

"They're still standing," he said, disconcerted. "Both targets."

A stunned pause.

"How about Eckers?"

"I can't see him," Harrison said.

"Kettering?"

Harrison had raised the glasses back to his eyes.

"No," he said.

The copilot looked at him again. "Shit," he said. "This is unbelievable."

Harrison shook his head.

"You read reports on that Sword op," he said. "There was nothing in them to indicate it would be simple."

Silence.

"How do we carry on?" said the copilot.

Harrison reached for the ignition and their engine revved.

"First we'll need to get on top of that boat," he said. "Then we need to decide."

His hands on the pontoon boat's wheel, Nimec glanced back over his shoulder and spotted the racer approaching from the vicinity of the underwater ledge. When he'd heard its outboards come to life only moments ago, it had been too far off to see with the naked eye. The pilot was pushing it hard.

"Annie," Nimec said. "Think you can hold us steady?"

Beside him in the pilot's station, Annie stood gripping the radio handset she'd used to contact Up-Link's temporary facility across the channel, providing its operators with Nimec's coded identifiers for emergency assistance. Nodding, she clipped it into place on the console, eased closer to him.

"I can try," she said. "What are you going to do?"

Nimec looked at her.

"This boat'll move at forty-five, fifty miles an hour if I really pour it on," he said. "The racer can double, maybe triple that speed."

"We won't be able to outdistance it."

"No," he said. "But we might not have to."

She shook her head to indicate her confusion.

"Think about it, Annie," he said. "Those guys on our tail are handcuffed as far as how they can finish their business, same as the ones who stayed aboard with us. Their whole setup depended on making it look like Blake ran us into the outcrop."

It took barely a second for understanding to flood Annie's eyes.

"They won't want to shoot," she said.

"That's what I'm betting," Nimec said. "And fast as their boat travels, ours is a lot bigger and heavier. They try to ram us, it'll be the racer that takes the worse beating."

Annie nodded. Then, not quite lost to their hearing under the growl of the vessel at their rear, a low moan rose from where Blake lay sprawled on deck.

"He needs a doctor," she said. "If we don't get him some medical help . . ."

"I know, Annie," Nimec said. "But we can't do anything for him until we shake loose that chase boat . . . and for that I need you to take the wheel."

She nodded again, shifted places with him.

"I've got us headed southeast toward that wilderness preserve Murthy talked about," Nimec said, and motioned toward the instrument panel's compass and GPS displays. "Keep us on course." He hesitated. "And if there's any gunfire, keep your head down."

Annie looked at him, fingers around the wheel now.

"I thought we're betting against that," she said.

Nimec squeezed her shoulder.

"Just in case," he said, and slid from behind the console.

Nimec examined the Steyr he'd taken from Annie's attacker and set its firing lever to full-automatic mode. He'd already ejected its magazine, determined it had plenty of rounds left, then palmed it back into its slot. If he was right and the chase team was still locked into its original plan, a few bullets would be all he needed.

He stood with his back to the pilot's station and looked out beyond the pontooner's stern. The speed-boat was close and getting closer, spray flying off to either side of its windscreen, water sheeting off its flanks, a white chop of foam trailing behind it. Seabirds squalled overhead or launched from the water in flapping clouds, terrified by the loud roar of its powerplants.

Nimec saw the racer angle off to starboard and hurried to the safety rail. Then he waited, his finger on the trigger.

The speedboat gained by the second. Came closer, closer, closer . . .

Finally it caught up, nosing past the stern, then rapidly pulling even with the pontooner's keel, continuing to surge forward until the two vessels were moving along side-by-side.

Nimec stood there waiting some more. The racer trimmed speed to avoid overshooting its target, then veered in sharply as if to broadside it, but Nimec knew that was bluff for the very reasons he'd given Annie. The lightweight strike boat would get the worst of any collision.

He kept watching the racer as it clipped along beside him, a slim band of water separating the two vessels now. He saw the racer's copilot move to its low portside gunwale, a Steyr in his hand. Then Nimec raised the barrel of his own gun to the safety rail's upper bar, tilted it upward, and fired a volley high across the racer's bow.

The copilot stared through his speed goggles, his gun pointed at Nimec over the gunwale. But Nimec didn't think he would return fire unless directly engaged . . . these men were pros and it would be clear that his salvo had been a warning.

His gunstock against his arm, he met the copilot's gaze and waited.

Whatever happened next, Nimec knew the call wasn't his to make.

"I'm pulling off them." Harrison said, his voice raised above the sound of the outboards.

The copilot glanced at him, his submachine gun still aimed at the pontoon boat.

278 Tom Clancy's Power Plays

"You're sure?" he asked.

Harrison nodded.

"Those shots were a message," he said. "He doesn't want a fight and our orders haven't changed."

The copilot understood. Eckers had stressed that they were to avoid using their guns on either the boat or the Sword man, were to refrain from firing at all absent a deadly and immediate threat—and even then there must be absolutely no other recourse. The mission's success hinged upon it looking like an accident.

He lowered the Steyr's barrel from the gunwale.

"What now?"

"We radio Beauchart," Harrison said.

"That gutless prick?"

Harrison nodded.

"Eckers is down," he said. "Gutless or not he's next in command."

The copilot frowned at him. "I don't like it," he said.

Harrison wrenched the wheel to his right and went sheering away from the pontooner.

"Beauchart can have the choppers pick this up or do whatever else he bloody well wants," he said. "It's out of our hands from here."

SEVEN

EASTERN CALIFORNIA
APRIL 2006

THEY HAD STARTED OUT IN THE DODGE COUPE from their appointed meeting place in Sonora and driven south on State Route 99 to cross the San Joaquin River some miles above Fresno. There Lathrop turned onto a series of local roads that took them eastward through the rolling dry country with its hills of eroded sandstone and occasional clumps of rough grass, sagebrush, and piñons on their dull, sunbaked faces.

The air conditioner worked well enough and they kept their windows shut as the temperature outside steadily climbed. Ricci sat in the passenger side saying very little, observing the monotonous scenery, and sipping coffee from the lid of the thermos bottle in the compartment between them. It had a thin, stale taste that got less palatable as they rode along, and was barely lukewarm by the time he noticed Lathrop slow the car coming up on a sign for some place called Amaranto.

Ricci remembered the smell of the coffee Julia Gordian had brought and how it had spread pleasantly in his dining room. Then he lowered his window partway, and as the hot air outside hit him, he extended his arm away from the flank of the car and sloshed what he had left in the plastic thermos lid onto the dusty blacktop.

Lathrop looked over at him.

"Don't like my brew?"

"No."

"Neither do I," Lathrop said. "But it's all we've got and I have to drive awhile longer."

Ricci didn't respond. He pressed the button to shut his window, put the lid back in place on the thermos, and glanced at the fuel gauge. The needle had fallen to just above the eighth-of-a-tank mark.

"We're low on gas," he said.

"I know."

Ricci motioned toward the road sign. It had a generic pump symbol below it.

"We should probably fill up," he said.

Lathrop shook his head.

"Not in Amaranto," he said. "Unless you want to find trouble."

"What sort of trouble?"

"The sort with eyes and ears connected to the Quiros family," Lathrop said.

Ricci grunted.

"Makes sense why you're riding heavy on the brakes," he said.

Lathrop gave him a small nod.

"I don't want to get stopped by any badges," he said. "They're the ones with the high-speed connections."

Ricci thought a moment. "How much farther to that ranch?"

"I told you, a while," Lathrop said. "About five minutes after we pass the town exit, there'll be an unmarked turnoff on the right. We'll have to take it north for fifteen, twenty miles through a whole lot of nothing."

Ricci leaned back, returned his eye to the fuel gauge.

"We're cutting it close," he said.

Lathrop shrugged, his hands on the wheel.

"Salvetti's expecting us," he said. "He'll be ready with whatever we need."

The turnoff led to a narrow, undivided road that ran away from the shoulders of the hills in meandering curves. Soon the ridges had almost disappeared behind them in the incessant flood of sunlight, and the surrounding landscape leveled into plains stubbled with more sagebrush, creosote shrubs, and, increasingly, widespread mats of those hardy grasses that somehow manage to thrive across the alkaline flats.

As they went on, the paved road became cracked and rutted from lack of maintenance and, with several bumps that seemed a final, rattling protest against this gradual but complete deterioration, surrendered to a hard dirt track that actually proved smoother by contrast. Looking out his window, Ricci saw brown- and white-fleeced goats grazing at the patches of grass in loosely defined groups, and then a weathered old barn with a couple of workhorses outside in a corral and chickens penned near some big, lounging mixed-breed watchdogs.

They rode for another three-quarters of a mile or so. Then Ricci spotted a vehicle up ahead in the glaring sun, a red open pickup truck. He could tell at once it wasn't moving and, as they got closer, realized it had been pulled across the track to block their advance.

Lathrop nosed the Dodge to within a few yards of the truck, stopped, cut the engine, and waited. The pickup's driver was its sole occupant, and a minute later he got out and approached the car. A solid, broad-shouldered man of about fifty with thick, neatly cut waves of salt-and-pepper hair, dark brown eyes, and a clean-shaven face with a firm, squarish chin, he wore a white T-shirt, dungarees, and cowboy boots.

Lathrop turned to Ricci.

"He's going to want to put a name on you," he said. "Any preferences?"

"Yeah," Ricci said. "Mine."

Lathrop shrugged and brought down his window as the man came around his side of the car, tugging a work glove off his right hand.

"Lathrop," he said, and leaned over toward the window. "Been a long time."

Lathrop nodded.

"Don't know how you always manage to look the same."

"That's for me to know, and you to find out."

"Sooner or later," Lathrop said, "I will."

The pickup driver grinned, reached his gloveless hand through the window, and gave Lathrop's shoulder a masculine squeeze, his eyes going to Ricci's face at the same time.

"Al Salvetti, Tom Ricci," Lathrop said. "Ricci, Al."

Salvetti took his hand off Lathrop's shoulder and stretched it over the back of his seat. He grasped Ricci's and shook it, holding his gaze on him a few seconds longer.

"Good to meet you," he said, then shifted his attention back to Lathrop. "I'll turn my truck around and you can follow me up to the house. Got some food in the fridge, and everything ready for working out the details of the flight."

Lathrop looked at him.

"We're on fumes," he said. "That old service station off the main road closed down and I wanted to steer clear of those sons of bitches in Amaranto."

"Can't blame you," Salvetti said. "Hang on, I'll bring a jerrican from the truck, put some gas in your tank to be on the safe side."

Salvetti turned and started back toward the pickup.

"Doesn't look like some boondocks rancher," Ricci said, watching him. "Or sound like one."

Lathrop faced him but didn't say anything.

"Chicago, south side," Ricci said. "I'd guess that's the accent."

Lathrop remained silent another moment and then shrugged.

"He is what he is," he said. "If he used to be something else and wants to tell you about it, it's up to him."

Salvetti's ranch house was a small, single-story building with rustic furnishings that looked as if they were mostly handcrafted. Its main room was off the kitchen and had a large trestle table with benches on either side, a Native American rug of some kind in the middle of the dark hardwood floor, and pine chests and chairs here and there around it. Ricci saw a computer in a hutch against one wall, a crowded bookshelf above it, and against the opposite wall a stereo with a turntable on a stand beside several stacked crates of vinyl albums. He didn't notice a television.

"I've got something for your stomachs," Salvetti said. He'd emerged from the kitchen with a tray of sandwiches and sweating ice-cold soda cans and set it at one end of the table. "Grab whatever you want; the bread and cheese are homemade."

Lathrop sat on a bench and reached for a sandwich. Ignoring the food, Ricci stepped toward the opposite end of the table to look at a pile of open and semi-unfolded maps.

"These for us?" he said.

Salvetti nodded, came around next to him.

"I had most of them handy, downloaded the rest off the Internet. Aerials, government topos, Triple-A road maps." He shuffled one out of the pile and fully outspread it. "This's a satellite closeup of that area out there south of Yosemite." He glanced over at Lathrop. "I circled off your major landmarks. The twin buttes, that creek . . . only thing I couldn't locate is the Miwok trail. If it's really there like the man told you, you'll have to sniff it out on your own."

Ricci looked at him.

"Miwok?"

"It's the name somebody or other gave the Sierra Nevada Indian tribes after they were happy to call themselves Ahwaneechee for four thousand years," Salvetti said.

"For God's sake," Lathrop said. "Listen to you."

Salvetti smiled a little.

"It pays to know your neighbors," he said. "Or at least to know who they are."

Lathrop rose from the bench and joined the other two, carrying his sandwich with him.

"You decide on someplace to put us down?" he asked.

Salvetti slid a finger over the map until he got to a site he'd inked a heavy black ring around, then tapped it twice.

"This mesa here should be perfect," he said. "It's low and wide so you can hardly notice its elevation. Pretty naked, too, and that's firsthand knowledge . . . I've flown over it before." He paused. "Brings you to within five miles of those buttes, the closest I can get."

Ricci looked at him again.

"Seems like it'd be a rough landing."

Salvetti seemed mildly surprised by his remark.

"I tell people I can bring them anywhere in my plane," he said. "They won't ever hear me guarantee it's going to be easy."

The moment he entered the hut, Pedro saw Marissa Vasquez watching him from her place on the floor. Always, she watched him. And always looking back into her eyes filled Pedro with a venom for this schooled and coddled daughter of privilege that only equaled his desire to have his way with her. It was as if the hateful resentment and lust fueled each other, and he wanted her to feel its relentless, intolerable inner burning just as he felt it. Physically feel its volcanic release inside her. And soon enough, when the time came, he would do it. He would treat her no better than the cheap Tijuana whores he left weeping in pain and degradation on their filthy sheets, on their bare backs, his crumpled bills reclaimed from the purses in which they had stuffed them. Treat her without even as much regard, for they did not ever think to stand up taller than he. Soon, yes, soon. Pedro would give her what roared within him like an angry, hungering beast, pound it into her, and as she fought and cried out in resistance, he would let her have still more of it. He would force upon her an education that not all her father's wealth could have provided, show her for once what it was to live in common flesh. And in that sharing Pedro would take something from her as well, for whatever long or short time she had left. And there, for him, would be the true and lasting satisfaction.

He stepped toward her in his combat-booted feet now, stood with hands on his hips. Her face was gaunt from weariness and anxiety, her hair hanging around it in tousled disarray. But her eyes were sharp and clear.

And they watched him

"I have good news, *hermosa,*" he said. And glanced at her constant guard. "If César has not already broken it."

288 Tom Clancy's Power Plays

Marissa said nothing. The guard shook his head slightly but did not otherwise move. He would, of course, never have taken it upon himself to tell her of the information that had reached them from Modesto.

"A man comes to free you," Pedro said. "As soon as today, I am led to believe."

She did not speak.

"He has been sent by your father," he said. "A gringo whose services the millionaire Esteban Vasquez has bought, as he always buys his adored *niña's* safety and comfort with his money."

She studied Pedro's masked face with restrained interest, as if not wishing to yield him the gratification of a perceived ruse. Her composed silence and stillness clawed at his stomach, made him impatient for the release he himself held tightly in check.

"Do you believe me about this?" he asked.

She did not speak.

"Do you believe me?" he repeated, an insistent edge in his voice.

Marissa finally shrugged.

"I'm not sure about anything my father will do," she said. "If someone comes, I suppose I'll know."

"Perhaps only after I throw your rescuer's dead body at your feet," Pedro said. "For the impressive gringo who comes for you, this one who is said to have delivered the daughter of a great and famous

American businessman from her own unfortunate captivity, has been betrayed by his *compañero* for the money of the millionaire who pays *me*." He showed a grin through the mouth opening of his balaclava. "We know where he will arrive. We know about when. And even now my men disperse to set their trap for him."

Marissa looked at him without answering.

Pedro's grin hardened. "So what do you think, *flora*?" he said. "Of how money brings us full circle, and the rest?"

She opened her mouth, closed it, opened it again, released a drawn out but steady breath.

"I don't know what to say that you would understand," she replied.

Pedro stared at the girl a second, feeling the angry urge to take her right there and then. On the ground, in the dirt, with his hands around her throat, he would add to her humiliation by doing it while César watched. But then he caught hold of himself. This affair was not over, not yet. If he was to collect on his own fee, he must still be bound to Juan Quiros's wishes.

He turned back through the hut entrance, suddenly perspiring under his full face hood, his mouth parched with thirst. Outside, he started to reach for the water canteen on his gear belt but changed his mind, his hand going instead to the metal flask of whiskey in his breast pocket.

The deep swig Pedro took quenched neither his thirst nor his seething rage. He had not expected that it would.

The slut's time was coming, he thought, and swiped a hand across his lips.

Not yet, no. Not yet.

But coming.

Salvetti drove them a short distance past his ranch house and then pulled the truck to a halt. Up ahead, a single-prop Grumman Tiger sat on a twelve-hundred-foot improved airstrip.

"That plane come with the ranch?" Ricci asked from the backseat.

Salvetti craned his head around.

"Uh-huh," he said. "The chickens also."

Ricci just looked at him.

Salvetti turned away, pushed open his door, glanced up at the cloudless sky, and checked his watch.

"Haul out your gear and I'll get us loaded aboard and flaps-down in the air," he said. "Under these flying conditions, we should be over the Sierra in a hop and a skip."

Pedro pushed through a tangle of manzanita and joined the three lookouts he'd posted on the other side. Then he gazed straight ahead northward, where the double buttes heaved up from the flat valley bottom, scored and knobbed with erosion, but stacked high above the surrounding landscape as if in a display of resistant strength.

After a moment Pedro turned to the man beside him. Leaving the hut out of sight had quieted his ache for their captive in a way the whiskey had not, but now he felt a restlessness to spring the ambush. It would, Juan Quiros had promised, be an action well worth his trouble.

"I take it the others are on the move, Lafé?" he asked.

"As you ordered," the guard said.

Pedro grunted with satisfaction, looked toward the buttes again. Though still washed in afternoon heat, he could barely wait for the chirping of the insects to announce dusk's arrival in the valley.

"The *maricone* will come for the girl from the direction of those spires," he said. "And he will go to his death under their shadows."

With its thirty-one-foot wingspan and high-rev Lycoming engine, the Tiger had been designed to be feather-light and fighter-powerful. And so it was as Salvetti piloted the little four-seater over an irregular terrain of jutting peaks, pine-forested upper slopes, and arid, shadow-splashed foothills and depressions studded with thickets of dryland scrub, all of it visible in panorama below vaporous white swags of low-altitude clouds.

Quiet since they had gone wheels-up, Ricci sat behind Salvetti trying to match what was depicted on the USGA map across his lap to what he saw through the aircraft's wide canopy and windows, occasionally glancing at the digital ground image on the avionic panel's navigational display for additional comparison. In the copilot's seat, Lathrop also kept his words to a minimum, but had seemed not once to look at the ground as he gazed outward into space.

Ricci observed this by chance and filed it away in his mind without particular inference.

Half an hour after takeoff, Salvetti pointed out the lined, wattled necks of the buttes projecting between the walls of a shallow valley or basin to his left.

"You're going thereabouts," he said, and then nodded his head toward the forward curve of the canopy. "Look out and you'll notice the land flatten in front of us almost like it's been smoothed over by giant rollers. A kind of dark rim around its edges, see?"

Ricci leaned forward.

"Shadows," he said.

Salvetti nodded.

"They outline the mesa's plateau, give you an idea how it barely rises over the plain," he said. "If this was around noontime instead of three in the afternoon, you'd have the bright sun overhead and might not even notice that it mounts." He paused, adjusted himself behind the controls. "You fellas better strap in—I'm going to drop down and run a couple of passes to scout a landing spot that won't throw our spines out of whack."

Lathrop reached for his seatbelt buckle.

"We hope," he said to finally break his long, staring silence.

It wasn't exactly easy. But it could have been much worse.

The Tiger grooved out of the sky to land with a jarring bump and then rumbled shakily on across the mesa's open table for several hundred feet, its propeller whipping up a cyclonic cloud of dust, its treaded wheels scraping out corrugated channels of parched earth and pebbles that tacked like hail against the underside of the airframe.

Inside the cabin, Salvetti had his lips puckered into a spout as he gripped the control column. Ricci couldn't hear him through the noise, but looking around his contoured headrest thought for a second that he might have been whistling.

Then there was another, lesser jolt. Ricci lurched forward against his seatbelt, and back against the leather upholstery, deceleration slapping his stomach like an iron hand in a furry mitt. Moments later the grating bombardment of dirt abated and the prop's blurry rotation slowed until its separate twin blades were distinguishable at the nose of the plane.

Salvetti rolled to a halt and exhaled a surge of

breath, his mouth wide open now, his knuckles relaxing around the column.

"Did it again," he said in a half whisper.

Then he took his hands off the controls, leaned back, and briefly closing his eyes, tipped a finger toward the heavens and crossed himself.

The five guerrillas came midway down the trail, where they could see the bend of the sluggish creek it followed winding away from the buttes. Then they took cover, three hiding in the snarled vegetation that bordered the trail on its right, two splitting off to its left.

They dumped their knapsacks, put their weapons down at their sides, and settled into position.

"There are still hours until sundown," one of them said to the man beside him in Spanish. He extracted a pack of cigarettes from his pocket and shook a couple out. They were unfiltered American Camels. "Nothing to fucking do but wait."

The man beside him nodded and accepted the cigarette that had been offered.

"It should be cooler soon," he said.

"Yes," said the other man, putting the rest of his cigarettes away and reaching for his Zippo lighter. "But then the biting flies come out."

"They are hateful creatures."

"Yes, that is the word. Hateful."

"I wish I could kill them. Kill every last one."

"I wish I could kill them all, too," said the man with the pack of smokes. He fired the cigarette in his mouth, then held the lighter to the tip of his companion's. "And I would like to kill both those fools who come for the girl."

"For making us sit out here in these bushes?"

"Yes. I ask you, what extra pay will we get for it?"

"Nothing." The man who'd been given the Camel puffed to get it started. "You have a point, but we can only kill the one."

"Yes."

"We are, unfortunately, limited."

"Yes, limited, I agree," said the man with the lighter in his hand. "That is another very good word."

He spit a fleck of loose tobacco from the tip of his tongue and then lapsed into silence, smoking and waiting for the dusk.

Outside the plane, Salvetti got their packs and other gear from the luggage hold and handed them off as they waited.

Ricci took his duffel, reached for his rifle case, and slung it over his shoulder. Then he turned to where Lathrop was on his haunches studying one of the maps, and walked over to him.

"We're basing what we're doing on something some small fry Quiros ringleader south of the border told you," he said. "You sure you weren't duped?"

Lathrop glanced up at Ricci. He had put on dark mirrored sunglasses that gleamed in the sunshine.

"It's late to be asking again," he said.

"Not too late yet."

Lathrop continued looking into the brightness.

"He knew what was at stake," he said. "I knew he was too scared to have lied."

Ricci stood there.

"Still haven't told me how his stake paid off for him," he said.

"And maybe that's how I want to keep it," Lathrop said. "But if I'd gone to Juan with anything besides the goods on Marissa Vasquez, he'd have laughed in my face. Instead he confirmed every piece of information I got and filled in blanks I left to see how it all fell in line."

"Because he thinks I'm the man who did whatever you won't tell me you did to his cousin down there in Baja," Ricci said.

Lathrop nodded.

"And because he thinks I hired you to help me grab the Vasquez girl back for her father," Ricci said.

Lathrop nodded.

"And because he thinks you're pulling a double-cross on me," Ricci said. "Setting me up for an ambush on that Indian trail. Dumb *blanco* that I am."

Lathrop nodded again.

"Except," Ricci said. "It isn't me who's being set up."

Lathrop's head went up and down a fourth and final time, the sunlight slipping across his lenses like quicksilver.

"Role reversal," he said. "With a twist."

Ricci looked at him awhile without saying anything more. Then they both heard Salvetti slam the door of the Tiger's baggage compartment.

Rising from his squat, Lathrop folded the map, stuffed it into his shirt pocket, and lifted his packs off the ground.

"We better get on the move," he said.

Sunset, the western sky bleeding red across the horizon. Ready now, the guerrillas increased their vigilance, the stocks of their HK G36 submachine guns tucked against their arms.

A last Camel was ground out in the scrub, dirt kicked hastily over its charred remnant.

The smoker cleared his throat of phlegm and swatted helplessly at the tiny winged biters as they swirled in, attracted to some chemical in human sweat.

"God damn this job," he said in a hushed tone. "I only want it to be over."

The man beside him nodded.

"What spares Lafé from coming out here?" he whispered. "Or even Manuel? It's as if his softness is being rewarded."

"He's already gotten his reward, or haven't you taken a look at the girl he seduced?"

"Of course I have. And between us, Pedro won't be satisfied until he takes his turn with her."

"Yes, I've noticed."

"He'll have it before all this is done, too, I would bet."

"Yes. You can see how he waits. In his eyes, you can see. It could happen very soon."

"Do you think so?"

"Yes," said the man who'd brought the cigarettes. "Yes, I do. While we're out here getting eaten up by bugs."

The other man frowned.

"You're right when you say this job stinks and must be gotten over with quickly," he said.

"And," said the man with the cigarettes, "keep in mind it hasn't even really begun."

Lathrop scuffed down the embankment, Ricci taking the moderately steep grade a little to his side, the two of them pausing there to orient themselves and catch their breaths, the weight of their gear pressing their backs and shoulders. Rocks and grit lay scattered around their boots. Within a few dozen feet of them to the left, the creek bed, more mud than water, serpentined north and east over the humped terrain. Straggly plants grew in a kind of apron around its banks, and higher up the valley ridges through which it wound its slow, undulant path away into the dis-

tance, ponderosa and blackjack pine grew in inter-
mingled and surprisingly dense terraces.

Not for the first time since they had left the mesa,
Lathrop pulled his map out of his shirt pocket, studied it, then studied the ground. The paper was damp
with his perspiration.

Several moments expired. Ricci waited in silence
under the lengthening shadows of the buttes as Lathrop raised his eyes from the map and stared out toward the creek, his lips slightly parted.

Then Lathrop turned to him, his finger pointing at
a slight angle from the languid waterway.

"Over there through the brush," he said. "That's
where I think we'll find the trail."

On inspection minutes later, he proved to be correct.

They didn't take it.

Crouched above the trail with his heels deep in a carpet of pine needles, Lathrop peered down between
the evergreen trunks with his binoculars, then handed
them off to Ricci.

"How many men you see?" he said in a hushed
voice.

"Five," Ricci whispered. "Three on this side, two
on the other. Bunched close together."

Lathrop nodded.

"Checks with what I saw," he said.

Still holding the binoculars, Ricci brought their fo-

cus up from the stony Indian trail, swept them across
the cut it followed through the blunt hillcrest. Then
he dropped the lenses from his eyes.

"You were on the money about the guns they'd be
toting," he said. "They're HK carbines. Five point
five-six mills."

Lathrop nodded. "Good thing I told you to bring
one of your own, isn't it?" he said.

Ricci looked at him, then motioned to the cleft's
opposite shoulder.

"I'll make my way around this rise, take out the
two from over there," he said. "You stay back and
handle the three."

Lathrop nodded again, lowered the strap of his rifle case, tapped the face of his wristwatch.

"We'd better synch up before you move off for
your boys," he said. "Does that UpLink watch you
wear tell time, or is it only for communicating with
Moon Maiden in her space coupe?"

Ricci was impassive.

"I'll need ten minutes," he said.

One minute and counting, Ricci thought. His eye was
against the scope of his carbine, taking advance measure of his targets.

Down below in the near twilight, their backs to
him, the pair of men in camouflage outfits was barely
hidden from sight in the thicket. *Your boys.* The trick
for him was to nail them exactly when Lathrop

sniped the others. Do it in a couple of accurate bursts, three at most, and mask Lathrop's rifle shots from however many of the kidnappers had remained behind with Marissa Vasquez. If the plan worked the way it was intended, they would mistake the sound of Ricci's HK firing at the ambushers for that of their guns shooting him as it echoed through the valley, think that Lathrop had led him into their ambush and *he'd* been the one who was erased.

He checked his watch now. Thirty-five seconds. Thirty-four, thirty-three . . .

Ricci's jaw tightened. A plan for success, he thought.

Except he did not like how it felt to kill men, and especially did not like how it felt shooting men in their backs. Not even men who had set themselves up to kill him.

Your boys.

His watch again. Its digital second readout ticking down the seconds.

Eleven left. Ten. Nine. Eight.

His heart pumped. He breathed through his front teeth. His finger steadied on the trigger.

Six, five, four, three, two . . .

His eye to the sight, the carbine rattled in Ricci's hand, its stock bucking against his shoulder.

Your boys.

Beneath him, his bullets ripped into their bodies, knocking them forward into the dirt, snuffing out their lives before they could have possibly known what hit them. And as he fired, Ricci could hear coordinated shots from the opposite slope.

But then, he was listening for them.

On his belly in the dirt, Lathrop relaxed his grip on the sound-suppressed SIG-Sauer SSG's trigger.

It had been neat and precise, just how he liked it. Three cracks of the rifle, three more pieces of dead meat to feed the crawling, wriggling, and buzzing local scavengers.

And making it all the more perfect, he'd ended up with a leftover round of ammunition in his clip.

Moments after he heard the stutter of the rifles, Pedro entered the hut and glanced knowingly at César. Then he let his eyes sink slowly down to Marissa Vasquez and meet her own disconcerted gaze.

"Gunfire," he said. "Do you recognize the sound of bullets spat from a gun?"

She kept silent.

"Perhaps you have never heard it in your town's favored streets. Or at the university you attend, eh?" He grinned, reached for his tin of whiskey, and uncapped it. "Let me know, *mi hermosa,* are such places too sheltered from the world's ugliness for such disturbances to their peace and quiet?"

She looked at him.

"I told you your father sent a rescuer," Pedro said. "And now I can tell you the rescuer is dead."

Marissa's gaze, filled with increasing dismay and confusion, finally lost its determined steadiness.

"No," she said, finally averting it from him.

Pedro's own eyes stayed on her, roving up and down, lingering in places. Then they went to César.

"Go outside and tell the men to bring their bloody carcass in here when they arrive," he said, and swigged deeply from the flask. "After that I want to be left alone . . . The other gringo can wait, am I understood?"

César nodded, left the hut, and Pedro turned back to Marissa.

"You would not believe me when I said someone was coming for you, but now you'll have a dead man for proof . . . and to keep us company," he said, taking another long drink, his eyes studying her again. "Who knows what may occur before his unseeing eyes? What acts we will perform that his mouth cannot speak of? Who, indeed, knows, *hermosa,* for the dead can tell no tales of what pleasures the living will soon enjoy."

"What's happening?" Manuel asked César. He had emerged from one of the other thatch shelters upon hearing the submachine gun salvos.

César paused on his way toward the brambles screening the trail head.

"They've got the one her father sent," he said. "*El jefe* wants his corpse brought into the hut."

Manuel looked at him.

"Why in there?" he said.

"I don't think about it," César said. "You shouldn't either."

He started forward, but Manuel reached out and grasped his arm.

"Let go of me," César said.

"Pedro's lost his mind," Manuel said. "He's turned this into something it wasn't supposed to be."

César's eyes bored into him.

"It isn't up to me what he does," he said. "I told you to let go."

Manuel held onto his elbow another moment, sighed, and then released his grip.

"We're all bastards," he said.

"And well-paid ones," César said, shrugging away from him to step toward the fold of brush.

As he did there was a muffled pop from behind it, another.

César grimaced and collapsed to the ground dripping blood, Manuel going down inches behind him.

And then the brush parted.

Pedro turned from Marissa Vasquez the moment he heard what he recognized as silenced shots outside, instantly reaching for the gun holstered on his belt.

His eyes landed on the two white men standing in the hut entrance, widened. One had a rifle strapped over his shoulder and, more importantly, a pistol in his right hand aimed at Pedro's chest. The other held a submachine gun.

Pedro straightened, staring at them, his fingers clenched around the butt of his own weapon.

"Fuck you," he said, and spat. "You might as well do it."

Lathrop centered his Glock on Pedro's chest, fired a third round from its barrel, and looked over his body into the hut as it fell.

"There's our girl," he said to Ricci. "Safe and sound."

Ricci saw Marissa Vasquez shackled on the floor at the rear of the hut and rushed through the entrance a half step behind Lathrop.

Then he noticed Lathrop drop back and halted, not thinking about why, or consciously thinking about why, just turning to look at him.

A cell phone had appeared in Lathrop's left hand.

"What the hell are you doing?" he said.

Lathrop flipped open the phone. "We need to contact Salvetti and tell him we're done," he said.

Ricci stood looking at him.

"That can wait," he said. "He'll find out when we get back to the mesa."

Lathrop held the cell phone open in his left hand. The Glock had remained in his right.

"The plane needs to get warmed up," he said.

"That plane can take off on a dime," Ricci said. "And you know it."

Lathrop's gaze went to his.

"I'm making my call."

"To Salvetti," Ricci said.

Their eyes remained locked.

"Or whoever I want," Lathrop said.

Ricci shook his head.

"What's the game this time?" he said. "You call Salvetti and he calls somebody else with a message? Or did you only toss his name at me on the spot."

Silence. Lathrop held the phone.

"Give it to me," Ricci said. "This isn't worth it."

Lathrop shook his head. "Sure it is," he said. "We can double our take on this job. Triple it. Doesn't hurt anybody or anything except some dope dealer's bankroll."

Ricci nodded toward Marissa Vasquez.

"How about her," he said.

Lathrop nodded, the phone raised in his left hand. Ricci had grown more aware of the Glock in his right.

"She just gets home a little later," Lathrop said. "All we have to do is play this out. Tell Esteban we saved his daughter's life and want something more for our efforts. He'll give us whatever we want of his dirty money. Any amount."

"A new play, new rules," Ricci said. "That it?"

Lathrop looked at him. "Explain why not," he said.

"Maybe because it would make us no better than the men we killed," Ricci said.

Another silence. The stillness of Ricci's eyes did not betray the close attention he was paying to the Glock.

"We made a deal and it isn't going to change for money we don't even know how to spend," he said. "Damn you, Lathrop, give me the phone and let's take her the hell out of here."

Lathrop looked at him a second longer.

"And what's my other choice?" he said.

Ricci nodded his chin slightly toward Lathrop's gun.

"Think you know," he said.

"Could be I do," Lathrop said. "But I want to hear you say it."

Ricci waited a beat, nodded toward the gun again.

"We see which one of us is quicker," he said.

Lathop stared at him for several long moments, his head angling a little to one side. Then his lips parted, took in air . . . and shaped themselves into the faintest of grins.

Keeping his Glock pointed down at the ground, he tossed the phone into Ricci's outstretched hand.

"You going to want my gun, too?" he said.

Ricci shook his head. "You might need it later on," he said, and then turned toward Marissa Vasquez.

Ricci stepped to the back of the hut, saw Marissa's expression, paused before he quite reached her. Her captors had used battery lanterns for lighting as dusk closed in around them, and their stark radiance had washed any hint of color from her face. She looked afraid, but mostly she looked to be in shock, her wide, glassy eyes seeming to stare at everything and nothing.

He crouched in front of her and glanced over at Lathrop, nodding toward the bodies of the men they'd killed. Lathrop began searching them for the keys to her restraints.

Ricci looked at her again.

"Marissa," he said. "We're taking you out of here."

Her gaze went to him. At first its remoteness, coupled with the strange, flat look on her face, made him feel only half in her attention. Then she appeared to draw it upon him with an effort.

"My boyfriend needs help," she said, her voice thin. "They're keeping Felipe here somewhere."

Ricci looked at her a moment, then shook his head.

"His name is Manuel Aguilera," he said slowly. "He was with them from the start."

She took a while to react. Ricci wasn't sure she'd grasped the meaning of what he had told her and gave it a while to sink in. But there was Lathrop behind him in the hut, and the possibility of stragglers outside from among the group who'd abducted her, and he could afford only so much time.

"No," she said at last.

Ricci kept looking at her.

"It's the truth," he said.

"No."

Ricci started to reach out a hand, saw her flinch back, and held it still.

"It hurts," he said. "But it's the truth."

Marissa Vasquez moved her head slightly from side to side.

"No."

Ricci hesitated.

"I'm not saying I know how he felt about you," he said. "He might've gotten to care, but maybe cared more about things you weren't part of. It isn't always one way or the other with people."

Though Marissa was shaking her head more vehemently now, Ricci saw tears gathering on the rims of her lower eyelids. She seemed to be trying to hold them back.

"His name is Felipe Escalona," she said.

Ricci looked at her.

"His name isn't what matters," he said. "What does is that he helped those men bring you here. And that I'm bringing you out."

She stared at him. Then her eyes sharpened on his face and she made a choking sound and began to sob, the tears running down her cheeks.

"I love him," she said, a desperate, pleading quality in her voice.

Ricci extended his hand a little further.

"There's a plane waiting for us," he said. "We're taking you home."

"I love him."

Ricci hesitated again, reaching his hand out until it was within an inch of hers.

"I know," he said. "But you need to trust me."

A moment passed, and then several more. Marissa Vasquez bent her head, crying hard, her entire body shaking with the release of emotion.

Ricci crouched in front of her without saying anything else, waiting, leaving his offered hand out there between them.

And then, finally, her chained hand came up and took it.

EIGHT

NIMEC BROUGHT THE PONTOONER IN TOWARD
the mangroves that hemmed the island's wild north-
western shore, getting it as far under the trees as he
could, sliding through their pale web of roots to finally pull beneath their arched, outspread limbs.

He throttled to a complete halt and turned toward
Annie. She was knelt over Blake, who had for the
past few minutes shown signs of awareness, if not
quite consciousness, squeezing his big hand weakly
around hers as she held it, once even half opening his
eyes to look at her face with seeming recognition.

"You holding up okay?" Nimec said.

"So far," she said. "There's nothing to do but try, I
suppose."

312 Tom Clancy's Power Plays

He ran a hand across his chin in thought, still looking at her. Unable to guess the severity of Blake's in-
jury, they had been careful not to move him from
where he'd fallen, and done little in the way of treat-
ing him other than to pat some of the blood off his
head with gauze from the boat's first-aid kit, then
gently ease it from the hard deck onto her folded
windbreaker, providing whatever minimal comfort
they could.

"Been about fifteen minutes since we radioed base
on the mainland," Nimec said. "The Skyhawks are
taking off out of San Fernando, and fast as those
birds travel, it'll be another ten or fifteen before they
show." He paused. "I'm guessing we can buy enough
time right here . . . or at least that right here's our best
chance."

Annie nodded her understanding. Overhead the
sky was almost unseen through the roof of branches,
cut into thin slivers of blue that scarcely showed between their interstices. In the Stingrays that patrolled
the island, men they could no longer trust—and had
every reason to want to elude—might very well be
out searching for them. And what blocked their view
of the sky would also block any view the chopper
crews might have of the pontoon boat from above.
That gave Annie some measure of hope. But she had
been a pilot most of her life, had flown above the at-
mosphere in a space shuttle and trained others to do

the same, and it had occurred to her there was more to be concerned about than visual observation.

"Pete," she said, her expression troubled. "If our people can fix on your GPS signal . . ."

He looked at her, and she let the sentence trail.

"Yeah, Annie," he said. "We'd have to figure theirs can, too."

Jarvis Lenard crouched in the shadows of the mangroves and wondered what was going on.

Drawn to the sound of the marine engine, he had picked his way through the undergrowth to investigate, gotten as close as he dared to peer at the approaching vessel from the gloom at the forest's edge. It was, he saw from his concealed position, a pontoon boat. *A pleasure boat*. To his knowledge, the Sunglasses would not come out looking for him in such a craft. Not unless they were trying some deception, no . . . but what would be its logic? The wilderness area was large, and he reasoned that it was unlikely they would stop the boat expecting he would be close enough to hear it, never mind be moved to risk being exposed to those aboard.

Which, Jarvis thought, was of course the very thing he had done. And perhaps that proved the Sunglasses were a step ahead of him, counting on his desperation to do him in, knowing the boat could tempt him to reveal himself this time when caution would have prevailed at another. Perhaps there were ten such boats, a dozen, set out into the marshes as lures.

Perhaps, yes . . .

And then again, perhaps not.

Jarvis flattened himself almost onto his belly and crawled further toward the shore, slipping among the low foliage and riblike air roots, his already soiled and tattered clothes muddying to stick clammily to his body. Then, a few yards from the boat, he paused again. A man in swim trunks and a jacket was moving from its pilot's station toward the middle part of the deck and Jarvis realized now that there was a woman with him, kneeling down over something—

His eyes widened.

No, he thought.

Not something.

Some*one*.

Jarvis inched still closer until he was chin-deep in the mire, hoping the insects and leeches in his company would not make a total feast of him. But on he went anyway—he had to get a better look at the person on that deck. It was a man, he saw now. A large man lying on his back, his head on what might have been a towel or jacket . . .

Suddenly Jarvis pulled in a breath.

There was blood all around that makeshift pillow. All around it, and all through it, and even smeared on the woman's swimsuit.

If these were Sunglasses and not people in
trouble . . . maybe even people with trouble akin to his
own, for why else would they have sought the forest in
a working boat rather than turn southward toward Los
Rayos, where the injured passenger could receive
medical attention . . . if these were Sunglasses, then he
was a brainless fool for wanting to help them, ah yeh.

An' help yah'self, ya want'a be honest, he thought.
For here might be a way off the island . . . a way to
reach someone of authority on the mainland before
he and his knowledge of Udonis's hidden shipping
files were made to disappear off the face of the earth,
like the oil shipped to far and unknown places on
those barges.

Dripping wet, spattered with muck, Jarvis put
aside his fear and weariness, got to his feet, and
started toward the boat—but had not taken more than
two steps forward when he heard a new sound that
momentarily froze him in his tracks.

Standing barely in the shadows of the trees, he
craned his head back, looked through the trees into a
broken sky, and saw three helicopters out over the
water, one on his left, the other two on his right, still
the size of wasps to his vision, but belting in with tra-
jectories that would lead them to converge directly
over the shore ahead of him.

Annie heard the chop of rotors and looked up, her
heart pounding in her chest.

"Pete," she said, and grabbed hold of his arm. "Pete, those *copters*—"

Nimec pointed up to their right.

"That one's theirs, Annie, I can tell from its shape," he said, and then swept his hand across to the left. "And those two . . . those two're ours."

The Stingray's pilot spotted the choppers coming on at breakneck speed from the south and turned toward the man beside him, his eyes surprised and dismayed behind his helmet visor.

"Warn those bloody bastards off, whoever they are," he said.

Still staring skyward at the choppers, Jarvis filled his lungs with what he thought must have been the deepest breath he'd taken in his entire life . . . and then prepared to make what he thought might be its greatest decision.

As fate would have it, the people he'd hoped would prove his salvation needed immediate rescuing themselves, needed to get immediately out of *sight* as well, for it was now beyond question that they too had fallen on the wrong side of the Sunglasses. Fallen in a way comparable to his own in terms of its threat to life and limb, if Jarvis could tell anything from the number of birds in the air.

And having reached these conclusions, how was he to act on them? What new demands of his conscience must he prepare to accept or reject? He exhaled. These were good enough questions in theory, no doubt. But however intimidating it might be, he must deal only with reality, as he had since his cousin was murdered, and then since his own aborted escape attempt on a boat, and all throughout his ordeal afterward. And however many questions he might choose to ask himself, Jarvis knew the choice before him was no different than it had been seconds earlier. He could retreat into the forest and whatever safety it provided, or do what he could for the passengers aboard that boat.

"Lord Almighty, do whatcha can to protect me," he muttered to himself, and plunged on ahead toward the water.

"You have entered restricted airspace," the Stingray's copilot said into his headset's mouthpiece, his radio tuned to a common frequency. "I repeat, this is a no-fly zone. Identify yourself and redirect—"

"We're UpLink International aircraft out of San Fernando," the lead Skyhawk's copilot responded in a calm voice. "And you can redirect your head up your ass, because we've got permission to approach from your government and are coming in whether you like it or not."

Jarvis Lenard emerged from the mangroves in an almost maniacal dash, splashing his bare feet into the open surf.

"Both of ya, come wit' me 'n' be quick," he yelled to the man and woman on the boat, cupping his hands over his mouth. "Getya injured fella int'a raft and come on where I can bring ya into hidin'!"

The Stingray's copilot looked over at the man flying the aircraft. "You think they've really gotten airspace clearance?" he said.

"They haven't had much time," the pilot said, his hand on the collective. "But we can't know for sure."

"What's our next move, then?"

The copilot thought, frowned.

"We aren't going to just let them through," he said.

"There are two of them—"

"I can count," said the pilot. "When can we expect some assistance up here?"

The copilot checked his graphic displays.

"It shouldn't be long," he said. "Beta-three-zero's closest, bearing in from the harbor. The others are also on course."

"Then hail Beauchart and give him the situation as it stands," the pilot said. "We stay with the intercept unless or until he call us off."

"Chopper alpha-one-zero reports a pair of UpLink choppers on a heading for the target vessel," the radioman said, his mouthpiece pulled slightly away from his face as he glanced up from the console.

"The intruders claim sanction from the mainland and our crew is asking how to proceed."

Standing to his right, Henri Beauchart bent his head toward his chest, closed his eyes, and rubbed them with his thumb and forefinger. What was he to do? Contact air traffic authorities in San Fernando to request they verify or deny the UpLink pilot's assertions? If the clearances proved legitimate, then those who afforded them certainly had been informed that the approaching helicopters were on an emergency rescue operation. How would he explain his position of wanting to turn them back? Even if he were able to come up with something to justify it, whatever he said would be disputed by UpLink. And the one *indisputable* fact was that Nimec and his wife had been able to send out a call for help. In the end, it wouldn't matter whether or not official permissions were given. If they were still to disappear, it could not be explained away. Eckers had staked everything on his accident scenario, and he, Beauchart, had been a willing accomplice—and now the scenario was dead. Along, perhaps, with Eckers.

Beauchart produced a long breath, feeling himself physically deflate. None of his options were good. It was all coming down. No matter what action he took, coming down around his head. A confrontation over the helicopters' right to approach would only help bury him deeper.

He opened his eyes, raised his head from where it had sunk, and turned to the radio operator.

"Order our pilots to disengage," he said. "The visitors are to be considered friendlies and allowed full entry."

The lead Skyhawk's pilot saw the Aug pulling off, turned to his partner, and grinned.

"I win the bet," he said. "Told you my bullshit story would work."

The copilot looked at him.

"Suckers," he said. "You gonna rub it in?"

"Just pay up and get me that date with your knockout cousin," he said. "I promise not to take *too* much advantage of her."

Nimec heard the man in ragged clothes screaming at them from the shore, looked his way, and then turned to Annie. The Stingray had veered off in the northerly direction of its approach, shrinking from sight even as the combined roar of UpLink's oncoming birds began to drown out whatever the stranger was shouting at the top of his lungs.

"What's he saying?" Annie said.

Nimec took a glance back over his shoulder as the Skyhawks swept in, then shrugged.

"Don't know," he said. "But for some reason or other, I'm sure we'll find out before too long."

EPILOGUE

SAN JOSE, CALIFORNIA

"OIL," VINCE SCULL SAID.

"*Rogue* oil," Nimec said. "Lots and lots of it."

"Going to Cuba and North Korea," Scull said. "Two countries on the government's long-term embargo list."

"And they were just the biggest customers," Nimec said, nodding. "There are others that've had temporary sanctions against the import of U.S. fuel products slapped on them. Foreign policy and national security reasons."

Scull put his hands over his ears.

"Enough, Petey," he said. "Here I am thinking it's love that makes the world go 'round, when you've got to show up and murder the idea."

Nimec gave him a faint smile. They were sitting in Scull's office at UpLink Sanjo, a medium-sized room adorned with photos of Vince at some of the many corporate sites where he'd been stationed over the years. Here he was with the founding crew members in Johor, here with his arm around a pretty female staffer in snowy Kaliningrad, there posing beside a pack mule against the mountain spires at Ghazni . . . Scull was well-traveled to say the least, his footloose leanings having very possibly worked to the extreme detriment of his three marriages, all of which had come to their crashing ends in acrimonious divorce proceedings.

Nimec had long wondered about the pictures of Vince's three ex-wives in a heart-shaped frame on his desk, each a smiling head shot. Was their sharing space in a single heart an example of typically crooked Scullian humor? Or could it be a window into something deep and sad?

One of these days, Nimec figured he'd find a tactful way to ask.

"It was some racket," he said now, and glanced at Scull across his desk. "A fifteen-hundred foot long oil tanker disguised as a container ship sets out from the oil field at Point Fortin with millions of gallons of refined aboard, anchors there in the water near Los Rayos to wait for feeders that've been converted to smaller oil barges. They get their fill-ups and head off to banned ports, or to rendezvous at sea with other smuggler ships." He paused. "We still don't know how often those runs were made, or exactly how long the operation was going before we caught onto it, or how much oil was moved in total, but the word is that it was all done on a scale nobody's ever seen. Not from a single producer."

Scull grunted.

"Gonna make a whole lot of high-priced international lawyers happy for a while," he said. "Nothing puts smiles on their faces faster than a big cloud of stink in the air, and the fumes from this scam reach from Washington across the Caribbean."

Nimec rubbed his chin, thinking about that. An oil field holder in Trinidad, members of the Trinidadian parliament, and a top Sedco Petroleum exec . . . these were just a few of the parties under investigation or indictment in the scandal, and more names were surfacing every day. The facts and figures relating to specific transactions had come from the records of Udonis Roberts, the Los Rayos shipping accountant who'd tipped off Megan in a sudden fit of conscience and gotten murdered for it during an attempt to flee the island . . . a hack job that left him and the Trinidadian runners he'd paid to take him away by boat stuffed into some Florida-bound air transport crates. The body parts had turned up at Miami International in an episode that made for some lurid tabloid headlines a while back, but it had taken the rogue oil discoveries for authorities to eventually tie the case to Los Rayos. And the connection still might never have been made if it wasn't for Roberts's cousin, Jarvis Lenard, hiding out there in the mangrove forest with his knowledge of where Roberts had stashed his evidence. Impressively to Nimec, he'd not only been able to elude the island's entire security force for weeks, but also a sort of elite ghost squad that did its dirty work—apparently the same group that had tried to off him, Annie, and Blake, then stage the pontooner's crackup. The information about this so-called Team Graywolf, as well as many of the key names attached to the oil scam, had been provided by Henri Beauchart after his arrest, when he'd immediately started singing to prosecutors in two countries with hopes of cutting deals.

Behind his desk, Scull sucked thoughtfully on his inner cheek a minute or two, then smoothed a hand over the crown of his mostly bald head.

"The thing I keep wondering about is that invite you got to Los Rayos from those Trinidadian officials," he said. "Between the e-mail to Meg and that islander being on the run from Beauchart's security goons, it couldn't've come at a worse time for the pols involved in the oil scheme. Or for the guy who gave Sedco distribution rights to what came out of his wells, and is supposed to have cooked up the smuggling operation with his pal on the Sedco board . . . Jean Claude Whatsisname."

"Morpaign," Nimec said, nodding. "I'm with you,

Vince, the timing would be some coincidence. And who knows, maybe it is. On the other hand, it could be the invitation came from parliament members that weren't in the mix, and had an idea what was happening at Los Rayos, and maybe even got the same tip-off Meg did sent to their Inboxes. With all the high level government and industrial types involved, and a corruption investigation sure to come, I can see how they wouldn't want to be known as finger pointers, and might decide it would be better for their careers setting me up to pull off the lid."

Scull chortled.

"No good for a politician to have a rep for honesty with his cronies, huh," he said.

"Either that or have somebody get even with him by looking into *his* rotten business affairs," Nimec said, and shrugged. "Hard enough finding a straight shooter in our own government, Vince. How much do we really know about what goes on behind closed doors in Trinidad?"

Scull looked at him a moment, then grunted again.

"Fucking Trinidad," he said. "You and the new missus take a boat ride and almost get turned into guppy food . . . helluva way to remember a vacation."

Nimec was silent. He thought about that long afternoon in the villa with Annie after he'd gone kiteboarding, thought about her lying with her head on the pillow beside him, both of them out of breath, their bodies relaxed and coated with sweat. *I think we did it, Pete,* she'd whispered in his ear. *Don't ask me how, but I've carried two children in my belly, and think I feel that we did.*

No, he told himself, Vince was wrong. Whatever bad had happened to him on Los Rayos, Nimec believed he would always remember it more for something else.

He rose from his chair now, stretched, and cracked his knuckles.

"Taking off on me so soon?" Scull said. "Where's the love gone, handsome?"

Nimec gave him a look. "Got a meeting with Rollie and Meg later," he said. "I need a chance to prepare."

Scull snorted.

"Your meeting about Ricci by any chance?" he said.

"Yeah," Nimec said, "Ricci."

He stood there a second, hoping Vince would leave it alone, thinking he really did want to ponder the matter some more before he talked about it with anyone.

"So's it gonna be thumbs-up or thumbs-down for your boy?" Scull said.

Nimec looked at him again, released a fatalistic sigh.

"Before this morning I'd pretty much decided we needed to cut him loose . . . he's going to stay out of touch, what can we do?" he said. "Then I see he left a voice mail on my cell phone last night, called right out of the blue, and I'm practically climbing right back on the fence."

Scull made a face.

"Hah!" he said. "Figures he'd show up exactly in time to make life complicated."

Nimec shrugged, turned toward the door.

"Not another step, Petey," Scull said. "You want to leave my premises, you first gotta tell me what Ricci *said* in his message."

Nimec paused halfway into the corridor, glanced over his shoulder.

"Just that he wants to talk," he said.

BONASSE, TRINIDAD

"You're positive the line's secure?" Baxter said.

The satphone to his ear, Jean Luc stood looking out the window at the men in flack jackets below, holding him under house arrest in his Bonasse mansion.

"Reed," he said with a dead calmness that surprised even himself. "Anything I hear stays right here with me in this room."

There was that odd, hollow silence in the earpiece distinctive of coded electronic communications.

"I had two visitors arrive at my office together first thing this morning," Baxter said. "One was a prosecutor from the Attorney General's office, a spic named Herrera attached to the Terrorist Financing

Task Force. The woman practically holding his dick in her hand was with Commerce. Ingrid Price. *Agent* Price, that is. The Export Enforcement Office." He paused. "How's this sounding to you so far?"

Jean Luc gazed past his police guards at the elegant topiary gardens out front, let his attention roam to the thick ruff of cedars sweeping around the foot of the hill. Then he turned toward his desk and the flintlock atop it.

"It sounds as if we've suddenly become very hot tickets with the law-enforcement set," Jean Luc said. "A whole lot of those people are waiting in line to see us."

"How you can make jest of this?" Baxter snapped. "Didn't you hear me use the word *terrorist*?"

Jean Luc sat down at the desk, studied the demon-headed stock of the pistol, and took a small wedge of flint from the objects arranged beside it.

"I heard," he said. "And rest assured, I'm able to grasp the seriousness of our problems."

"They've prepared an indictment to put before a grand jury," Baxter said. "Twenty counts, you should have heard that cunt rattle them off to me. Like she was reading a grocery list. Conspiracy to ship products to designated state sponsors of terrorism. Concealing shipments from authorities. Money laundering. And they're threatening to tack on murder conspiracy charges. The Secret Service, Internal Revenue, even the State Department . . . they're all jumping aboard."

Jean Luc lifted the gun and wedged the flint into the jaws of its hammer, slyly designed in the shape of a serpent's mouth.

"As I said, Reed, I understand," he said.

"I hope you do," Baxter said, his voice raspy with nerves. "Because if one of us goes down, the other goes with him. Like it or not, that's how it is."

Satisfied that the flint was securely in place, Jean Luc thumbed the pistol's hammer into a half-cocked position and reached for another of the items that had been laid out next to it, a leather flask he'd bought at an antique gun shop a while ago. He removed its stopper, poured some gunpowder from inside it down the barrel of the weapon, then picked up the ball and ramrod and loaded up.

"Reed, you border on insulting me, though I realize that isn't your intent," he said. Calmly again. "I know it's tough where you sit. I understand the pressures you've always been under better than you might think. In Washington, it's all in your face, all the time, and now more than ever I suppose it must be tempting to imagine it's somehow easier for me to cope here in my tropical paradise."

"I've never said anything to give you that idea," Baxter said. "You're putting words in my mouth."

"Not in your head, though," Jean Luc said. "I've developed a good sense of how you think, Reed. How you characterize our roles. You're the mover and shaker. The executive who needs to be at the office at nine A.M. and the boardroom by eleven. The insider that plays the *hard* part. And I've always been the flighty one. The rootless traveler, dilettante inheritor of land and oil fields who returns from his wanderings to reap the free-flowing rewards of the family enterprise. Or do you want go on insisting that I'm off the mark?"

"I'm not about to insist on anything," Baxter said. "Look, this isn't the time for either of us to be speculating about what's on the other's mind. Or arguing—"

"You're probably right," Jean Luc said. "But I still feel it might be worth reminding you there would be nothing without the oil. No shining office towers, no conference tables, nothing. And the same goes for every dollar that you've pocketed or gambled away or stuffed into the fingers of your expensive casino whores these past few years. The whole thing, Reed, all of it, has flowed from my wells. From *me* to you."

Andrew Reed Baxter made a harsh, dry sound in his throat. It had an unhealthy quality, as if he were straining for air.

"Damn it, Jean. Goddamn it. I don't know where you're coming from today," he said. "We are in the deepest shit possible and need to stick together. No, it's more than that. We're *bound* together by fucking history."

Jean Luc was silent, taking a moment to admire the pistol in his hand, the cool gleam of its barrel in the daylight pouring through his window. He slid his thumb appreciatively over the detail work on its butt plate, over the demon's head, and then his free hand went for the last of the implements he'd set out on his desk. It was a useful gadget that resembled an expensive brass cartridge pen, and a concession to modernity that hadn't been invented back when old Redbone had given the gun to his ancestor . . . but hadn't he once told Eckers he was a *now* kind of person?

Inserting its tip into the flintlock's pan, Jean Luc pushed down on the finely calibrated little primer to eject three pre-measured grains of gunpowder and finish his preparations.

In his ear, Baxter's voice was an abrasive croak. "Jean Luc, have you been listening? Did you hear what I've tried to explain?"

Jean Luc Morpaign fully cocked the gun's hammer now, raised the snout of the gun to the center of his forehead.

"Yes," he replied. "Yes I have."

"Then what's the score?" Baxter said. "What do you have to say about it?"

Jean Luc turned toward the window, smiled faintly to himself.

"Consider us unbound," he said, and then pulled the trigger on times present and long past.

BAY AREA, CALIFORNIA

Dressed in a tank top and jogging shorts, a digital music player clipped to her waistband, Julia Gordian was in her entry hall lacing her sneakers when she heard a car pull into the driveway.

She rose from her crouch, glanced out the side lights bordering her door, and then turned around to face the greyhounds.

"Hmm, kiddies," she said. "What have we here?"

The dogs stared back at her from the living room, Jill's teeth chattering a little, all of them showing the typical mix of fretfulness and anticipation with which they met any potential blip in their routine.

Julia looked at the car again. It was a small VW Jetta, and as its engine went quiet she saw Tom Ricci sit behind the wheel a moment, get out, reach in for a large white paper bag on the passenger seat, and start up her front walk.

Though her hair had been pulled into an operable ponytail, Julia paused to smooth it back anyway. Then she unlocked her door and opened it before he could buzz.

"Tom, hi," she said. "This is a surprise . . . how'd you find my house?"

Ricci looked at her.

"I remembered from last year," he said.

"Oh, right."

"When you were missing."

"Right," Julia said, and nodded. "I should have figured."

Ricci stood there on the doorstep holding his package.

"This a bad time for me show up?" he said.

"No, no . . ."

"I can go if it is."

"Really, it's fine." Julia waved her hands over herself. "Guess you can tell from these clothes I was about to head out for a jog . . . every other day, rain or shine, you know . . . but it isn't like I'm on the clock."

Ricci nodded. He held his bag out to her, standing there in a white T-shirt, navy sweat pants, and sneakers.

"I brought muffins from that place you like," he said.

"Michael's?"

Another nod.

"They're apricot and cherry," he said. "The ones with the macadamia nuts were sold out."

Julia took the bag, opened it, and made a minor performance of sniffing its contents.

"Yum-yum, I'll settle." She smiled. "Tom, this is really nice, but you didn't have to go out of your way . . ."

"I didn't," he said. "You did that for me last time."

Stuck for a response, Julia cleared her throat.

"Speaking of last time," she said, pretty much just to say *something*. "Did you enjoy your camping trip?"

Ricci hesitated.

"Got what I needed out of it," he said. Then he looked slightly down and past her. "Hi, girl," he said. "Good to see you."

Julia suddenly realized Vivian had managed to poke her head between her leg and the doorframe. She watched as Ricci slowly extended the back of his hand, keeping his knuckles loosely bent, giving Viv a chance to pick up whatever dogs did from his scent. After a few seconds she began licking and nuzzling his fingers.

"Now you're in trouble," Julia said. "That hound's an insatiable sponge when it comes to attention."

Ricci had crouched to scratch under Viv's chin.

"It's okay," he said, and brought his eyes up to Julia's face. "Everything she's been through in her life, she deserves it."

Julia looked at him silently a moment, not quite sure why she'd again found herself at a loss for words.

"Well," she said, hefting her bag of muffins. "I should probably bring these inside, brew us up some coffee . . ."

"Thought you were going for a jog," Ricci said.

Julia shrugged.

"No reason it can't wait," she said.

Ricci straightened, looked at her from where he stood in the morning sunlight.

"It's better to eat afterward," he said. "You don't want your stomach to cramp."

Julia shrugged again.

"Weren't you intending to join me?" she said.

"I was," Ricci said. He took in a breath, produced a long exhalation. "But I let myself get out of shape lately, figured maybe we could go jogging together first . . . that is, if you don't mind."

Julia noticed what he was wearing—*really* noticed—and came close to slapping her head.

"No," she said. "I don't."

"You're sure," he said.

"I'm positive," Julia said. "In fact, Viv and I would really like the company."

They looked at each other a while. Then Ricci nodded, and Julia opened the door wider for him.

"C'mon in," she said. "I need to put this bag away for when we get back."